CITY OF ENDLESS NIGHT

CITY OF ENDLESS NIGHT

BY

MILO HASTINGS

WITH A NEW INTRODUCTION BY

SAM MOSKOWITZ

HYPERION PRESS, INC.
WESTPORT, CONNECTICUT

Library of Congress Cataloging in Publication Data

Hastings, Milo, 1884-1957.
  City of endless night.

    Reprint of the ed. published by Dodd, Mead,
New York.
    I. Title.
PZ3.H2807Ci6   [PS3515.A8296]   813'.5'2   73-13257
ISBN 0-88355-112-8
ISBN 0-88355-141-1 (pbk.)

Published in 1920
by Dodd, Mead and Company, New York
Copyright 1919, 1920
by Dodd, Mead and Company, Inc.

Copyright © 1974 by Hyperion Press, Inc.

Hyperion reprint edition 1974

Library of Congress Catalogue Number 73-13257

ISBN 0-88355-112-8 (cloth ed.)
ISBN 0-88355-141-1 (paper ed.)

Printed in the United States of America

MILO HASTINGS:
Prophet of Totalitarianism

By Sam Moskowitz

Of the pioneering anti-Utopian novels, one of the finest and least known is *City of Endless Night* by Milo Hastings, first published in book form by Dodd, Mead in 1920. This unusual work, filled with uncanny prescience about impending events, was born out of the experience of World War I and the impact on Americans of imperial Germany's statist creed, which believed in the subjugation of the individual for the sake of the nation. On all counts of inventiveness, social significance, narrative flow and intrinsic worth, it ranks with *When the Sleeper Wakes* by H.G. Wells, *Messiah of the Cylinder* by Victor Rousseau and *We* by Eugene Zimiatin, all written and published about the same period.

Hastings' novel also represents the finest achievement of the *Physical Culture* school of science fiction, the only legitimate masterpiece to result from Bernarr McFadden's attempts to teach proper living and realistic standards of morality through fiction. Few are aware that for a period of twenty-five years, McFadden published science fiction as a regular feature of his magazine, *Physical Culture*. His obvious enthusiasm for science fiction explains why McFadden helped engineer the bankruptcy of Hugo Gernsback's Experimenter Publications and then seized control of *Amazing Stories*.

Most of the writers who wrote science fiction for McFadden were not well known, except for Upton Sinclair whose novel, *Prince Hagen*, was serialized in *Physical Culture*. With few exceptions, they produced propaganda tracts instead of genuine science fiction; their stories were preachy and moralistic, primarily designed to convert the reader to a special point of view. Milo Hastings — particularly in *City of Endless Night* — was the notable exception.

Hastings was also a physical culture enthusiast. His earliest signed contribution to *Physical Culture* appeared under what was apparently his real name, Milton Hastings, in the December, 1909 issue, and was entitled *An Experiment in Cooking.* The point of the article was that most cooking destroyed the nutrients in food; Hastings sought to teach his readers how to cook properly and retain the nutrients. The author's credentials as an authority on the subject were solid; he was then the physiological chemist for Christian's School of Applied Food Chemistry. Before that he had worked for the Bureau of Animal Industry at the U.S. Dept. of Agriculture; he was a graduate of the Kansas Agricultural College. A second article — this one by *Milo* Hastings — reflected his views on vegetarianism. Titled *The Case Against Meat as a Staple Food,* it ran in the April, 1910 issue

These initial efforts began Hastings' career as a contributor to *Physical Culture* and other McFadden publications, for which he would also serve, at various times, as a staff member. Hastings also became involved as an associate in some of the McFadden health homes and clinics.

Though diet and physical culture were central in Hastings' life, he had a secondary passion. An avid reader and collector of science fiction, he also ventured into the field as a writer of his own science fiction tales. *City of Endless Night,* the only one of his works to achieve book form, was by far his best, but another novel about a war of the future, *In the Clutch of the War God,* is of special interest. Its sub-title gives some of its unique flavor: "The tale of the Orient's invasion of the Occident, as chronicled in the Humaniculture Society's 'History of the Twentieth Century.'"

Bernarr McFadden himself wrote a signed blurb for it: "FOREWORD: In this strange story of another day, the author has 'dipped into the future' and viewed with his mind's eye the ultimate effect of America's self-satisfied complacency, and her persistent refusal to heed the lessons of Oriental progress. I can safely promise the reader who takes up this unique recital of the twentieth century warfare, that his interest will be sustained to the very end by the interesting deductions and keen insight into the possibilities of the present trend of international affairs exhibited by the author."

The story, briefly outlined, tells how Japan, bent on expansion and aided by a superior air force, attacks the United States and conquers portions of the American southwest. Japanese settlers follow hard on the heels of the military spearhead, for it is Japan's purpose to use the newly-gained territories to solve its own pressing problems of food shortages and excess population. The United States, which has employed its scientific knowledge mainly to serve the needs of the privileged few, is unable to mount an effective defense. Eventually, Japan also invades and occupies huge areas of the wheat-growing lands of the middle west, which are swiftly inhabited by Japanese farmers. To guard against potential American uprisings in the conquered territories, the new masters maintain a trim fleet of aircraft and a sufficient supply of bombs.

Hastings' best — and best known — work, *City of Endless Night*, also made its first appearance in serial form, but not under that title and not in the pages of *Physical Culture*. Its original title was *Children of "Kultur"*, and it was first published, oddly enough, in the pages of *True Story Magazine*, which would seem to be just as unlikely a publication as *Physical Culture* in which to find science fiction. The plain, perhaps astonishing fact, however, is that *True Story Magazine*, which is known primarily for sensational true-to-life stories about women, also published tales that qualify as bonafide science fiction. The magazine's receptivity to this kind of fiction was clearly stated in an enunciation of editorial policy, as written by editor John Brennan in its first issue of May, 1919: "The stories that it presents will be taken as nearly as possible from the actual experiences of life, and we believe they will be read with keener interest than the products of imagination, even when coming from inspired pens...*Our only deviation from the rule we have laid down will be in stories of the future.*" *Children of "Kultur"* was presented as a "Might-have-been or May-yet-be True Story." It ran in seven installments through to November, 1919.

As published in *True-Story Magazine*, the opening chapters of Hastings' original manuscript were cut and revised and a very long synopsis substituted for the text later to be found in the book. The original, uncut version, published in book form as *City of Endless Night*, must have been known to Hugo Gernsback, one of modern science fiction's outstanding pioneers. I drew this inference from a story told me in 1953 by Harvey Gernsback, Hugo's son, when he was the executive editor, and I the managing editor, of the magazine *Science-Fiction Plus*. Harvey told me that when he was very young a copy of Hastings' novel had been given to him as a present by a member of the family; the book had apparently made a deep impression on him. It was at Harvey Gernsback's urging that I began my subsequent research into Hastings' science fiction writings.

There seem to be two possible major antecedents of *City of Endless Night*. One is the famed novel *Underground Man* by Gabriel de Tarde, issued with an introduction by H. G. Wells in 1905 by Duckworth & Co., London. In de Tarde's work, mankind is forced underground and ingeniously manages to construct a civilization by finding methods of obtaining food and food substitutes, elements for clothing and other basics of life. The other is the apocalyptic novel, *The Nightland,* by William Hope Hodgsen, first published in 1912 by Everleigh Nash, London. In Hodgson's nightmare world, all remaining humanity lives many miles beneath the earth's surface inside an enormous pyramid that rises nearly eight miles high and is besieged by innumerable horrors from the surrounding region.

Hastings' novel is an extraordinary anticipation of the Nazi doctrine, which was soon to begin its meteoric rise in Germany. It even refers to an ideological work, *God's Anointed*, which contains striking parallels to Hitler's *Mein Kampf,* and to the concept of a Nordic super race that closely resembles the Aryan mystique of Naziism. As its main theme, *City of Endless Night* offers a prophetic vision of a totalitarian future, in which a nation, very much like that of fascist Germany, effects a stalemate in a World War and gradually creates a new, tightly controlled society under conditions of perpetual siege.

The influence exerted on Hastings by Bernarr McFadden's strong and advanced views on the hypocrisy and harmful results of sexual prudery were apparent in his treatment of how sex would be handled in a specialized society of the future, a subject usually glossed over in previous utopian or anti-Utopian novels. The author accomplishes this with skill and frankness.

The problem of excessive leisure time is dealt with in a completely modern manner. People of limited education and skills, who have narrow intellectual horizons and are trained to perform only a single function, have great difficulty coping in what for them becomes the burden of leisure.

In addition to all its other virtues, *City of Endless Night* has a driving narrative pace that sweeps the reader along through what is essentially a serious, thoughtful work. In my judgement, it will be increasingly recognized as a book far in advance of its times — truly a landmark in the history of science fiction.

CONTENTS

CITY OF ENDLESS NIGHT

CHAPTER I

THE RED AND BLACK AND GOLD STRUGGLE FOR SUPREMACY ON THE CHANGING MAP OF THE WORLD

1

WHEN but a child of seven my uncle placed me in a private school in which one of the so-called redeemed sub-sailors was a teacher of the German language. As I look back now, in the light of my present knowledge, I better comprehend the docile humility and carefully nurtured ignorance of this man. In his class rooms he used as a text a description of German life, taken from the captured submarine. From this book he had secured his own conception of a civilization of which he really knew practically nothing. I recall how we used to ask Herr Meineke if he had actually seen those strange things of which he taught us. To this he always made answer, " The book is official, man's observation errs."

2

" He can talk it," said my playmates who attended the public schools where all teaching of the language of the outcast nation was prohibited. They invariably elected me to be " the Germans," and locked me up in the old garage while they rained a stock of sun-dried clay bombs upon the roof and then came with a rush to " batter down the walls of Berlin " by breaking in the door, while I, muttering strange guttural oaths, would be led forth to be " exterminated."

On rainy days I would sometimes take my favoured playmates into my uncle's library where five great maps hung in ordered sequence on the panelled wall.

The first map was labelled " The Age of Nations — 1914," and showed the black spot of Germany, like in size to many of the surrounding countries, the names of which one recited in the history class.

The second map —" Germany's Maximum Expansion of the First World War — 1918 "— showed the black area trebled in size, crowding into the pale gold of France, thrusting a hungry arm across the Hellespont towards Bagdad, and, from the Balkans to the Baltic, blotting out all else save the flaming red of Bolshevist Russia, which spread over the Eastern half of Europe like a pool of fresh spilled blood.

Third came " The Age of the League of Nations, 1919 — 1983," with the gold of democracy battling with the spreading red of socialism, for the black of autocracy had erstwhile vanished.

The fourth map was the most fascinating and terrible. Again the black of autocracy appeared, obliterating the red of the Brotherhood of Man, spreading across half of Eurasia and thrusting a broad black shadow to the Yellow Sea and a lesser one to the Persian Gulf. This map was labelled " Maximum German Expansion of the Second World War, 1988," and lines of dotted white retreated in concentric waves till the line of 2041. This same year was the first date of the fifth map, which was labelled " A Century of the World State," and here, as all the sea was blue, so all the land was gold, save one black blot that might have been made by a single spattered drop of ink, for it was no bigger than the Irish Island. The persistence of this remaining black on the map of the world troubled my boyish mind, as it has troubled three generations of the United World, and strive as I might, I could not comprehend why the great blackness of the fourth map had been erased and this small blot alone remained.

3

When I returned from school for my vacation, after I had my first year of physical science, I sought out my uncle in his laboratory and asked him to explain the mystery of the little black island standing adamant in the golden sea of all the world.

" That spot," said my uncle, " would have been erased in two more years if a Leipzig professor had not discovered The Ray. Yet we do not know his name nor how he made his discovery."

" But just what is The Ray? " I asked.

" We do not know that either, nor how it is made.

We only know that it destroys the oxygen carrying power of living blood. If it were an emanation from a substance like radium, they could have fired it in projectiles and so conquered the earth. If it were ether waves like electricity, we should have been able to have insulated against it, or they should have been able to project it farther and destroy our aircraft, but The Ray is not destructive beyond two thousand metres in the air and hardly that far in the earth."

" Then why do we not fly over and land an army and great guns and batter down the walls of Berlin and be done with it? "

" That, as you know if you studied your history, has been tried many times and always with disaster. The bomb-torn soil of that black land is speckled white with the bones of World armies who were sent on landing invasions before you or I was born. But it was only heroic folly, one gun popping out of a tunnel mouth can slay a thousand men. To pursue the gunners into their catacombs meant to be gassed; and sometimes our forces were left to land in peace and set up their batteries to fire against Berlin, but the Germans would place Ray generators in the ground beneath them and slay our forces in an hour, as the Angel of Jehovah withered the hosts of the Assyrians."

" But why," I persisted, " do we not tunnel under the Ray generators and dig our way to Berlin and blow it up? "

My uncle smiled indulgently. " And that has

been tried too, but they can hear our borings with microphones and cut us off, just as we cut them off when they try to tunnel out and place new generators. It is too slow, too difficult, either way; the line has wavered a little with the years but to no practical avail; the war in our day has become merely a watching game, we to keep the Germans from coming out, they to keep us from penetrating within gunshot of Berlin; but to gain a mile of worthless territory either way means too great a human waste to be worth the price. Things must go on as they are till the Germans tire of their sunless imprisonment or till they exhaust some essential element in their soil. But wars such as you read of in your history, will never happen again. The Germans cannot fight the world in the air, nor in the sea, nor on the surface of the earth; and we cannot fight the Germans in the ground; so the war has become a fixed state of standing guard; the hope of victory, the fear of defeat have vanished; the romance of war is dead."

"But why, then," I asked, "does the World Patrol continue to bomb the roof of Berlin?"

"Politics," replied my uncle, "military politics, just futile display of pyrotechnics to amuse the populace and give heroically inclined young men a chance to strut in uniforms — but after the election this fall such folly will cease."

4

My uncle had predicted correctly, for by the time

I again came home on my vacation, the newly elected Pacifist Council had reduced the aerial activities to mere watchful patroling over the land of the enemy. Then came the report of an attempt to launch an airplane from the roof of Berlin. The people, in dire panic lest Ray generators were being carried out by German aircraft, had clamoured for the recall of the Pacifist Council, and the bombardment of Berlin was resumed.

During the lull of the bombing activities my uncle, who stood high with the Pacifist Administration, had obtained permission to fly over Europe, and I, most fortunate of boys, accompanied him. The plane in which we travelled bore the emblem of the World Patrol. On a cloudless day we sailed over the pock-marked desert that had once been Germany and came within field-glass range of Berlin itself. On the wasted, bomb-torn land lay the great grey disc — the city of mystery. Three hundred metres high they said it stood, but so vast was its extent that it seemed as flat and thin as a pancake on a griddle.

"More people live in that mass of concrete," said my uncle, " than in the whole of America west of the Rocky Mountains." His statement, I have since learned, fell short of half the truth, but then it seemed appalling. I fancied the city a giant ant-hill, and searched with my glass as if I expected to see the ants swarming out. But no sign of life was visible upon the monotonous surface of the sand-blanketed roof, and high above the range of naked vision hung the hawk-like watchers of the World Patrol.

The lure of unravelled secrets, the ambition for discovery and exploration stirred my boyish veins. Yes, I would know more of the strange race, the unknown life that surged beneath that grey blanket of mystery. But how? For over a century millions of men had felt that same longing to know. Aviators, landing by accident or intent within the lines, had either returned with nothing to report, or they had not returned. Daring journalists, with baskets of carrier pigeons, had on foggy nights dropped by parachute to the roof of the city; but neither they nor the birds had brought back a single word of what lay beneath the armed and armoured roof.

My own resolution was but a boy's dream and I returned to Chicago to take up my chemical studies.

CHAPTER II

I

W HEN I was twenty-four years old, my uncle was killed in a laboratory explosion. He had been a scientist of renown and a chemical inventor who had devoted his life to the unravelling of the secrets of the synthetic foods of Germany. For some years I had been his trusted assistant. In our Chicago laboratory were carefully preserved food samples that had been taken from the captured submarines in years gone by; and what to me was even more fascinating, a collection of German books of like origin, which I had read with avidity. With the exception of those relating to submarine navigation, I found them stupidly childish and decided that they had been prepared to hide the truth and not reveal it.

My uncle had bequeathed me both his work and his fortune, but despairing of my ability worthily to continue his own brilliant researches on synthetic food, I turned my attention to the potash problem, in which I had long been interested. My reading of early chemical works had given me a particular interest in the reclamation of the abandoned potash

8

mines of Stassfurt. These mines, as any student of chemical history will know, were one of the richest properties of the old German state in the days before the endless war began and Germany became isolated from the rest of the world. The mines were captured by the World in the year 2020, and were profitably operated for a couple of decades. Meanwhile the German lines were forced many miles to the rear before the impregnable barrier of the Ray had halted the progress of the World Armies.

A few years after the coming of the Ray defences, occurred what history records as " The Tragedy of the Mines." Six thousand workmen went down into the potash mines of Stassfurt one morning and never came up again. The miners' families in the neighbouring villages died like weevils in fumigated grain. The region became a valley of pestilence and death, and all life withered for miles around. Numerous governmental projects were launched for the recovery of the potash mines but all failed, and for one hundred and eleven years no man had penetrated those accursed shafts.

Knowing these facts, I wasted no time in soliciting government aid for my project, but was content to secure a permit to attempt the recovery with private funds, with which my uncle's fortune supplied me in abundance.

In April, 2151, I set up my laboratory on the edge of the area of death. I had never accepted the orthodox view as to the composition of the gas that issued from the Stassfurt mines. In a few months I was gratified to find my doubts confirmed. A short time after this I made a more unexpected and astonishing discovery. I found that this complex and hitherto misunderstood gas could, under the influence of certain high-frequency electrical discharges, be made to combine with explosive violence with the nitrogen of the atmosphere, leaving only a harmless residue. We wired the surrounding region for the electrical discharge and, with a vast explosion of weird purple flame, cleared the whole area of the century-old curse. Our laboratory was destroyed by the explosion. It was rebuilt nearer the mine shafts from which the gas still slowly issued. Again we set up our electrical machinery and dropped our cables into the shafts, this time clearing the air of the mines.

A hasty exploration revealed the fact that but a single shaft had remained intact. A third time we prepared our electrical machinery. We let down a cable and succeeded in getting but a faint reaction at the bottom of the shaft. After several repeated clearings we risked descent.

Upon arrival at the bottom we were surprised to find it free from water, save for a trickling stream. The second thing we discovered was a pile of huddled skeletons of the workmen who had perished over a century previous. But our third and most important discovery was a boring from which the poisonous gas was slowly issuing. It took but a few hours to provide an apparatus to fire this gas as fast as it issued, and the potash mines of Stassfurt were regained for the world. My associates were for beginning mining operations at once, but I had been granted a twenty years' franchise on the output of these mines, and I was in no such haste. The boring from which this poisonous vapour issued was clearly man-made; moreover I alone knew the formula of that gas and had convinced myself once for all as to its man-made origin. I sent for microphones and with their aid speedily detected the sound of machinery in other workings beneath.

It is easy now to see that I erred in risking my own life as I did without the precaution of confiding the secret of my discovery to others. But those were days of feverish excitement. Impulsively I decided to make the first attack on the Germans as a private enterprise and then call for military aid. I had my own equipment of poisonous bombs and my sapping and mining experts determined that the German workings were but eighty metres beneath us. Hastily, among the crumbling skeletons, we set up our electrical boring machinery and began sinking a one-metre shaft towards the nearest sound.

After twenty hours of boring, the drill head suddenly came off and rattled down into a cavern. We saw a light and heard guttural shouting below and the cracking of a gun as a few bullets spattered against the roof of our chamber. We heaved down our gas bombs and covered over our shaft. Within a few hours the light below went out and our microphones failed to detect any sound from the rocks beneath us. It was then perhaps that I should have called for military aid, but the uncanny silence of the lower workings proved too much for my eager curiosity. We waited two days and still there was no evidence of life below. I knew there had been ample time for the gas from our bombs to have been dissipated, as it was decomposed by contact with moisture. A light was lowered, but this brought forth no response.

I now called for a volunteer to descend the shaft. None was forthcoming from among my men, and against their protest I insisted on being lowered into the shaft. When I was a few metres from the bottom the cable parted and I fell and lay stunned on the floor below.

2

When I recovered consciousness the light had gone out. There was no sound about me. I shouted up the shaft above and could get no answer. The chamber in which I lay was many times my height and I could make nothing out in the dark hole above. For some hours I scarcely stirred and feared to burn my pocket flash both because it might reveal my presence to lurking enemies and because I wished to conserve my battery against graver need.

But no rescue came from my men above. Only recently, after the lapse of years, did I learn the cause of their deserting me. As I lay stunned from my

fall, my men, unable to get answer to their shout-
ings, had given me up for dead. Meanwhile the
apparatus which caused the destruction of the German gas had gone wrong. My associates, unable to
fix it, had fled from the mine and abandoned the
enterprise.

After some hours of waiting I stirred about and
found means to erect a rough scaffold and reach the
mouth of the shaft above me. I attempted to climb,
but, unable to get a hold on the smooth wet rock,
I gave up exhausted and despairing. Entombed in
the depths of the earth, I was either a prisoner of
the German potash miners, if any remained alive,
or a prisoner of the earth itself, with dead men for
company.

Collecting my courage I set about to explore my
surroundings. I found some mining machinery evidently damaged by the explosion of our gas bombs.
There was no evidence of men about, living or dead.
Stealthily I set out along the little railway track that
ran through a passage down a steep incline. As I
progressed I felt the air rapidly becoming colder.
Presently I stumbled upon the first victim of our gas
bombs, fallen headlong as he was fleeing. I hurried
on. The air seemed to be blowing in my face and
the cold was becoming intense. This puzzled me
for at this depth the temperature should have been
above that on the surface of the earth.

After a hundred metres or so of going I came into
a larger chamber. It was intensely cold. From
out another branching passage-way I could hear a

sizzling sound as of steam escaping. I started to turn into this passage but was met with such a blast of cold air that I dared not face it for fear of being frozen. Stamping my feet, which were fast becoming numb, I made the rounds of the chamber, and examined the dead miners that were tumbled about. The bodies were frozen.

One side of this chamber was partitioned off with some sort of metal wall. The door stood blown open. It felt a little warmer in here and I entered and closed the door. Exploring the room with my dim light I found one side of it filled with a row of bunks — in each bunk a corpse. Along the other side of the room was a table with eating utensils and back of this were shelves with food packages.

I was in danger of freezing to death and, tumbling several bodies out of the bunks, I took the mattresses and built of them a clumsy enclosure and installed in their midst a battery heater which I found. In this fashion I managed to get fairly warm again. After some hours of huddling I observed that the temperature had moderated.

My fear of freezing abated, I made another survey of my surroundings and discovered something that had escaped my first attention. In the far end of the room was a desk, and seated before it with his head fallen forward on his arms was the form of a man. The miners had all been dressed in a coarse artificial leather, but this man was dressed in a woven fabric of cellulose silk.

The body was frozen. As I tumbled it stiffly

back it fell from the chair exposing a ghastly face. I drew away in a creepy horror, for as I looked at the face of the corpse I suffered a sort of waking nightmare in which I imagined that I was gazing at my own dead countenance.

I concluded that my normal mind was slipping out of gear and proceeded to back off and avail myself of a tube of stimulant which I carried in my pocket.

This revived me somewhat, but again, when I tried to look upon the frozen face, the conviction returned that I was looking at my own dead self.

I glanced at my watch and figured out that I had been in the German mine for thirty hours and had not tasted food or drink for nearly forty hours. Clearly I had to get myself in shape to escape hallucinations. I went back to the shelves and proceeded to look for food and drink. Happily, due to my work in my uncle's laboratory, these synthetic foods were not wholly strange to me. I drank copiously of a non-alcoholic chemical liquor and warmed on the heater and partook of some nitrogenous and some starchy porridges. It was an uncanny dining place, but hunger soon conquers mere emotion, and I made out a meal. Then once more I faced the task of confronting this dead likeness of myself.

This time I was clear-headed enough. I even went to the miners' lavatory and, jerking down the metal mirror, scrutinized my own reflection and reassured myself of the closeness of the resemblance. My purpose framed in my mind as I did this.

Clearly I was in German quarters and was likely to remain there. Sooner or later there must be a rescuing party.

Without further ado, I set about changing my clothing for that of the German. The fit of the dead man's clothes further emphasized the closeness of the physical likeness. I recalled my excellent command of the German language and began to wonder what manner of man I was supposed to be in this assumed personality. But my most urgent task was speedily to make way with the incriminating corpse. With the aid of the brighter flashlight which I found in my new pockets, I set out to find a place to hide the body.

The cold that had so frightened me had now given way to almost normal temperature. There was no longer the sound of sizzling steam from the unexplored passage-way. I followed this and presently came upon another chamber filled with machinery. In one corner a huge engine, covered with frost, gave off a chill greeting. On the floor was a steaming puddle of liquid, but the breath of this steam cut like a blizzard. At once I guessed it. This was a liquid air engine. The dead engineer in the corner helped reveal the story. With his death from the penetrating gas, something had gone wrong with the engine. The turbine head had blown off, and the conveying pipe of liquid air had poured forth the icy blast that had so nearly frozen me along with the corpses of the Germans. But now the flow of liquid had ceased, and the last remnants were evap-

orating from the floor. Evidently the supply pipe
had been shut off further back on the line, and
I had little time to lose for rescuers were probably
on the way.

Along one of the corridors running from the engine room I found an open water drain half choked
with melting ice. Following this I came upon a
grating where the water disappeared. I jerked up
the grating and dropped a piece of ice down the
well-like shaft. I hastily returned and dragged
forth the corpse of my double and with it everything
I had myself brought into the mine. Straightening
out the stiffened body I plunged it head foremost
into the opening. The sound of a splash echoed
within the dismal depths.

I now hastened back to the chamber into which I
had first fallen and destroyed the scaffolding I had
erected there. Returning to the desk where I had
found the man whose clothing I wore, I sat down
and proceeded to search my abundantly filled pockets. From one of them I pulled out a bulky note-
book and a number of loose papers. The freshest
of these was an official order from the Imperial
Office of Chemical Engineers. The order ran as
follows:

Capt. Karl Armstadt
    Laboratory 186, E. 58.
Report is received at this office of the sound of sapping operations in potash mine D5. Go at once and verify the same
and report of condition of gas generators and make analyses
of output of the same.

Evidently I was Karl Armstadt and very happily a chemical engineer by profession. My task of impersonation so far looked feasible — I could talk chemical engineering.

The next paper I proceeded to examine was an identification folder done up in oiled fabric. Thanks to German thoroughness it was amusingly complete. On the first page appeared what I soon discovered to be *my* pedigree for four generations back. The printed form on which all this was minutely filled out made very clear statements from which I determined that my father and mother were both dead.

I, Karl Armstadt, twenty-seven years of age, was the fourteenth child of my mother and was born when she was forty-two years of age. According to the record I was the ninety-seventh child of my father and born when he was fifty-four. As I read this I thought there was something here that I misunderstood, although subsequent discoveries made it plausible enough. There was no further record of my plentiful fraternity, but I took heart that the mere fact of their numerical abundance would make unlikely any great show of brotherly interest, a presumption which proved quite correct.

On the second page of this folder I read the number and location of my living quarters, the sources from which my meals and clothing were issued, as well as the sizes and qualities of my garments and numerous other references to various details of living, all of which seemed painstakingly ridiculous at the time.

I put this elaborate identification paper back into its receptacle and opened the notebook. It proved to be a diary kept likewise in thorough German fashion. I turned to the last pages and perused them hastily. The notes in Armstadt's diary were concerned almost wholly with his chemical investigations. All this I saw might be useful to me later but what I needed more immediately was information as to his personal life. I scanned back hastily through the pages for a time without finding any such revelations. Then I discovered this entry made some months previously:

"I cannot think of chemistry tonight, for the vision of Katrina dances before me as in a dream. It must be a strange mixture of blood-lines that could produce such wondrous beauty. In no other woman have I seen such a blackness of hair and eyes combined with such a whiteness of skin. I suppose I should not have danced with her — now I see all my resolutions shattered. But I think it was most of all the blackness of her eyes. Well, what care, we live but once!"

I read and re-read this entry and searched feverishly in Armstadt's diary for further evidence of a personal life. But I only found tedious notes on his chemical theories. Perhaps this single reference to a woman was but a passing fancy of a man otherwise engrossed in his science. But if rescuers came and I succeeded in passing for the German chemist the presence of a woman in my new rôle of life would surely undo all my effort. If no personal acquaintance of the dead man came with the rescuing party I saw no reason why I could not for the time pass successfully as Armstadt. I should at least make the effort and I reasoned I could best do this by playing the malingerer and appearing mentally incompetent. Such a ruse, I reasoned, would give me opportunity to hear much and say little, and perhaps so get my bearings in the new rôle that I could continue it successfully.

Then, as I was about to return the notebook to my pocket, my hopes sank as I found this brief entry which I had at first scanning overlooked:

"It is twenty days now since Katrina and I have been united. She does not interfere with my work as much as I feared. She even lets me talk chemistry to her, though I am sure she understands not one word of what I tell her. I think I have made a good selection and it is surely a permanent one. Therefore I must work harder than ever or I shall not get on."

This alarmed me. Yet, if Armstadt had married he made very little fuss about it. Evidently it concerned him chiefly in relation to his work. But whoever and whatever Katrina was, it was clear that her presence would be disastrous to my plans of assuming his place in the German world.

Pondering over the ultimate difficulty of my situation, but with a growing faith in the plan I had evolved for avoiding immediate explanations, I fell into a long-postponed sleep. The last thing I remember was tumbling from my chair and sprawling out upon the floor where I managed to snap out my light before the much needed sleep quite overcame me.

3

I was awakened by voices, and opened my eyes to find the place brightly lighted. I closed them again quickly as some one approached and prodded me with the toe of his boot.

" Here is a man alive," said a voice above me.

" He is Captain Armstadt, the chemist," said another voice, approaching; " this is good. We have special orders to search for him."

The newcomer bent over and felt my heart. I was quite aware that it was functioning normally. He shook me and called me by name. After repeated shakings I opened my eyes and stared at him blankly, but I said nothing. Presently he left me and returned with a stretcher. I lay inertly as I was placed thereon and borne out of the chamber. Other stretcher-bearers were walking ahead. We passed through the engine room where mechanics were at work on the damaged liquid air engine. My stretcher was placed on a little car which moved swiftly along the tunnel.

We came into a large subterranean station and I was removed and brought before a bevy of white garbed physicians. They looked at my identification folder and then examined me. Through it all I lay limp and as near lifeless as I could simulate, and they succeeded in getting no speech out of me. The final orders were to forward me post haste to the Imperial Hospital for Complex Gas Cases.

After an eventless journey of many hours I was again unloaded and transferred to an elevator. For several hundred metres we sped upward through a shaft, while about us whistled a blast of cold, crisp air. At last the elevator stopped and I was carried out to an ambulance that stood waiting in a brilliantly lighted passage arched over with grey concrete. I was no longer beneath the surface of the earth but was somewhere in the massive concrete structure of the City of Berlin.

After a short journey our ambulance stopped and attendants came out and carried my litter through an open doorway and down a long hall into the spacious ward of a hospital.

From half closed eyes I glanced about apprehensively for a black-haired woman. With a sigh of relief I saw there were only doctors and male attendants in the room. They treated me most professionally and gave no sign that they suspected I was other than Capt. Karl Armstadt, which fact my papers so eloquently testified. The conclusion of their examination was voiced in my presence. " Physically he is normal," said the head physician, " but his mind seems in a stupor. There is no remedy, as the nature of the gas is unknown. All that can be done is to await the wearing off of the effect."

I was then left alone for some hours and my appetite was troubling me. At last an attendant approached with some savoury soup; he propped me up and proceeded to feed me with a spoon.

I made out from the conversation about me that the other patients were officers from the underground fighting forces. An atmosphere of military discipline pervaded the hospital and I felt reassured in the conclusion that all visiting was forbidden.

Yet my thoughts turned repeatedly to the black-eyed Katrina of Armstadt's diary. No doubt she had been informed of the rescue and was waiting in grief and anxiety to see him. So both she and I were awaiting a tragic moment — she to learn that her husband or lover was dead, I for the inevitable tearing off of my protecting disguise.

After some days the head physician came to my cot and questioned me. I gazed at him and knit my brows as if struggling to think.

" You were gassed in the mine," he kept repeating, " can you remember? "

" Yes," I ventured, " I went to the mine, there was the sound of boring overhead. I set men to watch; I was at the desk, I heard shouting, after that I cannot remember."

" They were all dead but you," said the doctor.

" All dead," I repeated. I liked the sound of this and so kept on mumbling " All dead, all dead."

4

My plan was working nicely. But I realized I could not keep up this rôle for ever. Nor did I wish to, for the idleness and suspense were intolerable and I knew that I would rather face whatever problems my recovery involved than to continue in this monotonous and meaningless existence. So I convalesced by degrees and got about the hospital, and was permitted to wait on myself. But I cultivated a slowness and brevity of speech.

One day as I sat reading the attendant announced, " A visitor to see you, sir."

Trembling with excitement and fear I tensely waited the coming of the visitor.

Presently a stolid-faced young man followed the attendant into the room. " You remember Holknecht," said the nurse, " he is your assistant at the laboratory."

I stared stupidly at the man, and cold fear crept over me as he, with puzzled eyes, returned my gaze.

" You are much changed," he said at last. " I hardly recognize you."

" I have been very ill," I replied.

Just then the head physician came into the room and seeing me talking to a stranger walked over to us. As I said nothing, Holknecht introduced himself. The medical man began at once to enlarge upon the peculiarities of my condition. " The unknown gas," he explained, " acted upon the whole nervous system and left profound effects. Never in the records of the hospital has there been so strange a case."

Holknecht seemed quite awed and completely credulous.

" His memory must be revived," continued the head physician, " and that can best be done by re-calling the dominating interest of his mind."

" Captain Armstadt was wholly absorbed in his research work in the laboratory," offered Holknecht.

" Then," said the physician, " you must revive the activity of those particular brain cells."

With that command the laboratory assistant was left in charge. He took his new task quite seriously. Turning to me and raising his voice as if to penetrate my dulled mentality, he began, " Do you not remember our work in the laboratory? "

" Yes, the laboratory, the laboratory," I repeated vaguely.

Holknecht described the laboratory in detail and gradually his talk drifted into an account of the chemical research. I listened eagerly to get the threads of the work I must needs do if I were to maintain my rôle as Armstadt.

Knowing now that visitors were permitted me, I again grew apprehensive over the possible advent of Katrina. But no woman appeared, in fact I had not yet seen a woman among the Germans. Always it was Holknecht and, strictly according to his orders, he talked incessant chemistry.

5

The day I resumed my normal wearing apparel I was shown into a large lounging room for conva-lescents. I seated myself a short distance apart from a group of officers and sat eyeing another group of large, hulking fellows at the far end of the room.   These I concluded to be common soldiers, for I heard the officers in my ward grumbling at the fact that they were quartered in the same hospital with men of the ranks.

Presently an officer came over and took a seat beside me.   "It is very rarely that you men in the professional service are gassed," he said.   "You must have a dull life, I do not see how you can stand it."

"But certainly," I replied, "it is not so dangerous."

"And for that reason it must be stupid — I, for one, think that even in the fighting forces there is no longer sufficient danger to keep up the military morale.   Danger makes men courageous — without danger courage declines — and without courage what advantage would there be in the military life?"

"Suppose," I suggested, "the war should come to an end?"

"But how can it?" he asked incredulously. "How can there be an end to the war? We cannot prevent the enemy from fighting."

"But what," I ventured, "if the enemy should decide to quit fighting?"

"They have almost quit now," he remarked with apparent disgust; "they are losing the fighting spirit — but no wonder — they say that the World State population is so great that only two per cent. of its men are in the fighting forces.   What I cannot see is how a people so peaceful can keep from utter degeneration. And they say that the World State soldiers are not even bred for soldiering but are picked from all classes. If they should decide to quit fighting, as you suggest, we also would have to quit — it would intolerable — it is bad enough now."

"But could you not return to industrial life and do something productive?"

"Productive!" sneered the fighter. "I knew that you professional men had no courage — it is not to be expected — but I never before heard even one of your class suggest a thing like that — a military man do something productive! Why don't you suggest that we be changed to women?" And with that my fellow patient rose and, turning sharply on his metal heel, walked away.

The officer's attitude towards his profession set me thinking, and I found myself wondering how far it was shared by the common soldiers. The next day when I came out into the convalescent corridor I walked past the group of officers and went down among the men whose garments bore no medals or insignia. They were unusually large men, evidently from some specially selected regiment. Picking out the most intelligent looking one of the group I sat down beside him.

"Is this the first time you have been gassed?" I inquired.

"Third time," replied the soldier.

"I should think you would have been discharged."

"Discharged," said the soldier, in a perplexed

tone, "why I am only forty-four years old, why should I be discharged unless I get in an explosion and lose a leg or something?"

"But you have been gassed three times," I said, "I should think they ought to let you return to civil life and your family."

The soldier looked hard at the insignia of my rank as captain. "You professional officers don't know much, do you? A soldier quit and do common labor, now that's a fine idea. And a family! Do you think I'm a Hohenzollern?" At the thought the soldier chuckled. "Me with a family," he muttered to himself, "now that's a fine idea."

I saw that I was getting on dangerous ground but curiosity prompted a further question: "Then, I suppose, you have nothing to hope for until you reach the age of retirement, unless war should come to an end?"

Again the soldier eyed me carefully. "Now you do have some queer ideas. There was a man in our company who used to talk like that when no officers were around. This fellow, his name was Mannteufel, said he could read books, that he was a forbidden love-child and his father was an officer. I guess he was forbidden all right, for he certainly wasn't right in his head. He said that we would go out on the top of the ground and march over the enemy country and be shot at by the flying planes, like the roof guards. If the officers had heard him they would surely have sent him to the crazy ward — why he said that the war would be over after that, and we would all go to the enemy country and go about as we liked, and own houses and women and flying planes and animals. As if the Royal House would ever let a soldier do things like that."

" Well," I said, " and why not, if the war were over? "

" Now there you go again — how do you mean the war was over, what would all us soldiers do if there was no fighting? "

" You could work," I said, " in the shops."

" But if we worked in the shops, what would the workmen do? "

" They would work too," I suggested.

The soldier was silent for a time. " I think I get your idea," he said. " The Eugenic Staff would cut down the birth rates so that there would only be enough soldiers and workers to fill the working jobs."

" They might do that," I remarked, wishing to lead him on.

" Well," said the soldier, returning to the former thought, " I hope they won't do that until I am dead. I don't care to go up on the ground to get shot at by the fighting planes. At least now we have something over our heads and if we are going to get gassed or blown up we can't see it coming. At least — "

Just then the officer with whom I had talked the day before came up. He stopped before us and scowled at the soldier who saluted in hasty confusion.

" I wish, Captain," said the officer addressing me,
" that you would not take advantage of these absurd
hospital conditions to disrupt discipline by fraterniz-
ing with a private."

At this the soldier looked up and saluted again.

" Well? " said the officer.

" He's not to blame, sir," said the soldier, " he's
off his head."

CHAPTER III

IN A BLACK UTOPIA THE BLOND BROOD BREEDS AND SWARMS

I

IT was with a strange mixture of eagerness and fear that I received the head physician's decision that I would henceforth recover my faculties more rapidly in the familiar environment of my own home.

A wooden-faced male nurse accompanied me in a closed vehicle that ran noiselessly through the vaulted interior streets of the completely roofed-in city. Once our vehicle entered an elevator and was let down a brief distance. We finally alighted in a street very like the one on which the hospital was located, and filed down a narrow passage-way. My companion asked for my keys, which I found in my clothing. I stood by with a palpitating heart as he turned the lock and opened the door.

The place we entered was a comfortably furnished bachelor's apartment. Books and papers were littered about giving evidence of no disturbance since the sudden leaving of the occupant. Immensely relieved I sat down in an upholstered chair while the nurse scurried about and put the place in order.

" You feel quite at home?" he asked as he finished his task.`

" Quite," I replied, " things are coming back to me now."

" You should have been sent home sooner," he said. " I wished to tell the chief as much, but I am only a second year interne and it is forbidden me to express an original opinion to him."

" I am sure I will be all right now," I replied.

He turned to go and then paused. " I think," he said, " that you should have some notice on you that when you do go out, if you become confused and make mistakes, the guards will understand. I will speak to Lieut. Forrester, the Third Assistant, and ask that such a card be sent you." With that he took his departure.

When he had gone I breathed joyfully and freely. The rigid face and staring eye that I had cultivated relaxed into a natural smile and then I broke into a laugh. Here I was in the heart of Berlin, unsuspected of being other than a loyal German and free, for the time at least, from problems of personal relations.

I now made an elaborate inspection of my surroundings. I found a wardrobe full of men's clothing, all of a single shade of mauve like the suit I wore. Some suits I guessed to be work clothes from their cheaper texture and some, much finer, were evidently dress apparel.

Having reassured myself that Armstadt had been the only occupant of the apartment, I turned to a pile of papers that the hospital attendant had picked up from the floor where they had dropped from a mail chute. Most of these proved to be the accumulated copies of a daily chemical news bulletin. Others were technical chemical journals. Among the letters I found an invitation to a meeting of a chemical society, and a note from my tailor asking me to call; the third letter was written on a typewriter, an instrument the like of which I had already discovered in my study. This sheet bore a neatly engraved head reading " Katrina, Permit 843 LX, Apartment 57, K Street, Level of the Free Women." The letter ran:

" Dear Karl: For three weeks now you have failed to keep your appointments and sent no explanation. You surely know that I will not tolerate such rude neglect. I have reported to the Supervisor that you are dropped from my list."

So this was Katrina! Here at last was the end of the fears that had haunted me.

2

As I was scanning the chemical journal I heard a bell ring and turning about I saw that a metal box had slid forth upon a side board from an opening in the wall. In this box I found my dinner which I proceeded to enjoy in solitude. The food was more varied than in the hospital. Some was liquid and some gelatinous, and some firm like bread or biscuit. But of natural food products there was nothing save a dish of mushrooms and a single sprig of green no longer than my finger, and which, like a feather in a boy's cap, was inserted conspicuously in the top of a synthetic pudding. There was one food that puzzled me, for it was sausage-like in form and sausage-like in flavour, and I was sure contained some real substance of animal origin. Presuming, as I did at that moment, that no animal life existed in Berlin, I ate this sausage with doubts and misgivings.

The dinner finished, I looked for a way to dispose of the dishes. Packing them back in the container I fumbled about and found a switch which set something going in the wall, and my dishes departed to the public dishwasher.

Having cleared the desk I next turned to Armstadt's book shelves. My attention was caught by a ponderous volume. It proved to be an atlas and directory of Berlin. In the front of this was a most revealing diagram which showed Berlin to be a city of sixty levels. The five lowest levels were underground and all were labelled " Mineral Industries." Above these were eight levels of Food, Clothing and Miscellaneous industries. Then came the seven workmen's residence levels, divided by trade groups. Above this were the four " Intellectual Levels," on one of which I, as a chemist had my abode. Directly above these was the " Level of Free Women," and above that the residence level for military officers. The next was the " Royal Level," double in height of the other levels of the city. Then came the " Administrative

Level," followed by eight maternity levels, then four levels of female schools and nine levels of male schools. Then, for six levels, and reaching to within five levels of the roof of the city, were soldiers' barracks. Three of the remaining floors were labelled " Swine Levels " and one " Green Gardens." Just beneath the roof was the defence level and above that the open roof itself.

It was a city of some three hundred metres in height with mineral industries at the bottom and the swine levels — I recalled the sausage — at the top. Midway between, remote from possible attack through mines or from the roof, Royalty was sheltered, while the other privileged groups of society were stratified above and below it.

Following the diagram of levels was a most informing chart arranged like a huge multiplication table. It gave after each level the words " permitted," " forbidden," and " permitted as announced," arranged in columns for each of the other levels. From this I traced out that as a chemist I was permitted on all the industrial, workmen's and intellectual levels, and on the Level of Free Women. I was permitted, as announced, on the Administrative and Royal Levels; but forbidden on the levels of military officers and soldiers' barracks, maternity and male and female schools.

I found that as a chemist I was particularly fortunate for many other groups were given even less liberty. As for common workmen and soldiers, they were permitted on no levels except their own.

The most perplexing thing about this system was the apparent segregation of such large groups of men from women. Family life in Germany was evidently wonderfully altered and seemingly greatly restricted, a condition inconsistent with the belief that I had always held — that the German race was rapidly increasing.

Turning to my atlas index I looked up the population statistics of the city, and found that by the last census it was near three hundred million. And except for the few millions in the mines this huge mass of humanity was quartered beneath a single roof. I was greatly surprised, for this population figure was more than double the usual estimates current in the outside world. Coming from a world in which the ancient tendency to congest in cities had long since been overcome, I was staggered by the fact that nearly as many people were living in this one city as existed in the whole of North America.

Yet, when I figured the floor area of the city, which was roughly oval in shape, being eight kilometres in breadth and eleven in length, I found that the population on a given floor area was no greater than it had been in the Island of Manhattan before the reform land laws were put into effect in the latter part of the Twentieth Century. There was, therefore, nothing incredible in these figures of total population, but what I next discovered was a severe strain on credence. It was the German population by sexes; the figures showed that there were nearly two and a half males for every female! According to the usual estimate of war losses the figure should have been at a ratio of six women living to about five men, and here I found them recorded as only two women to five men. Inspection of the birth rate showed an even higher proportion of males. I consulted further tables that gave births by sexes and groups. These varied somewhat but there was this great preponderance of males in every class but one. Only among the seventeen thousand members of Royalty did the proportion of the sexes approach the normal.

Apparently I had found an explanation of the careful segregation of German women — there were not enough to go around!

Turning the further pages of my atlas I came upon an elaborately illustrated directory of the uniforms and insignia of the various military and civil ranks and classes. As I had already anticipated, I found that any citizen in Berlin could immediately be placed in his proper group and rank by his clothing, which was prescribed with military exactness.

Various fabrics and shades indicated the occupational grouping while trimmings and insignia distinguished the ranks within the groups. In all there were many hundreds of distinct uniforms. Two groups alone proved exceptions to this iron clad rule; Royalty and free women were permitted to dress as they chose and were restricted only in that they were forbidden to imitate the particular uniforms of other groups.

I next investigated the contents of Armstadt's desk. My most interesting find was a checkbook, with receipts and expenditures carefully recorded on the stubs. From this I learned that, as Armstadt, I was in receipt of an income of five thousand marks, paid by the Government. I did not know how much purchasing value that would amount to, but from the account book I saw that the expenses had not equalled a third of it, which explained why there was a bank balance of some twenty thousand marks.

Clearly I would need to master the signature of Karl Armstadt so I searched among the papers until I found a bundle of returned clecks. Many of the larger checks had been made out to " Katrina," others to the " Master of Games," — evidently to cover gambling losses. The smaller checks, I found by reference to the stubs, were for ornaments or entertainment that might please a woman. The lack of the more ordinary items of expenditure was presently made clear by the discovery of a number of punch marked cards. For intermittent though necessary expenses, such as tonsorial service, clothing and books. For the more constant necessities of life, such as rent, food, laundry and transportation, there was no record whatever; and I correctly assumed that these were supplied without compensation and were therefore not a matter of personal choice or permissible variation. Of money in its ancient form of metal coins and paper, I found no evidence.

3

In my mail the next morning I found a card signed by Lieut. Forrester of the hospital staff. It read:

"The bearer, Karl Armstadt, has recently suffered from gas poisoning while defending the mines beneath enemy territory. This has affected his memory. If he is therefore found disobeying any ruling or straying beyond his permitted bounds, return him to his apartment and call the Hospital for Complex Gas Cases."

It was evidently a very kindly effort to protect a man whose loss of memory might lead him into infractions of the numerous rulings of German life. With this help I became ambitious to try the streets of Berlin alone. The notice from the tailor afforded an excuse.

Consulting my atlas to get my bearings I now ventured forth. The streets were tunnel-like passage-ways closed over with a beamed ceiling of whitish grey concrete studded with glowing light globes. In the residence districts the smooth side walls were broken only by high ventilating gratings and the narrow passage halls from which led the doors of the apartments.

The uncanny quiet of the streets of this city with its three hundred million inhabitants awed and oppressed me. Hurriedly I walked along occasionally passing men dressed like myself. They were pale men, with blanched or sallow faces. But nowhere were there faces of ruddy tan as one sees in a world of sun. The men in the hospital had been pale, but that had seemed less striking for one is used to pale faces in a hospital. It came to me with a sense of something lost that my own countenance blanched in the mine and hospital would so remain colourless like the faces of the men who now stole by me in their felted foot-wear with a cat-like tread.

At a cross street I turned and came upon a small group of shops with monotonous panelled display windows inserted in the concrete walls. Here I found my tailor and going in I promptly laid down his notice and my clothing card. He glanced casually at the papers, punched the card and then looking up he remarked that my new suit had been waiting some time. I began explaining the incident in the mine and the stay in the hospital; but the tailor was either disinterested or did not comprehend.

" Will you try on your new suit now? " he interrupted, holding forth the garments. The suit proved a trifle tight about the hips, but I hastened to assure the tailor that the fit was perfect. I removed it and watched him do it up in a parcel, open a wall closet, call my house number, and send my suit on its way through one of the numerous carriers that interlaced the city.

As I walked more leisurely back to my apartment by a less direct way, I found my analytical brain puzzling over the refreshing quality of the breezes that blew through those tunnel-like streets. With bits of paper I traced the air flow from the latticed faces of the elevator shafts to the ventilating gratings of the enclosed apartments, and concluded that there must be other shafts to the rear of the apartments for its exit. It occurred to me that it must take an enormous system of ventilating fans to keep this air in motion, and then I remembered the liquid air engine I had seen in the mine, and a realization of the economy and efficiency of the whole scheme dawned upon me. The Germans had solved the power problem by using the heat of the deeper strata of the earth to generate power through the agency of liquid air and the exhaust from their engines had automatically solved their ventilating problem. I recalled with a smile that I had seen no evidence of heating apparatus anywhere except that which the miners had used to warm their food. In this city cooling rather than heating facilities would evidently be needed, even in the dead of winter, since the heat generated by the inhabitants and the industrial processes would exceed the radiation from the exterior walls and roof of the city. Sunshine and " fresh air " they had not, but our own scientists had taught us for generations that heat and humidity and not lack of oxygen or sunshine was the cause of the depression experienced in indoor quarters. The air of Berlin was cool and the excess of vapor had been frozen out of it. Yes, the " climate " of Berlin should be more salubrious to the body, if not to the mind, than the fickle environment of capricious nature.

From my reasoning about these ponderous problems of existence I was diverted to a trivial matter. The men I observed on the streets all wore their hair clipped short, while mine, with six weeks' growth, was getting rather long.   I had seen several barber's signs but I decided to walk on for quite a distance beyond my apartment.   I did not want to confront a barber who had known Karl Armstadt, for barbers deal critically in the matter of heads and faces.   At last I picked out a shop. I entered and asked for a hair-cut.

"But you are not on my list," said the barber, staring at me in a puzzled way, "why do you not go to your own barber?"

Grasping the situation I replied that I did not like my barber.

"Then why do you not apply at the Tonsorial Administrative Office of the level for permission to change?"

Returning to my apartment I looked up the office in my directory, went thither and asked the clerk if I could exchange barbers.   He asked for my card and after a deal of clerical activities wrote thereon the name of a new barber.   With this official sanction I finally got my hair cut and my card punched, thinking meanwhile that the soundness of my teeth would obviate any amateur detective work on the part of a dentist.

Nothing, it seemed, was left for the individual to decide for himself.   His every want was supplied by orderly arrangement and for everything he must have an authoritative permit.   Had I not been classed as a research chemist, and therefore a man of some importance, this simple business of getting a hair-cut might have proved my undoing. Indeed, as I afterwards learned, the exclusive privacy of my living quarters was a mark of distinction. Had I been one of lower ranking I should have shared my apartment with another man who would have slept in my bed while I was at work, for in the sunless city was neither night nor day and the whole population worked and slept in prescribed shifts — the vast machinery of industry, like a blind giant in some Plutonic treadmill, toiled ceaselessly.

The next morning I decided to extend my travels to the medical level, which was located just above my own. There were stairs beside the elevator shafts but these were evidently for emergency as they were closed with locked gratings.

The elevator stopped at my ring. Not sure of the proper manner of calling my floor I was carried past the medical level. As we shot up through the three-hundred-metre shaft, the names of levels as I had read them in my atlas flashed by on the blind doors. On the topmost defence level we took on an officer of the roof guard —strangely swarthy of skin — and now the car shot down while the rising air rushed by us with a whistling roar.

On the return trip I called my floor as I had heard others do and was let off at the medical level. It was even more monotonously quiet than the chemical level, save for the hurrying passage of occasional ambulances on their way between the elevators and the various hospitals. The living quarters of the physicians were identical with those on the chemists' level. So, too, were the quiet shops from which the physicians supplied their personal needs.

Standing before one of these I saw in a window a new book entitled " Diseases of Nutrition." I went in and asked to see a copy. The book seller staring at my chemical uniform in amazement reached quickly under the counter and pressed a button. I became alarmed and turned to go out but found the door had been automatically closed and locked. Trying to appear unconcerned I stood idly glancing over the book shelves, while the book seller watched me from the corner of his eye.

In a few minutes the door opened from without and a man in the uniform of the street guard appeared. The book seller motioned toward me.

" Your identification folder," said the guard.

Mechanically I withdrew it and handed it to him. He opened it and discovered the card from the hospital. Smiling on me with an air of condescension, he took me by the arm and led me forth and conducted me to my own apartment on the chemical level. Arriving there he pushed me gently into a chair and stepped toward the switch of the telephone.

" Just a minute," I said, " I remember now. I was not on my level — that was not my book store."

" The card orders me to call up the hospital," said the guard.

" It is unnecessary," I said. " Do not call them."

The guard gazed first at me and then at the card. "It is signed by a Lieutenant and you are a Captain—" his brows knitted as he wrestled with the problem —"·I do not know what to do. Does a Captain with an affected memory outrank a Lieutenant?"

"He does," I solemnly assured him.

Still a little puzzled, he returned the card, saluted and was gone. It had been a narrow escape. I got out my atlas and read again the rules that set forth my right to be at large in the city. Clearly I had a right to be found in the medical level — but in trying to buy a book there I had evidently erred most seriously. So I carefully memorized the list of shops set down in my identification folder and on my cards.

For the next few days I lived alone in my apartment unmolested except by an occasional visit from Holknecht, the laboratory assistant, who knew nothing but chemistry, talked nothing but chemistry, and seemed dead to all human emotions and human curiosity. Applying myself diligently to the study of Armstadt's books and notes, I was delighted to find that the Germans, despite their great chemical progress, were ignorant of many things I knew. I saw that my knowledge discreetly used, might enable me to become a great man among them and so learn secrets that would be of immense value to the outer world, should I later contrive to escape from Berlin.

By my discoveries of the German workings in the

potash mines I had indeed opened a new road to
Berlin. It was up to me by further discoveries to
open a road out again, not only for my own escape,
but perhaps also to find a way by which the World
Armies might enter Berlin as the Greeks entered
Troy. Vague ambitious dreams were these that
filled and thrilled me, for I was young in years, and
the romantic spirit of heroic adventure surged in
my blood.

These days of study were quite uneventful, except for a single illuminating incident; a further
example of the super-efficiency of the Germans. I
found the meals served me at my apartment rather
less in quantity than my appetite craved. While
there was a reasonable variety, the nutritive value
was always the same to a point of scientific exactness,
and I had seen no shops where extra food was
available. After I had been in my apartment about
a week, some one rang at the door. I opened it
and a man called out the single word, " Weigher."
Just behind him stood a platform scale on small
wheels and with handles like a go-cart. The
weigher stood, note-book in hand, waiting for me
to act. I took the hint and stepped upon the scales.
He read the weight and as he recorded it, remarked:
" Three kilograms over."

Without further explanation he pushed the scales
toward the next door. The following day I noticed
that the portions of food served me were a trifle
smaller than they had been previously. The original Karl Armstadt had evidently been of such

build that he carried slightly less weight than I, which fact now condemned me to this light diet.

However, I reasoned that a light diet is conducive to good brain work, and as I later learned, the object of this systematic weight control was not alone to save food but to increase mental efficiency, for a fat man is phlegmatic and a lean one too excitable for the best mental output. It would also help my disguise by keeping me the exact weight and build of the original Karl Armstadt.

After a fortnight of study, I felt that I was now ready to take up my work in the laboratory, but I feared my lack of general knowledge of the city and its ways might still betray me. Hence I began further journeyings about the streets and shops of those levels where a man of my class was permitted to go.

4

After exhausting the rather barren sport of walking about the monotonous streets of the four professional levels I took a more exciting trip down into the lower levels of the city where the vast mechanical industries held sway. I did not know how much freedom might be allowed me, but I reasoned that I would be out of my supposed normal environment and hence my ignorance would be more excusable and in less danger of betraying me.

Alighting from the elevator, I hurried along past endless rows of heavy columns. I peered into the workrooms, which had no enclosing walls, and discovered with some misgiving that I seemed to have come upon a race of giants. The men at the machines were great hulking fellows with thick, heavy muscles such as one would expect to see in a professional wrestler or weight-lifter. I paused and tried to gauge the size of these men: I decided that they were not giants for I had seen taller men in the outer world. Two officials of some sort, distinguishable by finer garb, walking among them, appeared to be men of average size, and the tops of their heads came about to the workers' chins. That there should be such men among the Germans was not unbelievable, but the strange thing was that there should be so many of them, and that they should be so uniformly large, for there was not a workman in the whole vast factory floor that did not over-top the officials by at least half a head.

" Of course," I reasoned, " this is part of German efficiency "; — for the men were feeding large plates through stamping mills —" they have selected all the large men for this heavy work." Then as I continued to gaze it occurred to me that this bright metal these Samsons were handling was aluminum!

I went on and came to a different work hall where men were tending wire winding machinery, making the coils for some light electrical instruments. It was work that girls could easily have done, yet these men were nearly, if not quite, as hulking as their mates in the stamping mill. To select such men for light-fingered work was not

efficiency but stupidity,— and then it came to me
that I had also thought the soldiers I had seen in
the hospital to be men picked for size, and that in
a normal population there could not be such an
abundance of men of abnormal size. The meaning
of it all began to clear in my mind — the pedigree
in my own identification folder with the numerous
fraternity, the system of social castes which my atlas
had revealed, the inexplicable and unnatural proportion of the sexes. These gigantic men were not
the mere pick from individual variation in the
species, but a distinct breed within a race wherein
the laws of nature, that had kept men of equal
stature for countless centuries, even as wild animals
were equal, had been replaced by the laws of scientific breeding. These heavy and ponderous labourers were the Percherons and Clydesdales of a domesticated and scientifically bred human species. The
soldiers, somewhat less bulky and more active, were,
no doubt, another distinct breed. The professional
classes which had seemed quite normal in physical
appearance — were they bred for mental rather
than physical qualities? Otherwise why the pedigree, why the rigid castes, the isolation of women?
I shuddered as the whole logical, inevitable explanation unfolded. It was uncanny, unearthly, yet perfectly scientific; a thing the world had speculated
about for centuries, a thing that every school boy
knew could be done, and yet which I, facing the fact
that it had been done, could only believe by a
strained effort at scientific coolness.

I walked on and on, absorbed, overwhelmed by these assaulting, unbelievable conclusions, yet on either side as I walked was the ever present evidence of the reality of these seemingly wild fancies. There were miles upon miles of these endless workrooms and everywhere the same gross breed of great blond beasts.

The endless shops of Berlin's industrial level were very like those elsewhere in the world, except that they were more vast, more concentrated, and the work more speeded up by super-machines and excessive specialization. Millions upon millions of huge, drab-clad, stolid-faced workmen stood at their posts of duty, performing over and over again their routine movements as the material of their labors shuttled by in endless streams.

Occasionally among the workmen I saw the uniforms of the petty officers who acted as foremen, and still more rarely the administrative offices, where, enclosed in glass panelled rooms, higher officials in more bespangled uniforms poured over charts and plans.

In all this colossal business there was everywhere the atmosphere of perfect order, perfect system, perfect discipline. Go as I might among the electrical works, among the vast factories of chemicals and goods, the lighter labor of the textile mills, or the heavier, noisier business of the mineral works and machine shops the same system of colossal coordinate mechanism of production throbbed ceaselessly. Materials flowed in endless streams, feeding electric furnaces, mills, machines; passing out to packing tables and thence to vast store rooms. Industry here seemed endless and perfect. The bovine humanity fitted to the machinery as the ox to the treadmill. Everywhere was the ceaseless throbbing of the machine. Of the human variation and the free action of man in labour, there was no evidence, and no opportunity for its existence.

Turning from the mere monotonous endlessness of the workshops I made my way to the levels above where the workers lived in those hours when they ceased to be a part of the industrial mechanism of production; and everywhere were drab-coloured men for these shifts of labour were arranged so that no space at any time was wholly idle. I now passed by miles of sleeping dormitories, and other miles of gymnasiums, picture theatres and gaming tables, and, strikingly incongruous with the atmosphere of the place, huge assembly rooms which were labelled " Free Speech Halls." I started to enter one of these, where some kind of a meeting was in progress, but I was thrust back by a great fellow who grinned foolishly and said: " Pardon, Herr Captain, it is forbidden you."

Through half-darkened streets, I again passed by the bunk-shelved sleeping chambers with their cavernous aisles walled with orderly rows of lockers. Again I came to other barracks where the men were not yet asleep but were straggling in and sitting about on the lowest bunks of these sterile makeshift homes.

I then came into a district of mess halls where a meal was being served. Here again was absolute economy and perfect system. The men dined at endless tables and their food like the material for their labours, was served to the workers by the highly efficient device of an endless moving belt that rolled up out of a slot in the floor at the end of the table after the manner of the chained steps of an escalator.

From the moving belts the men took their portions, and, as they finished eating, they cleared away by setting the empty dishes back upon the moving belt. The sight fascinated me, because of the adaptation of this mechanical principle to so strange a use, for the principle is old and, as every engineer knows, was instrumental in founding the house of Detroit Vehicle Kings that once dominated the industrial world. The founder of that illustrious line gave the poorest citizen a motor car and disrupted the wage system of his day by paying his men double the standard wage, yet he failed to realize the full possibilities of efficiency for he permitted his men to eat at round tables and be served by women! Truly we of the free world very narrowly escaped the fetish of efficiency which finally completely enslaved the Germans.

Each of the long tables of this Berlin dining hall, the ends of which faced me, was fenced off from its neighbours. At the entrance gates were signs which read " 2600 Calories," " 2800 Calories," " 3000 Calories "— I followed down the line to the sign which read " Maximum Diet, 4000 Calories." The next one read, " Minimum Diet 2000 Calories," and thence the series was repeated. Farther on I saw that men were assembling before such gates in lines, for the meal there had not begun. Moving to the other side of the street I walked by the lines which curved out and swung down the street. Those before the sign of " Minimum Diet " were not quite so tall as the average, although obviously of the same breed. But they were all gaunt, many of them drooped and old, relatively the inferior specimens and their faces bore a cowering look of fear and shame, of men sullen and dull, beaten in life's battle. Following down the line and noting the improvement in physique as I passed on, I came to the farthest group just as they had begun to pass into the hall. These men, entering the gate labelled " Maximum Diet, 4000 Calories," were obviously the pick of the breed, middle-aged, powerful, Herculean,— and yet not exactly Herculean either, for many of them were overfull of waistline, men better fed than is absolutely essential to physical fitness. Evidently a different principle was at work here than the strict economy of food that required the periodic weighing of the professional classes.

Turning back I now encountered men coming out of the dining hall in which I had first witnessed the meal in progress. I wanted to ask questions and yet was a little afraid. But these big fellows were seemingly quite respectful; except when I started to enter the Free Speech Hall, they had humbly made

way for me.   Emboldened by their deference I now
approached a man whom I had seen come out of a
" 3800 Calories " gate, and who had crossed the
street and stood there picking his teeth with his finger nail.

He ceased this operation as I approached and was
about to step aside.   But I paused and smiled at
him, much, I fear, as one smiles at a dog of unknown
disposition, for I could hardly feel that this ungainly
creature was exactly human.   He smiled back and
stood waiting.

" Perhaps, I stammered, " you will tell me about
your system of eating; it seems very interesting."

" I eat thirty-eight," he grinned, " pretty good,
yes?   I am twenty-five years old and not so tall
either."

I eyed him up — my eyes came just to the top
button of his jacket.

" I began thirty," continued the workman, " I
came up one almost every year, one year I came up
two at once.   Pretty good, yes?   One more to
come."

" What then? " I asked.

The big fellow smiled with a childish pride, and
doubling up his arm, as huge as an average man's
thigh, he patted his biceps.   " I get it all right.   I
pass examination, no flaws in me, never been to
hospital, not one day.   Yes, I get it."

" Get what? "

" Paternity," said the man in a lower voice, as
he glanced about to see if any of his fellows was

listening. " Paternity, you know? Women!"
I thought of many questions but feared to ask
them. The worker waited for some men to pass,
then he bent over me, grinning sardonically. " Did
you see them? You have seen women, yes?"
" Yes," I ventured, " I have seen women."
" Pretty good, beautiful, yes?"
" Yes," I stammered, " they are very beautiful."
But I was getting nervous and moved away. The
workman, hesitating a little, then followed at my
side.

" But tell me," I said, " about these calories.
What did you do to get the big meals? Why do
some get more to eat than others?"

" Better man," he replied without hesitation.

" But what makes a better man?"

" You don't know; of course, you are an intellectual and don't work. But we work hard. The
harder we work the more we eat. I load aluminum
pigs on the elevator. One pig is two calories, nineteen hundred pigs a day, pretty good, yes? All
kind of work has its calories, so many for each thing
to do.

" More work, more food it takes to do it. They
say all is alike, that no one can get fat. But all
work calories are not alike because some men get
fatter than others. I don't get fat; my work is
hard. I ought to get two and a half calories for
each pig I load. Still I do not get thin, but I do not
play hard in gymnasium, see? Those lathe men,
they got it too easy and they play hard in gymna-

sium. I don't care if you do report. I got it mad at them; they got it too easy. One got paternity last year already, and he is not as good a man as I am. I could throw him over my shoulder in wrestling. Do you not think they get it too easy?"

"Do the men like this system," I asked; "the measuring of food by the amount of work one does? Do any of them talk about it and demand that all be fed alike?"

"The skinny minimum eaters do," said the workman with a sneer," when we let them talk, which isn't often, but when they get a chance they talk Bellamism. But what if they do talk, it does them no good. We have a red flag, we have Imperial Socialism; we have the House of Hohenzollern. Well, then, I say, let them talk if they want to, every man must eat according to his work; that is socialism. We can't have Bellamism when we have socialism."

This speech, so much more informative and evidencing a knowledge I had not anticipated, quite disturbed me. "You talk about these things," I ventured, "in your Free Speech Halls?"

The hitherto pleasant face of the workingman altered to an ugly frown.

"No you don't," he growled, "you don't think because I talk to you, that you can go asking me what is not your right to know, even if you are an officer?"

I remained discreetly silent, but continued to walk

at the side of the striding giant.   Presently I asked:
" What do you do now, are you going to work? "
" No," he said, looking at me doubtfully, " that
was dinner, not breakfast.   I am going now to the
picture hall."
" And then," I asked, " do you go to bed? "
" No," he said, " we then go to the gymnasium
or the gaming tables.   Six hours' work, six hours'
sleep, and four hours for amusement."
" And what do you do," I asked, " the remainder
of the day? "
He turned and stared at me.   " That is all we
get here, sixteen hours.   This is the metal workers'
level.   Some levels get twenty hours.   It depends
on the work."
" But," I said, " a real day has twenty-four
hours."
" I've heard," he said, " that it does on the upper
levels."
" But," I protested, " I mean a real day — a day
of the sun.   Do you understand that? "
" Oh yes," he said, " we see the pictures of the
Place in the Sun.   That's a fine show."
" Oh," I said, " then you have pictures of the
sun? "
" Of course," he replied, " the sun that shines
upon the throne.   We all see that."
At the time I could not comprehend this refer-
ence, but I made bold to ask if it were forbidden
me to go to his picture hall.
" I can't make out," he said, " why you want to

see, but I never heard of any order forbidding it.

"I go here," he remarked, as we came to a picture theatre.

I let my Herculean companion enter alone, but followed him shortly and found a seat in a secluded corner. No one disputed my presence.

The music that filled the hall from some hidden horn was loud and, in a rough way, joyous. The pictures — evidently carefully prepared for such an audience — were limited to the life that these men knew. The themes were chiefly of athletic contests, of boxing, wrestling and feats of strength. There were also pictures of working contests, always ending by the awarding of honours by some much bespangled official. But of love and romance, of intrigue and adventure, of pathos and mirth, these pictures were strangely devoid,— there was, in fact, no woman's likeness cast upon the screen and no pictures depicting emotion or sentiment.

As I watched the sterile flittings of the picture screen I decided, despite the glimmering of intelligence that my talking Hercules had shown in reference to socialism and Bellamism and the secrets of the Free Speech Halls, that these men were merely great stupid beasts of burden.

They worked, they fed, they drank, they played exuberantly in their gymnasiums and swimming pools, they played long and eagerly at games of chance. Beyond this their lives were essentially blank. Ambition and curiosity they had none beyond the narrow circle of their round of living.

But for all that they were docile, contented and, within their limitations, not unhappy. To me they seemed more and more to b; like well cared for domestic animals, and I found myself wondering, as I left the hall, why we of the outer world had not thought to produce pictures in similar vein to entertain our dogs and horses.

5

As I returned to my own quarters, I tried to recall the description I had read of the " Children of the Abyss," the dwellers in ancient city slums. There was a certain kinship, no doubt, between those former submerged workers in the democratic world and this labour breed of Berlin. Yet the enslaved and sweated workers of the old régime were always depicted as suffering from poverty, as undersized, ill-nourished and afflicted with disease. The reformers of that day were always talking of sanitary housing, scientific diet and physical efficiency. But here was a race of labourers whose physical welfare was as well taken care of as if they had been prize swine or oxen. There was a paleness of countenance among these labourers of Berlin that to me seemed suggestive of ill health, but I knew that was merely due to lack of sun and did not signify a lack of physical vitality. Mere sun-darkened skin does not mean physiological efficiency, else the negro were the most efficient of races. Men can live without sun, without rain, without contact with the soil, without nature's greenery and the brotherhood of fellow species in wild haunts. The whole climb of civilization had been away from these primitive things. It had merely been an artificial perfecting of the process of giving the living creature that which is needed for sustenance and propagation in the most concentrated and most economical form, the elimination of Nature's superfluities and wastes.

As I thought of these things it came over me that this unholy imprisonment of a race was but the logical culmination of mechanical and material civilization. This development among the Germans had been hastened by the necessities of war and siege, yet it was what the whole world had been driving toward since man first used a tool and built a hut. Our own freer civilization of the outer world had been achieved only by compromises, by a stubborn resistance against the forces to which we ascribed our progress. We were merely not so completely civilized, because we had never been wholly domesticated.

As I now record these thoughts on the true significance of the perfected civilization of the Germans I realize that I was even more right than I then knew, for the sunless city of Berlin is of a truth a civilization gone to seed, its people are a domesticated species, they are the logical outcome of science applied to human affairs, with them the prodigality and waste of Nature have been eliminated, they have stamped out contagious diseases of every kind, they have substituted for the laws of Nature the laws that man may pick by scientific theory and experiment from the multitude of possibilities. Yes, the Germans were civilized. And as I pondered these things I recalled those fairy tales that naturalists tell of the stagnant and fixed society of ants in their subterranean catacombs. These insect species credited for industry and intelligence, have in their lesser world reached a similar perfection of civilization. Ants have a royal house, they have a highly specialized and fixed system of caste, a completely socialized state — yes, a Utopia — even as Berlin was a Utopia, with the light of the sun and the light of the soul, the soul of the wild free man, forever shut out. Yes, I was walking in Utopia, a nightmare at the end of man's long dream — Utopia — Black Utopia — City of Endless Night — diabolically compounded of the three elements of civilization in which the Germans had always been supreme — imperialism, science and socialism.

CHAPTER IV

I GO PLEASURING ON THE LEVEL OF FREE WOMEN AND DRINK SYNTHETIC BEER

I

I HAD returned from my adventure on the labour levels in a mood of sombre depression. Alone again in my apartment I found difficulty in getting my mind back upon chemical books. With a sense of relief I reported to Holknecht that I thought myself sufficiently recovered to return to work.

My laboratory I found to be almost as secluded as my living quarters. I was master there, and as a research worker I reported to no man until I had finished the problem assigned me. From my readings and from Holknecht's endless talking I had fairly well grasped the problem on which I was supposed to be working, and I now had Holknecht go carefully over the work he had done in my absence and we prepared a report. This I sent to headquarters with a request for permission to start work on another problem, the idea for which I claimed to have conceived on my visit to the attacked potash mines.

Permission to undertake the new problem was promptly granted. I now set to work to reproduce in a German laboratory the experiments by which I had originally conquered the German gas that had successfully defended those mines from the world for over a century. Though loath to make this revelation, I knew of no other " Discovery " wherewith to gain the stakes for which I was playing.

Events shaped themselves most rapidly along the lines of my best hopes. The new research proved a blanket behind which to hide my ignorance. We needed new material, new apparatus, and new data and I encouraged Holknecht to advise me as to where to obtain these things and so gained requisite working knowledge.

The experiments and demonstrations finished, I made my report. My immediate superior evidently quickly recognized it as a matter too important for his consideration and dutifully passed it up to his own superiors. In a few days I was notified to prepare for a demonstration before a committee of the Imperial Chemical Staff.

They came to my small laboratory with much eager curiosity. From their manner of making themselves known to me I realized with joy that they were dealing with a stranger. Indeed it was improbable that it should have been otherwise for there were upwards of fifty thousand chemists of my rank in Berlin.

The demonstration went off with a flourish and the committee were greatly impressed. Means were at once taken to alter the gas with which the Stassfurt mines were flooded, but I realized that meant nothing since I believed that my companions had abandoned the enterprise and the secret that had enabled me to invade mines had not been shared with any one in the outer world.

As I anticipated, my revelation was accepted by the Chemical Staff as evidence of profound scientific genius. It followed as a logical matter that I should be promoted to the highest rank of research chemists with the title of Colonel. Because of my youth the more was made of the honour. This promotion entitled me to double my previous salary, to a larger laboratory and larger and better living quarters in a distant part of the city.

My assistant would now be of the rank I had previously been and as Holknecht was not eligible to such promotion I was removed entirely from all previous acquaintances and surroundings and so greatly decreased the chance of discovery of my true identity.

2

After I had removed to my new quarters I was requested to call at the office of the Chemical Staff to discuss the line of research I should next take up. My adviser in this matter was the venerable Herr von Uhl, a white haired old patriarch whose jacket was a mass of decorations. The insignia on the left breast indicating the achievements in chemical science were already familiar to me, but those on the right breast were strange.

Perhaps I stared at them a little, for the old

man, noting my interest, remarked proudly, " Yes, I have contributed much glory to the race and our group,— one hundred and forty-seven children,— one hundred and four of them sons, fifty-eight already of a captain's rank, and twenty-nine of them colonels — my children of the second and third generation number above two thousand. Only three men living in Berlin have more total descendants — and I am but seventy-eight years of age. If I live to be ninety I shall break all records of the Eugenic Office. It all comes of good breeding and good work. I won my paternity right, when I was but twenty-eight, just about your age. If you pass the physical test, perhaps you can duplicate my record. For this early promotion you have won qualifies you mentally."

Astonished and alarmed beyond measure I could find no reply and sat staring dumbly, while Herr von Uhl, beginning to speak of chemical matters, inquired if I had any preference as to the problem I should now take up. Incapable of any clear thinking I could only ask if he had any to suggest.

Immediately the old man's face brightened. " A man of your genius," he said, " should be permitted to try his brain with the greatest problems on which the life of Germany depends. The Staff discussed this and has assigned you to original research for the finding of a better method of the extraction of protium from the ore. To work on this assignment you must of necessity share grave secrets, which, should they be disclosed, might create profound fears, but your professional honour is a sufficient guarantee of secrecy. In this research you will compete with some of the most distinguished chemists in Berlin. If you should be successful you will be decorated by His Majesty and you will receive a liberal pension commensurate with the value of your discovery."

I was profoundly impressed. Evidently I had stumbled upon something of vital importance, the real nature of which I did not in the least comprehend, and happily was not supposed to. The interview was ended by my being entrusted with voluminous unpublished documents which I was told to take home and study. Two armed men were ordered to accompany me and to stand alternate guard outside my apartment while I had the documents in my possession.

3

In the quiet of my new abode I unsealed the package. The first sheet contained the official offer of the rewards in store for success with the research. The further papers explained the occasion for the gravity and secrecy, and outlined the problem.

The colossal consequence of the matter with which I was dealing gripped and thrilled me. Protium, it seemed, was the German name for a rare element of the radium group, which, from its atomic weight and other properties, I recognized as being known to the outside world only as a laboratory curiosity of no industrial significance.

But, as used by the Germans, this element was the essence of life itself, for by the influence of its emanations, they had achieved the synthesis of protein capable of completely nourishing the human body — a thing that could be accomplished in the outside world only through the aid of natural protein derived from plants and animals.

How I wished, as I read, that my uncle could have shared with me this revelation of a secret that he had spent his life in a fruitless effort to unravel. We had long since discovered how the Germans had synthesized the carbohydrate molecule from carbon dioxide and water and built therefrom the sugars, starches and fat needed for human nutrition. We knew quite as well how they had created the simpler nitrogen compounds, that this last step of synthesizing complete food proteins — a step absolutely essential to the support of human life wholly from synthetic foods — the chemists of the outer world had never mastered.

But no less interesting than the mere chemistry of all this was the history of it all, and the light it threw on the larger story of how Germany had survived when the scientists of the world had predicted her speedy annihiliation. The original use of protium had, I found, been discovered late in the Twentieth Century when the protium ores of the Ural Mountains were still available to the German

chemists.   After Russia had been won by the World
Armies, the Germans for a time suffered chronic
nitrogen starvation, as they depended on the protium derived from what remained of their agriculture and from the fisheries in the Baltic.   As the
increasing bombardment from the air herded them
within their fast building armoured city, and drove
them beneath the soil in all other German territory
and from the surface of the sea in the Baltic; they
must have perished miserably but for the discovery
of a new source of protium.

This source they had found in the uninhabited
islands of the Arctic, where the formation of the
Ural Mountains extends beneath the sea.   Sending
their submarines thence in search of platinum ores
they had not found platinum but a limited supply
of ore containing the even more valuable protium.   By this traffic Germany had survived for a
century and a half.   The quantity of the rare element needed was small, for its effect, like that of
radium, was out of all proportion to its bulk.   But
this little they must have, and it seems that the supply of ore was failing.

Nor was that all to interest me.   How did the
German submarine get to the Arctic since the World
State had succeeded, after half a century of effort,
in damming the Baltic by closing up several passes
among the Danish Islands and the main pass of
the sound between Zealand and Sweden?   I remember, as a youngster, the great Jubilee that celebrated
the completion of that monumental task, and the

joy that hailed from the announcement that the world's shipping would at last be freed from an ancient scourge.

But little had we of the world known the magnitude of the German fears as the Baltic dam neared completion. We had thought merely to protect our commerce from German piracy and perhaps to stop them from getting a little copper and rubber in some remote corner of the earth. But we did not realize that we were about to cut them off from an essential element without which that conceited and defiant race must have speedily run up the white flag of absolute surrender or have died to the last man, like rats in a neglected trap.

But the completion of the Baltic dam evidently had not shut off the supply of Arctic ore, for the annual importation of ore was given right up to date though the Baltic had been closed for nearly a score of years. Eagerly I searched my papers for an item that would give some hint as to how the submarines got out of the dammed-up Baltic. But on that point the documents before me were silent. They referred to the Arctic ore, gave elaborate details as to mineralogy and geology of the strata from which it came, but as to the ways of its coming into Berlin there was not the slightest suggestion. That this ore must come by submarine was obvious. If so, the submarine must be at large in the Atlantic and Arctic seas, and those occasional reports of periscopes sighted off the coast of Norway, which have never been credited, were really true. The

submarines, or at least their cargoes, must reach
Berlin by some secret passage. Here indeed was a
master mystery, a secret which, could I unravel it
and escape to the outer world with the knowledge,
would put unconditionally within the power of the
World State the very life of the three hundred millions of this unholy race that was bred and fed by
science in the armoured City of Berlin, or that, working like blind moles of the earth, held the world at
bay from off the sterile and pock-marked soil of all
that was left of the one-time German Empire.

That night I did not sleep till near the waking
hour, and when the breakfast container bumped into
the receiving cupboard I was nodding over the chemical papers amid strange and wonderful dreams.

4

Next day with three assistants, themselves chemists of no mean rank, I set to work to prepare apparatus for repeating all the known processes in
the extraction and use of the rare and vital element.
This work absorbed me for many weeks, during
which time I went nowhere and saw no one and slept
scarce one hour out of four.

But the steady application told upon me, and, by
way of recreation, I decided to spend an evening
on the Level of Free Women, a place to which, much
though it fascinated me, I had not yet mustered the
courage to go.

My impression, as I stepped from the elevator,
was much as that of a man who alights from a train

in a strange city on a carnival night.   Before me, instead of the narrow, quiet streets of the working and living quarters of the city, there spread a broad and seemingly endless hall of revelry, broken only by the massive grey pillars that held up the multi-floored city.   The place was thronged with men of varied ranks and professions.   But more numerous and conspicuous were the women, the first and only women that I had seen among the Germans — the Free Women of Berlin, dressed in gorgeous and daring costumes; women of whom but few were beautiful, yet in whose tinted cheeks and sparkling eyes was all the lure of parasitic love.

The multi-hued apparel of the throng dazzled and astonished me.   Elsewhere I had found a sterile monotony of dress and even of stature and features. But here was resplendent variety and display.   Men from all the professional and military classes mingled indiscriminately, their divers uniforms and decorations suggesting a dress ball in the capital of the world.   But the motley costumes of the women, who dressed with the license of unrestrained individuality, were even more startling and bizarre — a kaleidoscopic fantastic masquerade.

I wondered if the rule of convention and tyranny of style had lost all hold upon these women.   And yet I decided, as I watched more closely, that there was not an absence of style but rather a warfare of styles.   The costumes varied from the veiled and beruffled displays, that left one confounded as to what manner of creature dwelt therein, to the other extreme of mere gaudily ornamented nudity. I smiled as I recalled the world-old argument on the relative modesty of much or little clothing, for here immodesty was competing side by side in both extremes, both seemingly equally successful.

But it was not alone in the matter of dress that the women of the Free Level varied. They differed even more strikingly in form and feature, for, as I was later more fully to comprehend, these women were drawn from all the artificially specialized breeds into which German science had wrought the human species. Most striking and most numerous were those whom I rightly guessed to be of the labour strain. Proportionally not quite so large as the males of the breed, yet they were huge, full-formed, fleshly creatures, with milky white skin for the most part crudely painted with splashes of vermilion and with blued or blackened brows. The garishness of their dress and ornament clearly bespoke the poorer quality of their intellect, yet to my disgust they seemed fully as popular with the men as the smaller and more refined types, evidently from the intellectual strains of the race.

Happily these ungainly women of the labour strain were inclined to herd by themselves and I hastened to direct my steps to avoid as much as possible their overwhelming presence.

The smaller women, who seemed to be more nearly human, were even more variegated in their features and make-up. They were not all blondes, for some of them were distinctively dark of hair and skin, though I was puzzled to tell how much of this was inborn and how much the work of art. Another thing that astonished me was the wide range of bodily form, as evidently determined by nutrition. Clearly there was no weight-control here, for the figures varied from extreme slenderness to waddling fatness. The most common type was that of mild obesity which men call " plumpness," a quality so prized since the world began that the women of all races by natural selection become relatively fatter than men.

For the most part I found these women unattractive and even repellent, and yet as I walked about the level I occasionally caught fleeting glimpses of genuine beauty of face and form, and more rarely expressions of a seeming high order of intelligence.

This revelling multitude of men and girls was uproariously engaged in the obvious business of enjoying themselves by means of every art known to appeal to the mind of man — when intelligence is abandoned and moral restraint thrown to the winds.

I wended my way among the multitude, gay with colour, noisy with chatter and mingled music, redolent with a hundred varieties of sensuous perfume. I came upon a dancing floor. Whirling and twisting about the columns, circling around a gorgeous scented and iridescent fountain, officers and scientists, chemists and physicians, each clasping in his arms a laughing girl, danced with abandon to languorous music.

As I watched the dance I overheard two girls

commenting upon the appearance of the dancers. Whirling by in the arms of a be-medalled officer, was a girl whose frizzled yellow hair fell about a dun-brown face.

" Did you see that, Fedora, tanned as a roof guard and with that hair! "

" Well, you know," said the other, " it's becoming quite the fashion again."

" Why don't you try it? Three baths would tan you adorably and you do have the proper hair."

" Oh, yes, I have the hair, all right, but my skin won't stand it. I tried it three years ago and I blistered outrageously."

The talk drifted to less informing topics and I moved on and came to other groups lounging at their ease on rugs and divans as they watched more skilful girls squirming through some intricate ballet on an exhibition platform.

Seeing me stand apart, a milk-white girl with hair dyed pink came tugging at my arm. Her opalescent eyes looked from out her chalky countenance; but they were not hard eyes, indeed they seemed the eyes of innocence. As I shook my head and rebuffed her cordial advance I felt, not that I was refusing the proffered love of a painted woman, but rather that I was meanly declining a child's invitation to join her play. In haste I edged away and wandered on past endless gaming tables where men in feverish eagerness whirled wheels of chance, while garishly dressed girls leaned on their shoulders and hung about their necks.

Announced by shouts and shrieking laughter I came upon a noisy jumble of mechanical amusement devices where men and girls in whirling upholstered boxes were being pitched and tumbled about.

Beyond the noise of the childish whirligigs I came into a space where the white ceiling lights were dimmed by crimson globes and picture screens were in operation. It did not take long for me to grasp the essential difference between these pictured stories and those I had seen in the workmen's level. There love of woman was entirely absent from the screen. Here it was the sole substance of the pictures. But unlike the love romances of the outer world, there were no engagement rings, no wedding bells, and never once did the face or form of a child appear.

In seating myself to see the pictures I had carefully chosen a place where there was only room for myself between a man and one of the supporting columns. At an interlude the man arose to go. The girl who had been with him arose also, but he pushed her back upon the bench, saying that he had other engagements, and did not wish her company. The moment he was gone the girl moved over and proceeded to crowd caressingly against my shoulder. She was a huge girl, obviously of the labour strain. She leaned over me as if I had been a lonely child and she a lonelier woman. Crowded against the pillar I could not escape and so tried to appear unconcerned.

" Did you like that story ? " I asked, referring to the picture that had just ended.

" No," she replied, " the girl was too timid. She could never have won a roof guard captain in that fashion. They are very difficult men, those roof guard officers."

" And what kind of pictures do you prefer? " I asked.

" Quartettes," she answered promptly. " Two men and two girls when both girls want the other man, and both men want the girl they have. That makes a jolly plot. Or else the ones where there are two perfect lovers and the man is elected to paternity and leaves her. I had a man like that once and it makes me sad to see such a picture."

" Perhaps," I said, speaking in a timorous voice, " you wanted to go with him and be the mother of his children? "

She turned her face toward me in the dim light. " He talked like that," she said, " and then, I hated him. I knew then that he wanted to go and leave me. That he hadn't tried to avoid the paternity draft. Yes, he wanted to sire children. And he knew that he would have to leave me. And so I hated him for ever loving me."

A strange thrill crept over me at the girl's words. I tried to fathom her nature, to separate the tangle of reality from the artificial ideas ingrained by deliberate mis-education. " Did you ever see children? Here, I mean. Pictures of them, perhaps, on the screen? "

" Never," said the girl, drawing away from me and straightening up till my head scarce reached her shoulder. "And I never want to. I hate the thought of them. I wish I never had been one. Why can't we — forget them?"

I did not answer, and the labour girl, who, for some technical flaw in her physique had been rejected for motherhood, arose and walked ponderously away.

After this baffling revelation of the struggle of human souls caught in the maw of machine-made science, I found the picture screen a dull dead thing, and I left the hall and wandered for miles, it seemed, past endless confusion of meaningless revelry. Everywhere was music and gaming and laughter. Men and girls lounged and danced, or spun the wheels of fortune or sat at tables drinking from massive steins, a highly flavoured variety of rather ineffectual synthetic beer. Older women served and waited on the men and girls, and for every man was at least one girl and sometimes as many as could crowd about him. And so they sang, and banged their mugs and sloshed their frothy beverage.

A lonely stranger amidst the jostling throngs, I wandered on through the carnival of Berlin's Level of Free Women. Despite my longing for human companionship I found it difficult to join in this strange recrudescent paganism with any ease or grace.

Girls, alone or in groups, fluttered about me with many a covert or open invitation to join in their merry-making, but something in my halting manner and constrained speech seemed to repulse them, for they would soon turn away as if condemning me as a man without appreciation of the value of human enjoyment.

My constraint and embarrassment were increased by a certain sense of guilt, a feeling which no one in this vast throng, either man or woman, seemed to share. The place had its own standard of ethics, and they were shocking enough to a man nurtured in a human society founded on the sanctification of monogamous marriage. But merely to condemn this recreational life of Germany, by likening it to the licentious freedom that exists in occasional unrestrained amusement places in the outer world, would be to give a very incorrect interpretation of Berlin's Level of Free Women. As we know such places elsewhere in the world there is always about them some tacit confession of moral delinquency, some pretence of apology on the part of the participants. The women who so revel in the outer world consider themselves under a ban of social disapproval, while the men are either of a type who have no sense of moral restraint or men who have for the time abandoned it.

But for this life in Berlin no guilt was felt, no apology offered. The men considered it as quite a normal and proper part of their life, while the women looked upon it as their whole life, to which they had been trained and educated and set apart by the Government; they accepted the rôle quite as did the scientist, labourer, soldier, or professional mother.   The state had decreed it to be.   They did not question its morality.   Hence the life here was licentious and yet unashamed, much, as I fancy was the life in the groves of Athens or the baths of ancient Rome.

CHAPTER V

I

MY research was progressing nicely and I had discovered that in this field of chemistry also my knowledge of the outer world would give me tremendous advantages over all competitors. Eagerly I worked at the laboratory, spending most of my evenings in study. Occasionally I attended the educational pictures or dined on the Level of Free Women with my chemical associates and spent an hour or so at dancing or at cards.

My life had settled into routine unbroken by adventure. Then I received a notice to report for the annual examination at the Physical Efficiency Laboratory. I went with some misgivings, but the ordeal proved uneventful. A week later I received a most disturbing communication, a bulky and official looking packet bearing the imprint of the Eugenic Office. I nervously slit the envelope and drew forth a letter:

" You are hereby notified that you have reached a stage of advancement in your professional work that marks you a man of superior gifts, and, having been reported as physically perfect you are hereby honoured with the high privilege and sacred duties of election to paternity. Full instructions for your conduct in this duty to the State will be found in the enclosed folder."

In nervous haste I scanned the printed folder:

"Your first duty will be to visit the boys' school for which passport is here enclosed. The purpose of this is to awaken the paternal instincts that you may better appreciate and feel the holy obligation and privilege conferred upon you. You will also find enclosed cards of introduction to three women whom the Eugenic Office finds to be fitted as mothers of your children. That natural selection may have a limited play you are permitted to select only one woman from each three assigned. Such selection must be made and reported within thirty days, after which a second trio will be assigned you. Until such final selection has been recorded you are expressly forbidden to conduct yourself toward these women in an amorous manner."

Next followed a set of exacting rules for the proper deportment, in the carrying out of these duties to which the State had assigned me.

A crushing sense of revulsion, a feeling of loathing and uncleanliness overwhelmed me as I pushed aside the papers. Coming from a world where the right of the individual to freedom and privacy in the matrimonial and paternal relations was recognized as a fundamental right of man, I found this officious communication, with its detailed instruction, appalling and revolting.

A man cravenly clings to life and yet there are instincts in his soul which will cause him to sell life defiantly for a mere conception of a moral principle. To become by official mandate a father of a numerous German progeny was a thing to which I could not and would not submit. Many times that day as I automatically pursued my work, I resolved to go to some one in authority and give myself up to be sent to the mines as a prisoner of war, or more likely to be executed as a spy. Cold reason showed me the futility of neglecting or attempting to avoid an assigned duty. It was a military civilization and I had already seen enough of this ordered life of Berlin to know that there was no middle ground of choice between explicit obedience and open rebellion. Nor need I concern myself with what punishment might be provided for this particular disobedience for I saw that rebellion for me would mean an investigation that would result in complete tearing away of the protecting mask of my German identity.

But after my first tumultuous feeling subsided I realized that something more than my own life was at stake. Already possessed of much intimate knowledge of the life within Berlin I believed that I was in a way to come into possession of secrets of vast and vital importance to the world. To gain these secrets, to escape from the walls of Berlin, was a more than personal ambition; it was an ambition for mankind.

After a day or two of deliberation I therefore decided against any rash rebellion. Moreover, as nothing compromising was immediately required of me, I detached and mailed the four coupons provided, having duly filled in the time at which I should make the preliminary calls.

2

On the day and hour appointed I presented the school card to the elevator operator, who punched it after the manner of his kind, and duly deposited me on the level of schools for boys of the professional groups. A lad of about sixteen met me at the elevator and conducted me to the school designated.

The master greeted me with obsequious gravity, and waved me to the visitor's seat on a raised platform. " You will be asked to speak," he said, " and I beg that you will tell the boys of the wonderful chemical discoveries that won you the honours of election to paternity."

" But," I protested, as I glanced at the boys who were being put through their morning drill in the gymnasium, " I fear the boys of such age will not comprehend the nature of my work."

" Certainly not," he replied, " and I would rather you did not try to simplify it for their undeveloped minds, merely speak learnedly of your work as if you were addressing a body of your colleagues. The less the boys understand of it the more they will be impressed with its importance, and the more ambitious they will be to become great chemists."

This strange philosophy of education annoyed me,

but I did not have time to argue further for the bell had rung and the boys were filing in with strict military precision. There were about fifty of them, all in their twelfth year, and of remarkable uniformity in size and development. The blanched skin, which marked the adult faces of Berlin, was, in the pasty countenance of those German boys, a more horrifying spectacle. Yet they stood erect and, despite their lack of colour, were evidently a well nourished, well exercised group of youngsters.

As the last boy reached his place the master motioned with his hand and fifty arms moved in unison in a mechanical salute.

"We have with us this morning," said the master, "a chemist who has won the honours of paternity with his original thought. He will tell you about his work which you cannot understand — you should therefore listen attentively."

After a few more sentences of these paradoxical axioms on education, the master nodded, and, as I had been instructed, I proceeded to talk of the chemical lore of poison gases.

"And now," said the master, when I resumed my seat, "we will have a review lesson. You will first recite in unison the creed of your caste."

"We are youth of the super-race," began the boys in a sing-song and well timed chorus. "We belong to the chemical group of the intellectual levels, being born of sires who were great chemists, born of great chemists for many generations. It is our duty to learn while we are yet young all that we may ever need to know, to keep our minds free from forbidden knowledge and to resist the temptation to think on unnecessary things. So we may be good Germans, loyal to the House of Hohenzollern and to the worship of the old German God and the divine blood of William the Great."

The schoolmaster, who had nodded his head in unison with the rhythm of the recitation, now smiled in satisfaction. "That was very good," he said. " I did not hear one faltering voice. Now you may recite individually in your alphabetical order.

"Anton, you may describe the stages in the evolution of the super-man."

Anton, a flaxen-haired youngster, arose, saluted like a wooden soldier, and intoned the following monologue:

"Man is an animal in the process of evolving into a god. The method of this evolution is a struggle in which the weak perish and the strong survive. First in this process of man's evolution came the savage, who lived with the lions and the apes. In the second stage came the dark races who built the so-called ancient civilizations, and fought among themselves to possess private property and women and children. Third came the barbarian Blond Brutes, who were destined to sire the super-race, but the day had not yet come, and they mixed with the dark races and produced the mongrel peoples, which make the fourth. The fifth stage is the pure bred Blond Brutes, uncontaminated by inferior races, which are the men, who under God's direction, built the Armoured City of Berlin in which to breed the Supermen who are to conquer the mongrel peoples. The sixth, last and culminating stage of the evolution of man is the Divinity in human form which is our noble House of Hohenzollern, descended physically from William the Great, and spiritually from the soul of God Himself, whose statue stands with that of the Mighty William at the portals of the Emperor's palace."

It had been a noble effort for so young a memory and as the proud master looked at me expectantly I could do nothing less than nod my appreciation.

The master now gave Bruno the following cue:

" Name the four kinds of government and explain each."

From the sad-eyed youth of twelve came this flow of wisdom:

" The first form of government is monarchy, in which the people are ruled by a man who calls himself a king but who has no divine authority so that the people sometimes failed to respect him and made revolutions and tried to govern themselves. The second form of government is a republic, sometimes called a democracy. It is usually co-existent with the lawyer, the priest, the family and the greed for gold. But in reality this government is by the rich men, who let the poor men vote and think they have a share in the government, thus to keep them contented with their poverty. The third form of government is proletariat socialism in which the people, having abolished kings and rich men, attempt to govern themselves; but this they cannot do for the same reason that a man cannot lift himself by his shoestraps —"

At this point Bruno faltered and his face went chalky white. The teacher being directly in front of the standing pupil did not see what had happened, while I, with fleeting memory of my own school days, suppressed my mirth behind a formal countenance, as the stoic Bruno resumed his seat.

The master marked zero on the roll and called upon Conrad, next in line, to finish the recitation.

" The fourth and last form of government," recited Conrad, " is autocratic socialism, the perfect government that we Germans have evolved from proletariat socialism which had destroyed the greed for private property and private family life, so that the people ceased to struggle individually and were ready to accept the Royal House, divinely appointed by God to govern them perfectly and prepare them to make war for the conquest of the world."

The recitations now turned to repetitions of the pedigree and ranking of the various branches of the Royal House. But it was a mere list of names like the begats of Genesis and I was not able to profit much by this opportunity to improve my own neglected education. As the morning wore on the parrot-like monologues shifted to elementary chemistry.

The master had gone entirely through the alphabet of names and now called again the apt Anton for a more brilliant demonstration of his system of teaching. "Since we have with us a chemist who has achieved powers of original thought, I will permit you, Anton, to demonstrate that even at the tender age of twelve you are capable of original thought."

Anton rose gravely and stood at attention. "And what shall I think about?" he asked.

"About anything you like," responded the liberal minded schoolmaster, "provided it is limited to your permitted field of psychic activity."

Anton tilted back his head and gazed raptly at a portrait of the Mighty William. "I think," he said, "that the water molecule is made of two atoms of hydrogen and one of oxygen."

A number of the boys shook their heads in disapproval, evidently recognizing the thought as not being original, but the teacher waited in respectful silence for the founts of originality to burst forth in Anton's mind.

"And I think," continued Anton, "that if the water molecule were made of four atoms of nitrogen and one of oxygen, it would be a great economy, for after we had bathed in the water we could evaporate it and make air and breath it, and after we had breathed it we could condense it again and use it to drink —"

"But that would be unsanitary," piped a voice from the back of the room.

To this interruption Anton, without taking his gaze from the face of William, replied, "Of course it would if we didn't sterilize it, but I was coming to that. We would sterilize it each time."

The master now designated two boys to take to the guardhouse of the school the lad who had spoken without permission. He then produced a red cardboard cross adorned with the imperial eagle and crossed test-tubes of the chemists' insignia and I was honoured by being asked to decorate Anton for his brilliant exploit in original thought.

" Our intellectual work of the day is over," resumed the master, " but in honour of our guest we will have, a day in advance, our weekly exercises in emotion. Heinrich, you may recite for us the category of emotions."

" The permitted emotions," said Heinrich, " are: First, anger, which we should feel when a weak enemy offends us. Second, hate, which is a higher form of anger, which we should feel when a powerful enemy offends us. Third, sadness, which we should feel when we suffer. Fourth, mirth, which we should feel when our enemy suffers. Fifth, courage, which we feel at all times because we believe in our strength. Sixth, humility, which we should feel only before our superiors. Seventh, and greatest, is pride, which we should feel at all times because we are Germans.

" The forbidden emotions are very numerous. The chief ones which we must guard against are: First, pity, which is a sadness when our enemy sufers; to feel this is exceedingly wicked. Second, envy, which is a feeling that some one else is better than we are, which we must not feel at all because it is destructive of pride. Third, fear, which is a lack of courage. Fourth, love, which is a confession of weakness, and is permissible only to women and dogs."

"Very good," said the. master, "I will now grant you permission to feel some of the permitted emotions. We will first conduct a chemical experiment. I have in this bottle a dangerous explosive and as I drop in this pellet it may explode and kill us all, but you must show courage and not fear." He held the pellet above the mouth of the bottle, but his eyes were on his pupils. As he dropped the pellet into the bottle, he knocked over with his foot a slab of concrete, which fell to the floor with a resounding crash. A few of the boys jumped in their seats, and the master gravely marked them as deficient in courage.

"You now imagine that you are adult chemists and that the enemy has produced a new form of gas bomb, a gas against which we have no protection. They are dropping the gas bombs into our ventilating shafts and are killing our soldiers in the mines. You hate the enemy — hate hard — make your faces black with hate and rage. Adolph, you are expressing mere anger. There, that is better. You never can be a good German until you learn to hate.

"And now we will have a permitted emotion that you all enjoy; the privilege to feel mirth is a thing for which you should be grateful.

" An enemy came flying over Berlin — and this is a true story. I can remember when it happened. The roof guard shot at him and winged his plane, and he came down in his parachute, which missed the roof of the city and fell to the earth outside the walls but within the first ring of the ray defences. He knew that he could not pass beyond this and he wandered about for many days within range of the glasses of the roof guards. When he was nearly starved he came near the wall and waved his white kerchief, which meant he wished to surrender and be taken into the city."

At this point one of the boys tittered, and the master stopped his story long enough to mark a credit for this first laugh.

" As the enemy aviator continued to walk about waving his cowardly flag another enemy plane saw him and let down a line, but the roof guards shelled and destroyed the plane. Then other planes came and attempted to pick up the man with lines. In all seven planes were destroyed in attempting to rescue one man. It was very foolish and very comical. At last the eighth plane came and succeeded in reaching the man a line without being winged. The roof batteries shot at the plane in vain — then the roof gunners became filled with good German hate, and one of them aimed, not at the plane, but at the man swinging on the unstable wire line two thousand metres beneath. The shell exploded so near that the man disappeared as by magic, and the plane flew off with the empty dangling line."

As the story was finished the boys who had listened with varying degrees of mechanical smiles now broke out into a chorus of raucous laughter. It was a forced unnatural laughter such as one hears from a bad actor attempting to express mirth he does not feel.

When the boys had ceased their crude guffaws the master asked, " Why did you laugh? "

" Because," answered Conrad, " the enemy were so stupid as to waste seven planes trying to save one man."

" That is fine," said the master; " we should always laugh when our enemy is stupid, because then he suffers without knowing why he suffers. If the enemy were not stupid they would cease fighting and permit us to rule them and breed the stupidity out of them, as it has been bred out of the Germans by our good old God and the divine mind of the House of Hohenzollern."

The boys were now dismissed for a recess and went into the gymnasium to play leap frog. But the sad-eyed Bruno promptly returned and saluted.

" You may speak," said the master.

" I wish, Herr Teacher," said Bruno, " to petition you for permission to fight with Conrad."

" But you must not begin a fight," admonished the master, " unless you can attach to your opponent the odium of causing the strife."

" But he did cause the odium," said Bruno; " he stuck it into my leg with a pin while I was reciting. The Herr Father saw him do it,"— and the boy turned his eyes towards me in sad and serious appeal.

The schoolmaster glanced at me inquiringly and I corroborated the lad's accusation.

" Then," said the master, " you have a *casus belli* that is actually true, and if you can make Conrad admit his guilt I will exchange your mark for his." Bruno saluted again and started to leave. Then he turned back and said, " But Conrad is two kilograms heavier than I am, and he may not admit it."

" Then," said the teacher, " you must know that I cannot exchange the marks, for victory in a fight compensates for the fault that caused it. But if you wish I will change the marks now, but then you cannot fight."

" But I wish to fight," said Bruno, " and so does Conrad. We arranged it before recitation that he was to stick me with the pin."

" Such diplomacy! " exulted the master when the lad had gone, " and to think that they can only be chemists! "

3

As the evening hour drew near which I had set for my call on the first of the potential mothers assigned me by the Eugenic Staff, I re-read the rules for my conduct:

" On the occasion of this visit you must wear a full dress uniform, including all orders, decorations and badges of rank and service to which you are entitled. This is very important and you should call attention thereto and explain the full dignity and importance of your rank and decorations.

" When you call you will first present the card of authorization. You will then present your identification folder and extol the worth and character of your pedigree.

" Then you will ask to see the pedigree of the woman, and will not fail to comment favourably thereon. If she be already a mother you will inquire in regard to her children. If she be not a mother, you will supplicate her to speak of her potential children. You will extol the virtue of her off-spring — or her visions thereof,— and will not fail to speak favourably of their promise of becoming great chemists whose service will redound to the honour of the German race and the Royal House.

" After the above mentioned matters have been properly spoken of, you may compliment the mother upon her own intelligence and fitness as a mother of scientists. But you will refrain from all reference to her beauty of person, lest her thoughts be diverted from her higher purpose to matters of personal amours.

" You will not prolong your call beyond the hours consistent with dignity and propriety, nor permit the mother to perceive your disposition toward her."

Surely nothing in such formal procedure could be incompatible with my own ideals of propriety. Taking with me my card of authorization bearing the name " Frau Karoline, daughter of Ernest Pfeiffer, Director of the Perfume Works," I now ventured to the Level of Maternity.

Countless women passed me as I walked along. They were erect of form and plain of feature, with expressions devoid of either intelligence or passion. Garbed in formless robes of sombre grey, like saints of song and story, they went their way with solemn resignation. Some of them led small children by the hand; others pushed perambulators containing white robed infants being taken to or from the nurseries for their scheduled stays in the mothers' individual apartments.

The actions of the mothers were as methodical as well trained nurses. In their faces was the cold, pallid light of the mother love of the madonnas of art, uncontaminated by the fretful excitement of the mother love in a freer and more uncertain world.

Even the children seemed wooden cherubim. They were physically healthy beyond all blemish, but they cooed and smiled in a subdued manner. Already the ever present "*verboten*" of an ordered life seemed to have crept into the small souls and repressed the instincts of anarchy and the aspirations of individualism. As I walked among these madonnas of science and their angelic offspring, I felt as I imagined a man of earthly passions would feel if suddenly loosed in a mediaeval and orthodox heaven; for everything about me breathed peace, goodness, and coldness.

At the door of her apartment Frau Karoline greeted me with formal gravity. She was a young woman of twenty years, with a high forehead and piercing eyes. Her face was mobile but her manner possessed the dignity of the matron assured of her importance in the world. Her only child was at the nursery at the time, in accordance with the rules of the level that forbids a man to see his step-children. But a large photograph, aided by Frau Karoline's fulsome description and eulogies, gave me a very clear picture of the high order of the young chemist's intelligence though that worthy had but recently passed his first birthday.

The necessary matters of the inspection of pedigrees and the signing of my card of authorization had been conducted by the young mother with the cool self-possession of a well disciplined school-mistress. Her attitude and manner revealed the thoroughness of her education and training for her duties and functions in life. And yet, though she relieved me so skilfully of what I feared would be an embarrassing situation, I conceived an intense dislike for this most exemplary young mother, for she made me feel that a man was a most useless and insignificant creature to be tolerated as a necessary evil in this maternal world.

"Surely," said Frau Karoline, as I returned her pedigree, "you could not do better for your first born child than to honour me with his motherhood. Not only is my pedigree of the purest of chemical lines, reaching back to the establishment of the eugenic control, but I myself have taken the highest honours in the training for motherhood."

"Yes," I acknowledged, "you seem very well trained."

"I am particularly well versed," she continued,

" in maternal psychology; and I have successfully cultivated calmness.   In the final tests before my confirmation for maternity I was found to be entirely free from erotic and sentimental emotions."

" But," I ventured, " is not maternal love a sentimental emotion? "

" By no means," replied Frau Karoline.   " Maternal love of the highest order, such as I possess, is purely intellectual; it recognizes only the passions for the greatness of race and the glory of the Royal House.   Such love must be born of the intellect; that is why we women of the scientific group are the best of all mothers.   Thus, were I not wholly free from weak sentimentality, I might desire that my second child be sired by the father of my first, but the Eugenic Office has determined that I would bear a stronger child from a younger father, therefore I acquiesced to their change of assignment without emotion, as becomes a proper mother of our well bred race.   My first child is extremely intellectual but he is not quite perfect physically, and a mother such as I should bear only perfect children.   That alone is the supreme purpose of motherhood.   Do you not see that I am fitted for perfect motherhood? "

" Yes," I replied, as I recalled that my instructions were to pay compliments, " you seem to be a perfect mother."

But the cold and logical perfection of Frau Karoline dampened my curiosity and oppressed my spirit of adventure, and I closed the interview with all

possible speed and fled headlong to the nearest elevator that would carry me from the level.

4

In my first experience I had suffered nothing worse
than an embarrassing half hour, so, with more confidence I pressed the bell the second evening, at the
apartment of Frau Augusta, daughter of Gustave
Schnorr, Authority on Synthetic Nicotine.

Frau Augusta was a woman of thirty-five. She
was well-preserved, more handsome and less coldly
inhuman than the younger woman.

" We will get the formalities over since you have
been told they are necessary," said Frau Augusta,
as she reached for my card and folder and, at the
same time, handing me her own pedigree.

Peering over the top of the chart that recorded
the antecedents of Gustave Schnorr, I saw his daughter going through my own folder with the business-
like dispatch of a society dowager examining the
" character " of a new housemaid.

" Ah, yes," she said, raising her brows. " I
thought I knew the family. Your Uncle Otto was
my second mate. He is the father of my third son
and my twin girls. I have no more promising children. Have you ever met him? He is in the
aluminum tempering laboratories."

I could only stare stupidly, struck dumb with embarrassment.

" No, I suppose not," went on Frau Augusta,
" it is hardly to be expected since you have upwards

of a hundred uncles." She arose and, going toward a shelf where half a dozen pictures of half a dozen men reposed in an orderly row, took the second one of the group and handed it to me.

" He is a fine man," she said, with a very full degree of pride for a past and partial possession. " I fear the Staff erred in transferring him, but then of course the twin girls were most unexpected and unfortunate since the Armstadt line is supposed to sire seventy-five per cent. male offspring.

" What do you think? Isn't the Eugenic Office a little unfair at times? My fifth man thought so. He said it was a case of politics. I don't know. I thought politics was something ancient that they had in old books like churches and families."

" I am sure I do not know," I murmured, as I fumbled the portrait of my putative uncle.

" Of course," continued the voluble Frau Augusta, " you must not think I am criticizing the authorities. It is all very necessary. And for the most part I think they have done very well by me. My ten children have six fathers. All of them but the first were men of most gracious manner and superior intelligence. The first one had his paternity right revoked, so I feel satisfied on that score, even if his son is not gifted — and yet the boy has beautiful hair — I think he would make an excellent violinist. But then perhaps he wouldn't have been able to play, so maybe it is all right, though I would think music would be more easily learned than chemistry. But then since I cannot read either I ought not to

judge.   I will show you his picture.   I may as well
show you all their pictures.   I don't see why you
elected fathers should not see our children — but
then I suppose it might produce quarrels.   Some
women are so foolish and insist on talking about
the children they have already borne in a way that
makes a man feel that his own children could never
come up to them.   Now I never do that.   Why
should one?   The future is always more interesting
than the past.   I haven't a single child that has not
won the porcelain cross for obedience.   Even my
youngest — he is only fourteen months — obeys as
if he were a full grown man.   Some say mental and
physical excellence are not correlated — but that is
a prejudice because of those great labour beasts.
There isn't one of my children that has fallen below
the minimum growth standards, except my third
daughter, and her father was undersized, so it is no
fault of mine."

As the loquacious mother chattered on, she produced an album, through which I now turned, in-
specting the annual photographs of her blond brood,
each of which was labelled with the statistics of physical growth and the tests of psychic development.

Strive as I might I could think of no comments
to make, but the mother came to the rescue.   Un-
fastening the binding of the loose leaf album she
hastily shuffled the sheets and brought into an orderly array on the table before me ten photographs
all taken at the age of one year.   "That is the
only fair way to view them," she said, " for of course

one cannot compare the picture of a boy of fifteen with an infant of one year. But at an equal age the comparison is fair to all and now you can surely tell me which is the most intelligent."

I gazed hopelessly at the infantile portraits which, despite their varied paternity, looked as alike as a row of peas in a pod.

"Oh, well," said Frau Augusta, "after all is it fair to ask you, since the twins are your cousins?"

Desperately I wondered which were the twins.

"They resemble you quite remarkably, don't you think so? Except that your hair is quite dark for an Armstadt." Frau Augusta turned and glanced furtively at my identification folder. "Of course! your mother. I had almost forgotten who your mother was, but now I remember, she had most remarkably dark hair. It will probably prove a dominant characteristic and your children will also be dark haired. Now I should like that by way of a change."

I became alarmed at this turn of the conversation toward the more specific function of my visit, and resolved to make my exit with all possible speed "consistent with dignity and propriety."

Meanwhile, as she reassembled the scattered sheets of the portrait album, the official mother chattered on concerning her children's attributes, while I shifted uneasily in my chair and looked about the room for my hat — forgetting in my embarrassment that I was dwelling in a sunless, rainless city and possessed no hat.

At last there was a lull in the monologue and I arose and said I must be going.

Frau Augusta looked pained and I recalled that I had not yet complimented her upon her intelligence and fitness to be the mother of coming generations of chemical scientists, but I stubbornly resolved not to resume my seat.

"You are young," said Frau Augusta, who had risen and shifted her position till she stood between me and the door. "Surely you have not yet made many calls on the maternity level." Then she sighed, "I do not see why they assign a man only three names to select from. Surely they could be more liberal." She paused and her face hardened. "And to think that you men are permitted to call as often as you like upon those degenerate hussies who have been forbidden the sacred duties of motherhood. It is a very wicked institution, that level of lust — some day we women — we mothers of Berlin — will rise in our wrath and see that they are banished to the mines, for they produce nothing but sin and misery in this man-made world."

"Yes," I said, "the system is very wrong, but —"

"But the authorities, you need not say it, I have heard it all before, the authorities, always the authorities. Why should men always be the authorities? Why do we mothers of Berlin have no rights? Why are we not consulted in these matters? Why must we always submit?"

Then suddenly, and very much to my surprise, she placed her hands upon my shoulders and said hoarsely: "Tell me about the Free Level. Are the women there more beautiful than I?"

"No," I said, "very few of them are beautiful, and those of the labour groups are most gross and stupid."

"Then why," wailed Frau Augusta, "was I not allowed to go? Why was I penned up here and made to bear children when others revel in the delights of love and song and laughter?"

"But," I said, shocked at this unexpected revelation of character, "yours is the more honourable, more virtuous life. You were chosen for motherhood because you are a woman of superior intelligence."

"It's a lie," cried Frau Augusta. "I have no intelligence. I want none. But I am as beautiful as they. But no, they would not let me go. They penned me up here with these saintly mothers and these angelic children. Children, children everywhere, millions and millions of them, and not a man but doctors, and you elected fathers who are sent here to bring us pain and sorrow. You say nothing of love — your eyes are cold. The last one said he loved me — the brute! He came but thrice, when my child was born he sent me a flower. But that is the official rule. And I hate him, and hate his child that has his lying eyes."

The distraught woman covered her face with her hands and burst into violent weeping.

When she had ceased her sobs I tried to explain to her the philosophy of contentment with life's lot. I told her of the seamy side of the gown that cloaks licentiousness and of the sorrows and bitterness of the ashes of burned out love.   With the most irides-cent words at my command I painted for her the halo of the madonna's glory, and translated for her the English verse that informs us that there is not a flower in any land, nor a pearl in any sea, that is as beautiful and lovely as any child on any mother's knee.

But I do not think I altogether consoled Frau Augusta for my German vocabulary was essentially scientific, not poetic.   But I made a noble effort and when I left her I felt very much the preacher, for the function of the preacher, not unlike death, is to make us cling to those ills we have when we would fly to others that we know not of.

5

There remained but one card unsigned of the three given me.

Frau Matilda, daughter of Siegfried Oberwinder, Analine Analyst, was registered as eighteen and evi-dently an inexperienced mother-elect as I was a father-elect.   The nature of the man is to hold the virgin above the madonna, and in starting on my third journey to the maternity level, I found hitherto inexperienced feelings tugging at my heartstrings and resolved that whatever she might be, I would be dignified and formal yet most courteous and kind.

My ring was answered by a slender, frightened girl.   She was so shy that she could only nod for me to enter. I offered my card and folder, smiling to reassure her, but she retreated precipitously into a far corner and sat staring at me beseechingly with big grey eyes that seemed the only striking feature of her small pinched face.

"I am sorry if I frighten you," I said, "but of ꞏurse you know that I am sent by the eugenic authorities. I will not detain you long. All that is really necessary is for you to sign this card."

She timidly signed the card and returned it to the corner of the table.

I felt extremely sorry for the fluttering creature; and, knowing that I could not alter her lot, I sought to speak words of encouragement. "If you find it hard now," I said, "it is only because you are young and a stranger to life, but you will be recompensed when you know the joys of motherhood."

At my words a look of consecrated purpose glowed in the girl's white face. "Oh, yes," she said eagerly. "I wish very much to be a mother. I have studied so hard to learn. I wish only to give myself to the holy duties of maternity. But I am so afraid."

"But you need not be afraid of me," I said. "This is only a formal call which I have made because the Eugenic Staff ordered it so. But it seems to me that some better plan might be made for these meetings. Some social life might be arranged so that you would become acquainted with the men who are to be the fathers of your children under less embarrassing circumstances."

" I try so hard not to be afraid of men, for I know they are necessary to eugenics."

" Yes," I said dryly, " I suppose they are, though I think I would prefer to put it that the love of man and woman is necessary to parenthood."

" Oh, no," she said in a frightened voice, " not that, that is very wicked."

" So you were taught that you should not love men? No wonder you are afraid of them."

" I was taught to respect men for they are the fathers of children," she replied.

" Then," I asked, deciding to probe the philosophy of the education for maternity, " why are not the fathers permitted to enjoy their fatherhood and live with the mother and the children? "

Frau Matilda now gazed at me with open-mouthed astonishment. " What a beautiful idea! " she exclaimed with rapture.

" Yes, I rather like it myself — the family —"

" The family! " cried the girl in horror.

" That is what we were talking about."

" But the family is forbidden. It is very wrong, very uneugenic. You must be a wicked man to speak to me of that."

" You have been taught some very foolish ideas," I replied.

" How dare you! " she cried, in alarm. " I have been taught what is right, and I want to do what is right and loyal. I passed all my examinations. I am a good mother-elect, and you say these forbidden things to me. You talk of love and families. You

insult me. And if you select me, I shall — I shall
claim exemption,—" and with that she rose and
darted through the inner door.

I waited for a time and then gently approached
the door, which I saw had swung to with springs
and had neither latch nor lock. My gentle rap upon
the hollow panel was answered by a muffled sob. I
realized the hopelessness of further words and silently turned from the door and left the apartment.

The streets of the level were almost deserted for
the curfew had rung and the lights glowed dim as
in a hospital ward at night. I hurried silently along,
shut in by enclosing walls and the lowering ceiling
of the street. From everywhere I seemed to feel
upon me the beseeching, haunting grey eyes of Frau
Matilda. My soul was troubled, for it seemed to
stagger beneath the burden of its realization of a
lost humanity. And with me walked grey shadows
of other men, felt-footed through the gloom, and
they walked hurriedly as men fleeing from a house
of death.

6

My next duty as a German father-elect was to report to the Eugenic Office. There at least I could
deal with men; and there I went, nursing rebellion
yet trying my utmost to appear outwardly calm.

To the clerk I offered my three signed cards by
way of introduction.

" And which do you select? " asked the oldish man
over his rimless glasses.

" None."

" Ah, but you must."

" But what if I refuse to do so? "

" That is most unusual."

" But does it ever happen? "

" Well, yes," admitted the clerk, " but only by Petition Extraordinary to the Chief of the Staff. But it is most unusual, and if he refuses to grant it you may be dishonoured even to the extent of having your election to paternity suspended, may be even permanently cancelled."

" You mean "— I stammered.

" Exactly — you refuse to accept any one of the three women when all are most scientifically selected for you.   Does it not throw some doubts upon your own psychic fitness for mating at all? If I may suggest, Herr Colonel — it would be wiser for you to select some one of the three — you have yet plenty of time."

" No," I said, trying to hide my elation.   " I will not do so.   I will make the Petition Extraordinary to your chief."

" Now? " stammered the clerk.

" Yes, now; how do I go about it? "

" You must first consult the Investigator."

After a few formalities I was conducted to that official.

" You refuse to make selection? " inquired the Investigator.

" Yes."

" Why? "

" Because," I replied, " I am engaged upon some chemical research of most unusual nature —"

" Yes," nodded the Investigator, " I have just looked that up. The more reason you should be honoured with paternity."

" Perhaps," I said, " you are not informed of the grave importance of the research. If you will consult Herr von Uhl of the Chemical Staff —"

" Entirely unnecessary," he retorted; " paternity is also important. Besides it takes but little time. No more than you need for recreation."

" But I do not find it recreation. I have not been able to concentrate my mind on my work since I received notice of my election to paternity."

" But you were warned against this," he said; " you have no right to permit the development of disturbing romantic emotions. They may be bad for your work, but they are worse for eugenics. So, if you have made romantic love to the mothers of Berlin, your case must be investigated."

" But I have not."

" Then why has this disturbed you? "

" Because," I replied, " this system of scientific paternity offends my instincts."

The investigator ogled me craftily. " What system would you prefer instead? " he asked.

I saw he was trying to trap me into disloyal admissions. " I have nothing to propose," I stated. " I only know that I find the paternity system offensive to me, and that the position I am placed in incapacitates me for my work."

The investigator made some notes on a pad. " That is all for the present," he said. " I will refer your case to the Chief."

Two days later I received an order to report at once to Dr. Ludwig Zimmern, Chief of the Eugenic Staff.

The Chief, with whom I was soon cloistered, was a man of about sixty years. His face revealed a greater degree of intelligence than I had yet observed among the Germans, nor was his demeanour that of haughty officiousness, for a kindly warmth glowed in his soft dark eyes.

" I have a report here," said Dr. Zimmern, " from my Investigator. He recommends that your rights of paternity be revoked on the grounds that he believes yours to be a case of atavistic radicalism. In short he thinks you are rebellious by instinct, and that you are therefore unsafe to father the coming generation. It is part of the function of this office to breed the rebellious instinct out of the German race. What have you to say in answer to these charges? "

" I do not want to seem rebellious," I stammered, " but I wish to be relieved of this duty."

" Very well," said Zimmern, " you may be relieved. If you have no objection I will sign the recommendation as it stands."

Surely, I thought, this man does not seem very bitter toward my traitorous instincts.

Zimmern smiled and eyed me curiously. " You know," he said, " that to possess a thought and to

speak of it indiscreetly are two different things."
" Certainly," I replied, emboldened by his words.
" A man cannot do original work in science if he
possesses a mind that never thinks contrary to the
established order of things."
The clerks in the outer office must have thought
my case a grievous one for I was closeted with their
chief for nearly an hour. Though our conversation
was vague and guarded, I knew that I had discovered in Dr. Ludwig Zimmern, Chief of the Eugenic
Staff, a man guilty himself of the very crime of
possessing rebellious instincts for which he had decided me unfit to sire German children. And when
I finally took my leave I carried with me his private
card and an invitation to call at his apartment to
continue our conversation.

7

In the weeks that followed, my acquaintance with
the Chief of the Eugenic Staff ripened rapidly into
a warm friendship. The frank manner in which he
revealed his dissatisfaction with the state of affairs
in Germany pleased me greatly. Zimmern was interested in my chemical researches and quickly com-
prehended their importance.
" I know so little of chemistry," he deplored, " yet
on it our whole life hangs. That is why I am so
glad of an opportunity to talk to you. I do not
approve of so much ignorance of each other's work
on the part of our scientists. Our old university
system was better. Then a scientist in any field

knew something of the science in all fields.   But now
we are specialized from childhood.   Take, for example, yourself.   You are at work on a great problem by which all of our labour stands to be undone
if you chemists do not solve it, and yet you do not
understand how we will all be undone.   I think you
should know more of what it means, then you will
work better.   Is it not so? "

" Perhaps," I said, " but I have little time.   I am
working too hard now."

" Then," said Zimmern, " you should spend more
time in pleasure on the Free Level.   Two days ago
I conferred with the Emperor's Advisory Staff, and
I learned that grave changes are threatened.   That
is one reason I am so interested in this protium
on which you chemists are working.   If you do not
solve this problem and replenish the food supply,
the Emperor has decided that the whole Free Level
with its five million women must be abolished.   His
Majesty will have no half-way measures.   He is
afraid to take part of these women away, lest the
intellectual workers rebel like the labourers did in
the last century when their women were taken away
piecemeal."

" But what will His Majesty do with these five
million women? " I inquired, eagerly desirous to
learn more.

" Do?   What can he do with the women? " exclaimed Dr. Zimmern in a low pitched but vibrant
voice.   " He thinks he will make workers of them.
He does not seem to appreciate how specialized they

are for pleasure.   He will make machine tenders of
them to relieve the workmen, who are to be made
soldiers.   He would make surface soldiers out of
these blind moles of the earth, put amber glasses on
them and train them to run on the open ground and
carry the war again into the sunlight.   It is folly,
sheer folly, and madness.   His Majesty, I fear,
reads too much of old books.   He always was historically inclined."

On a later occasion Zimmern gave me the broad
outlines of the history of German Eugenics.

" Our science of applied Eugenics," he said, " began during the Second World War.   Our scientists
had long known that the same laws of heredity by
which plants and animals had been bred held true
with man, but they had been afraid to apply those
laws to man because the religion of that day taught
that men had souls and that human life was something too sacred to be supervised by science.   But
William III was a very fearless man, and he called
the scientists together and asked them to outline a
plan for the perfection of the German race.

" At first all they advocated was that paternity
be restricted to the superior men.   This broke up
the old-fashioned family where every man chose his
own wife and sired as many children as he liked.
There were great mutterings about that, and if we
had not been at war, there would have been rebellion.   The Emperor told the people it was a military necessity.   The death toll of war then was great
and there was urgent need to increase the birth rate,

so the people submitted and women soon ceased to complain because they could no longer have individual husbands.   The children were supported by the state, and if they had legitimate fathers of the approved class they were left in the mothers' care. As all women who were normal and healthy were encouraged to bear children, there was a great increase in the birth rate, which came near resulting in the destruction of the race by starvation.

" As soon as a sufficient number of the older generation that had believed in the religious significance of the family and marriage system had died out, the ambitious eugenists set about to make other reforms. The birth rate was cut down by restricting the privilege of motherhood to a selected class of women. The other women were instructed in the arts of pleasing man and avoiding maternity, and that is where we have the origin of our free women.   In those days they were free to associate with men of all classes.   Indeed any other plan would at first have been impossible.

" A second fault was that the superior men for whom paternity was permitted were selected from the official and intellectual classes.   The result was that the quality of the labourers deteriorated.   So two strains were established, the one for the production of the intellectual workers, and the other for producing manual workers.   From time to time this specialization has increased until now we have as many strains of inheritance as there are groups of useful characteristics known to be hereditary.

"We have produced some effects," mused Zimmern, "which were not anticipated, and which have been calling forth considerable criticism. His Majesty sends me memorandums nearly every year, after he reviews the maternity levels, insisting that the feminine beauty of the race is, as a whole, deteriorating. And yet this is logical enough. With the exception of our small actor-model strain, the characteristics for which we breed have only the most incidental relation to feminine beauty. The type of the labour female is, as you have seen, a buxom, fleshly beauty; youth and full nutrition are essential to its display, and it soon fades. In the scientific strains it seems that the power of original thought correlates with a feminine type that is certainly not beautiful. Doubtless not understanding this you may have felt that you were discriminated against in your assignment. But the clerical mind with its passion for monotonous repetition of petty mental processes seems to correlate with the most exquisite and refined feminine features. Those scintillating beauties on the Free Level who have ever at their beck our wisest men are from our clerical strain,— but of course they are only the rejects. It is unfortunate that you cannot see the more privileged specimens in the clerical maternity level.

" But I digress to that which is of no consequence. The beauty of women is unimportant but the number of women is very important. When some women were specialized for motherhood then there were surplus women. At first they made workers of them.   The war was then conducted on a larger scale than now.   We had not yet fully specialized the soldier class.   All the young men went to war; and, when they came back and went to work, they became bitterly jealous of the women workers and made an outcry that those who could not fight should not work.   The men workers drove the women from industry, hoping thereby each to possess a mistress.   As a result the great number of unproductive women was a drain upon the state.   All sorts of schemes were proposed to reduce the number of female births but most of these were unscientific. In studying the records it was found that the offspring of certain men were predominantly males. By applying this principle of selection we have, with successive generations, been able to reduce the proportion of female births to less than half the old rate.

"But the sexual impulse of the labourers made them restless and rebellious, and the support of the free women for these millions of workers was a great economic waste.   When animals had been bred to large size and great strength their sexuality had decreased, while their power as beasts of burden increased.   The same principle applied to man has resulted in more docile workers.   By beginning with the soldiers and mine workers, who were kept away from women, and by combining proper training with the hereditary selection, we solved that problem and removed all knowledge of women from the minds of the workmen."

" But how about paternity among the workers? "
I asked.

" Those who are selected are removed to special isolated quarters. They are told they are being taken to serve as His Majesty's body guard; and they never go back to mingle with their fellows."

I then related for the doctor my conversation with the workman who asked me about women.

" So," said Zimmern, " there has been a leak somewhere; knowledge is hard to bottle. Still we have bottled most of it and the labourer accepts his loveless lot. But it could not be done with the intellectual worker."

Dr. Zimmern smiled cynically. " At least," he added, " we don't propose to admit that it can be done. And that, Col. Armstadt, is what I was remarking about the other evening. Unless you chemists can solve the protium problem, Germany must cut her population swiftly, if we do not starve out altogether. His Majesty's plan to turn the workmen into soldiers and make workers of the free women will not solve it. It is too serious for that. The Emperor's talk about the day being at hand is all nonsense. He knows and we know that these mongrel herds, as he calls the outside enemy, are not so degenerate.

" We may have improved the German stock in some ways by our scientific breeding, but science cannot do much in six generations, and what we have accomplished, I as a member of the Eugenist Staff, can assure you has really been attained as much by training as by breeding, though the breeding is given the credit.   Our men are highly specialized, and once outside the walls of Berlin they will find things so different that this very specialization will prove a handicap.   The mongrel peoples are more adaptable.   Our workmen and soldiers are large in physique, but dwarfed of intellect.   The enemy will beat us in open war, and, even if we should be victorious in war, we could not rule them.   Either we solve this food business or we all turn soldiers and go out into the blinding sunlight and die fighting."

I ventured as a wild remark: " At least, if we get outside there will be plenty of women."

The older man looked at me with the superiority of age towards youth.   " Young man," he said, " you have not read history; you do not understand this love and family doctrine; it exists in the outside world today just as it did two centuries ago.   The Germans in the days of the old surface wars made too free with the enemy's women, and that is why they ran us into cover here and penned us up. These mongrel people will fight for their women when they will fight for nothing else.   We have not bred all the lust out of our workmen either.   It is merely dormant.   Once they are loosed in the outer world they will not understand this thing and they will again make free with the enemy's women, and then we shall all be exterminated."

Dr. Zimmern got up and filled a pipe with synthetic tobacco and puffed energetically as he walked about the room.   " What do you say about this protium ore?" he asked; "will you be able to solve the problem?"

"Yes," I said, "I think I shall."

"I hope so," replied my host, "and yet sometimes I do not care; somehow I want this thing to come to an end. I want to see what is outside there. I think, perhaps, I would like to fly.

"What troubles me is that I do not see how we can ever do it. We have bred and trained our race into specialization and stupidity. We wouldn't know how to go out and join this World State if they would let us."

Dr. Zimmern paced the room in silence for a time. "Do you know," he said, "I should like to see a negro, a black man with kinky hair — it must be queer."

"Yes," I answered, "there must be many queer things out there."

CHAPTER VI

I

WHEN I told Dr. Zimmern that I should solve the problem of the increase of the supply of protium I may have been guilty of speaking of hopes as if they were certainties. My optimism was based on the discovery that the exact chemical state of the protium in the ore was unknown, and that it did not exist equally in all samples of the ore.

After some further months of labour I succeeded in determining the exact chemical ingredients of the ore, and from this I worked rapidly toward a new process of extraction that would greatly increase the total yield of the precious element. But this fact I kept from my assistants whose work I directed to futile researches while I worked alone after hours in following up the lead I had discovered.

During the progress of this work I was not always in the laboratory. I had become a not infrequent visitor to the Level of the Free Women. The continuous carnival of amusement had an attraction for me, as it must have had for any tired and lonely man. But it was not merely the lure of sensuous

pleasures that appealed to me, for I was also fascinated with the deeper and more tragic aspect of life
beneath the gaudy surface of hectic joy.

Some generalities I had picked up from observation and chance conversations. As a primary essential to life on the level I had quickly learned that
money was needed, and my check book was in fre-
quent demand. The bank provided an aluminum
currency for the pettier needs of the recreational
life, but neither the checks nor the currency had had
value on other levels, since there all necessities were
supplied without cost and luxuries were unobtain-
able. This strange retention of money circulation
and general freedom of personal conduct exclusively
on the Free Level puzzled me. Thus I found that
food and drink were here available for a price, a
seeming contradiction to the strict limitations of the
diet served me at my own quarters. At first it
seemed I had discovered a way to defeat that
limitation — but there was the weigher to be considered.

It was a queer ensemble, this life in the Black
Utopia of Berlin, a combination of a world of rigid
mechanistic automatism in the regular routine of
living with rioting individual license in recreational
pleasure. The Free Level seemed some ancient
Bagdad, some Bourbon Court, some Monte Carlo set
here, an oasis of flourishing vice in a desert of sterile
law-made, machine-executed efficiency and puritan-
ically ordered life. Aided by a hundred ingenious
wheels and games of chance, men and women gam-

bled with the coin and credit of the level.   These games were presided over by crafty women whose years were too advanced to permit of a more personal means of extracting a living from the grosser passions of man.   Some of these aged dames were, I found, quite highly regarded and their establishments had become the rendezvous for many younger women who by some arrangement that I could not fathom plied their traffic in commercialized love under the guidance of these subtler women who had graduated from the school of long experience in preying upon man.

But only the more brilliant women could so establish themselves for the years of their decline.   There were others, many others, whose beauty had faded without an increase in wit, and these seemed to be serving their more fortunate sisters, both old and young, in various menial capacities.   It was a strange anachronism in this world where men's more weighty affairs had been so perfectly socialized, to find woman retaining, evidently by men's permission, the individualistic right to exploit her weaker sister.

The thing confounded me, and yet I recalled the well known views of our sociological historians who held that it was woman's greater individualism that had checked the socialistic tendencies of the world. Had the Germans then achieved and maintained their rigid socialistic order by retaining this incongruous vestige of feminine commercialism as a safety valve for the individualistic instincts of the race?

They called it the Free Level, and I marvelled at the nature of this freedom. Freedom for licentiousness, for the getting and losing of money at the wheels of fortune, freedom for temporary gluttony and the mild intoxication of their flat, ill-flavoured synthetic beer. A tragic symbol it seemed to me of the ignobility of man's nature, that he will be a slave in all the loftier aspects of living if he can but retain his freedom for his vices and corruptions. Had the Germans then, like the villain of the moral play, a necessary part in the tragedy of man; did they exist to show the other races of the earth the way they should not go? But the philosophy of this conception collapsed when I recalled that for more than a century the world had lost all sight of the villain and yet had not in the least deteriorated from a lack of the horrible example.

From these vaguer speculations concerning the Free Level of Berlin that existed like a malformed vestigial organ in the body of that socialized state, my mind came back to the more human, more personal side of the problem thus presented me. I wanted to know more of the lives of these women who maintained Germany's remnant of individualism.

To what extent, I asked myself, have the true instincts of womanhood and the normal love of man and child been smothered out of the lives of these girls? What secret rebellions are they nursing in their hearts? I wondered, too, from what source they came, and why they were selected for this life, for Zimmern had not adequately enlightened me on this point.

Pondering thus on the secret workings in the hearts of these girls, I sat one evening amid the sensuous beauty of the Hall of Flowers. I marvelled at how little the Germans seemed to appreciate it, for it was far less crowded than were the more tawdry places of revelry. Here within glass encircling walls, preserved through centuries of artificial existence, feeding from pots of synthetic soil and stimulated by perpetual light, marvellous botanical creations flourished and flowered in prodigal profusion. Ponderous warm-hued lilies floated on the sprinkled surface of the fountain pool. Orchids, dangling from the metal lattice, hung their sensuous blossoms in vapour-laden air. Luxurious vines, climatized to this unreal world, clambered over cosy arbours, or clung with gripping fingers to the mossy concrete pillars.

2

I was sitting thus in moody silence watching the play of the fountain, when, through the mist, I saw the lonely figure of a girl standing in the shadows of a viny bower. She was toying idly with the swaying tendrils. Her hair was the unfaded gold of youth. Her pale dress of silvery grey, unmarred by any clash of colour, hung closely about a form of wraith-like slenderness.

I arose and walked slowly toward her. As I approached she turned toward me a face of flawless girlish beauty, and then as quickly turned away as if seeking a means of escape.

" I did not mean to intrude," I said.

She did not answer, but when I turned to go, to my surprise, she stepped forward and walked at my side.

" Why do you come here alone? " she asked shyly, lifting a pensive questioning face.

" Because I am tired of all this tawdry noise. But you," I said, " surely you are not tired of it? You cannot have been here long."

" No," she replied, " I have not. Only thirty days "; and her blue eyes gleamed with childish pride.

" And that is why you seem so different from them all? "

Timidly she placed her hand upon my arm. " So you," she said gratefully, " you understand that I am not like them — that is, not yet."

" You do not act like them," I replied, " and what is more, you act as if you did not want to be like them. It surely cannot be merely that you are new here. The other girls when they come seem so eager for this life, to which they have long been trained. Were you not trained for it also? "

" Yes," she admitted, " they tried to train me for it, but they could not kill my artist's soul, for I was not like these others, born of a strain wherein women can only be mothers, or, if rejected for that, come here. I was born to be a musician, a group where women may be something more than mere females."

" Then why are you here? " I asked.

" Because," she faltered, " my voice was imperfect. I have, you see, the soul of an artist but lack the physical means to give that soul expression. And so they transferred me to the school for free women, where I have been courted by the young men of the Royal House. But of course you understand all that."

" Yes," I said, " I know something of it; but my work has always so absorbed me that I have not had time to think of these matters. In fact, I come to the Free Level much less than most men."

For a moment, it seemed, her eyes hardened in cunning suspicion, but as I returned her intent gaze I could fathom only the doubts and fears of childish innocence.

" Please let us sit down," I said; " it is so beautiful here; and then tell me all about yourself, how you have lived your childhood, and what your problems are. It may be that I can help you."

" There is not much to tell," she sighed, as she seated herself beside me. " I was only eight years old when the musical examiners condemned my voice and so I do not remember much about the music school. In the other school where they train girls for the life on the Free Level, they taught us dancing, and how to be beautiful, and always they told us that we must learn these things so that the men would love us. But the only men we ever saw were

the doctors.   They were always old and serious and
I could not understand how I could ever love men.
But our teachers would tell us that the other men
would be different.   They would be handsome and
young and would dance with us and bring us fine
presents.   If we were pleasing in their sight they
would take us away, and we should each have an
apartment of our own, and many dresses with beautiful colours, and there would be a whole level full
of wonderful things and we could go about as we
pleased, and dance and feast and all life would be
love and joy and laughter.

"Then, on the 'Great Day,' when we had our
first individual dresses — for before we had always
worn uniforms — the men came.   They were young
military officers and members of the Royal House
who are permitted to select girls for their own exclusive love.   We were all very shy at first, but many
of the girls made friends with the men and some of
them went away that first day.   And after that the
men came as often as they liked and I learned to
dance with them, and they made love to me and
told me I was very beautiful.   Yet somehow I did
not want to go with them.   We had been told that
we would love the men who loved us.   I don't know
why, but I didn't love any of them.   And so the
two years passed and they told me I must come here
alone.   And so here I am."

"And now that you are here," I said, "have you
not, among all these men found one that you could
love?"

" No," she said, with a tremor in her voice, " but they say I must."

" And how," I asked, " do they enforce that rule?   Does any one require you — to accept the men ? "

" Yes," she replied.   " I must do that — or starve."

" And how do you live now ? " I asked.

" They gave me money when I came here, a hundred marks.   And they make me pay to eat and when my money is gone I cannot eat unless I get more.   And the men have all the money, and they pay.   They have offered to pay me, but I refused to take their checks, and they think me stupid."

The child-like explanation of her lot touched the strings of my heart.   " And how long," I asked, " is this money that is given you when you come here supposed to last ? "

" Not more than twenty days," she answered.

" But you," I said, " have been here thirty days! "

She looked at me and smiled proudly.   " But I," she said, " only eat one meal a day.   Do you not see how thin I am ? "

The realization that any one in this scientifically fed city could be hungry was to me appalling.   Yet here was a girl living amidst luxurious beauty, upon whom society was using the old argument of hunger to force her acceptance of the love of man.

I rose and held out my hand.   " You shall eat again today," I said.

" I would rather not," she demurred. " I have not yet accepted favours from any man."

" But you must. You are hungry," I protested. " The problem of your existence here cannot be put off much longer. We will go eat and then we will try and find some solution."

Without further objection she walked with me. We found a secluded booth in a dining hall. I ordered the best dinner that Berlin had to offer.

During the intervals of silence in our rather halting dinner conversation, I wrestled with the situation. I had desired to gain insight into the lives of these girls. Yet now that the opportunity was presented I did not altogether relish the rôle in which it placed me. The apparent innocence of the confiding girl seemed to open an easy way for a personal conquest — and yet, perhaps because it was so obvious and easy, I rebelled at the unfairness of it. To rescue her, to aid her to escape — in a free world one might have considered these more obvious moves, but here there was no place for her to escape to, no higher social justice to which appeal could be made. Either I must accept her as a personal responsibility, with what that might involve, or desert her to her fate. Both seemed cowardly — yet such were the horns of the dilemma and a choice must be made. Here at least was an opportunity to make use of the funds that lay in the bank to the credit of the name I bore, and for which I had found so little use. So I decided to offer her money, and to insist that it was not offered as the purchase price of love.

" You must let me help you," I said, " you must let me give you money."

" But I do not want your money," she replied. " It would only postpone my troubles. Even if I do accept your money, I would have to accept money from other men also, for you cannot pay for the whole of a woman's living."

" Why not," I asked, " does any rule forbid it ? "

" No rule, but can so young a man as you afford it ? "

" How much does it take for you to live here ? "

" About five marks a day."

I glanced rather proudly at my insignia as a research chemist of the first rank. " Do you know," I asked, " how much income that insignia carries ? "

" Well, no," she admitted, " I know the income of military officers, but there are so many of the professional ranks and classes that I get all mixed up."

" That means," I said, " ten thousand marks a year."

" So much as that ! " she exclaimed in astonishment. " And I can live here on two hundred a month, but no, I did not mean that — you wouldn't, — I couldn't — let you give me so much."

" Much ! " I exclaimed; " you may have five hundred if you need it."

" You make love very nicely," she replied with aloofness.

" But I am not making love," I protested.

" Then why do you say these things ? Do you

prefer some one else? If so why waste your funds on me?"

"No, no!" I cried, "it is not that; but you see I want to tell you things; many things that you do not know. I want to see you often and talk to you. I want to bring you books to read. And as for money, that is so you will not starve while you read my books and listen to me talk. But you are to remain mistress of your own heart and your own person. You see, I believe there are ways to win a woman's love far better than buying her cheap when she is starved into selling in this brutal fashion."

She looked at me dubiously. "You are either very queer," she said, "or else a very great liar."

"But I am neither," I protested, piqued that the girl in her innocence should yet brand me either mentally deficient or deceitful. "It is impossible to make you understand me," I went on, "and yet you must trust me. These other men, they approve the system under which you live, but I do not. I offer you money, I insist on your taking it because there is no other way, but it is not to force you to accept me but only to make it unnecessary for you to accept some one else. You have been very brave, to stand out so long. You must accept my money now, but you need never accept me at all — unless you really want me. If I am to make love to you I want to make love to a woman who is really free; a woman free to accept or reject love, not starved into accepting it in this so-called freedom."

"It is all very wonderful," she repeated; "a minute ago I thought you deceitful, and now I want to believe you. I can not stand out much longer and what would be the use for just a few more days?"

"There will be no need," I said gently, "your courage has done its work well — it has saved you for yourself. And now," I continued, "we will bind this bargain before you again decide me crazy."

Taking out my check book I filled in a check for two hundred marks payable to —" To whom shall I make it payable?" I asked.

" To Bertha, 34 R 6," she said, and thus I wrote it, cursing the prostituted science and the devils of autocracy that should give an innocent girl a number like a convict in a jail or a mare in a breeder's herd book.

And so I bought a German girl with a German check — bought her because I saw no other way to save her from being lashed by starvation to the slave block and sold piecemeal to men in whom honour had not even died, but had been strangled before it was born.

With my check neatly tucked in her bosom, Bertha walked out of the café clinging to my arm, and so, passing unheeding through the throng of indifferent revellers, we came to her apartment.

At the door I said, " Tomorrow night I come again. Shall it be at the café or here?"

" Here," she whispered, " away from them all."

I stooped and kissed her hand and then fled into the multitude.

3

I had promised Bertha that I would bring her books, but the narrow range of technical books permitted me were obviously unsuitable, nor did I feel that the unspeakably morbid novels available on the Level of Free Women would serve my purpose of awakening the girl to more wholesome aspirations. In this emergency I decided to appeal to my friend, Zimmern.

Leaving the laboratory early, I made my way toward his apartment, puzzling my brain as to what kind of a book I could ask for that would be at once suitable to Bertha's childlike mind and also be a volume which I could logically appear to wish to read myself. As I walked along the answer flashed into my mind — I would ask for a geography of the outer world.

Happily I found Zimmern in. " I have come to ask," I said, " if you could loan me a book of description of the outer world, one with maps, one that tells all that is known of the land and seas and people."

" Oh, yes," smiled Zimmern, " you mean a geography. Your request," he continued, " does me great honour. Books telling the truth about the world without are very carefully guarded. I shall be pleased to get the geography for you at once. In fact I had already decided that when you came again I would take you with me to our little secret library. Germany is facing a great crisis, and I know no better way I can serve her than doing my part to help prepare as many as possible of our scientists to cope with the impending problems. Unless you chemists avert it, we shall all live to see this outer world, or die that others may."

Dr Zimmern led the way to the elevator. We alighted on the Level of Free Women. Instead of turning towards the halls of revelry we took our course in the opposite direction along the quiet streets among the apartments of the women. We turned into a narrow passage-way and Dr. Zimmern rang the bell at an apartment door. But after waiting a moment for an answer he took a key from his pocket and unlocked the door.

"I am sorry Marguerite is out," he said, as he conducted me into a reception room. The walls were hung with seal-brown draperies. There were richly upholstered chairs and a divan piled high with fluffy pillows. In one corner stood a bookcase of burnished metal filigree.

Zimmern waved his hand at the case with an expression of disdain. "Only the conventional literature of the level, to keep up appearances," he said; "our serious books are in here"; and he thrust open the door of a room which was evidently a young lady's boudoir.

Conscious of a profane intrusion, I followed Dr. Zimmern into the dainty dressing chamber. Stepping across the room he pushed open a spacious wardrobe, and thursting aside a cleverly arranged shield of feminine apparel he revealed, upon some improvised shelves, a library of perhaps a hundred volumes. He ran his hand fondly along the bindings. "No other man of your age in Berlin," he said, "has ever had access to such a complete fund of knowledge as is in this library."

I hope the old doctor took for appreciation the smile that played upon my face as I contrasted his pitiful offering with the endless miles of book stacks in the libraries of the outer world where I had spent so many of my earlier days.

"Our books are safer here," said Zimmern, "for no one would suspect a girl on this level of being interested in serious reading. If perchance some inspector did think to perform his neglected duties we trust to him being content to glance over the few novels in the case outside and not to pry into her wardrobe closet. There is still some risk, but that we must take, since there is no absolute privacy anywhere. We must trust to chance to hide them in the place least likely to be searched."

"And how," I asked, "are these books accumulated?"

"It is the result of years of effort," explained Zimmern. "There are only a few of us who are in this secret group but all have contributed to the collection, and we come here to secure the books that the others bring. We prefer to read them here, and so avoid the chance of being detected carrying forbidden books. There is no restriction on the callers a girl may have at her apartment; the authorities of the level are content to keep records only of her monetary transactions, and that fact we take advantage of. Should a man's apartment on another level be so frequently visited by a group of men an inquiry would be made."

All this was interesting, but I inferred that I would again have opportunity to visit the library and now I was impatient to keep my appointment with Bertha. Making an excuse for haste, I asked Zimmern to get the geography for me. The stiff back of the book had been removed, and Zimmern helped me adjust the limp volume beneath my waistcoat.

" I am sorry you cannot remain and meet Marguerite tonight," he said as I stepped toward the door. " But tomorrow evening I will arrange for you to meet Colonel Hellar of the Information Staff, and Marguerite can be with us then. You may go directly to my booth in the café where you last dined with me."

4

After a brief walk I came to Bertha's apartment, and nervously pressed the bell. She opened the door stealthily and peered out, then recognizing me, she flung it wide.

" I have brought you a book," I said as I entered; and, not knowing what else to do, I went through the ridiculous operation of removing the geography from beneath my waistcoat.

" What a big book," exclaimed Bertha in amazement. However, she did not open the geography

but laid it on the table, and stood staring at me
with her child-like blue eyes.

"Do you know," she said, "that you are the first
visitor I ever had in my apartment? May I show
you about?"

As I followed her through the cosy rooms, I
chafed to see the dainty luxury in which she was
permitted to live while being left to starve. The
place was as well adapted to love-making as any
other product of German science is adapted to its
end. The walls were adorned with sensual prints;
but happily I recalled that Bertha, having no education in the matter, was immune to the insult.

Anticipating my coming she had ordered dinner,
and this was presently delivered by a deaf-and-dumb
mechanical servant, and we set it forth on the dainty
dining table. Since the world was young, I mused,
woman and man had eaten a first meal together
with all the world shut out, and so we dined amid
shy love and laughter in a tiny apartment in the
heart of a city where millions of men never saw
the face of woman — and where millions of babies
were born out of love by the cold degree of science.
And this same science, bartering with licentious
iniquity, had provided this refuge and permitted us
to bar the door, and so we accepted our refuge
and sanctified it with the purity that was within our
own hearts — such at least was my feeling at the
time.

And so we dined and cleared away, and talked
joyfully of nothing. As the evening wore on Ber-

tha, beside me upon the divan, snuggled contentedly against my shoulder. The nearness and warmth of her, and the innocence of her eyes thrilled yet maddened me.

With fast beating heart, I realized that I as well as Bertha was in the grip of circumstances against which rebellion was as futile as were thoughts of escape. There was no one to aid and no one to forbid or criticize. Whatever I might do to save her from the fate ordained for her would of necessity be worked out between us, unaided and unhampered by the ethics of civilization as I had known it in a freer, saner world.

In offering Bertha money and coming to her apartment I had thrust myself between her and the crass venality of the men of her race, but I had now to wrestle with the problem that such action had involved. If, I reasoned, I could only reveal to her my true identity the situation would be easier, for I could then tell her of the rules of the game of love in the world I had known. Until she knew of that world and its ideals, how could I expect her to understand my motives? How else could I strengthen her in the battle against our own impulses?

And yet, did I dare to confess to her that I was not a German? Would not deep-seated ideals of patriotism drilled into the mind of a child place me in danger of betrayal at her hands? Such a move might place my own life in jeopardy and also destroy my opportunity of being of service to the world, could I contrive the means of escape from Berlin with the knowledge I had gained.   Small though the possibilities of such escape might be, it was too great a hope for me to risk for sentimental reasons.   And could she be expected to believe so strange a tale? And so the temptation to confess that I was not Karl Armstadt passed, and with its passing, I recalled the geography that I had gone to so much trouble to secure, and which still lay unopened upon the table.   Here at least was something to get us away from the tumultuous consciousness of ourselves and I reached for the volume and spread it open upon my knees.

"What a funny book!" exclaimed Bertha, as she gazed at the round maps of the two hemispheres. "Of what is that a picture?"

"The world," I answered.

She stared at me blankly. "The Royal World?" she asked.

"No, no," I replied.   "The world outside the walls of Berlin."

"The world in the sun," exclaimed Bertha, "on the roof where they fight the airplanes?   A roof-guard officer" she paused and bit her lip —

"The world of the inferior races," I suggested, trying to find some common footing with her pitifully scant knowledge.

"The world underground," she said, "where the soldiers fight in the mines?"

Baffled in my efforts to define this world to her, I began turning the pages of the geography, while

Bertha looked at the pictures in child-like wonder, and I tried as best I could to find simple explanations.

Between the lines of my teaching, I scanned, as it were, the true state of German ignorance. Despite the evident intended authoritativeness of the book — for it was marked " Permitted to military staff officers "— I found it amusingly full of erroneous conceptions of the true state of affairs in the outer world.

This teaching of a child-like mind the rudiments of knowledge was an amusing recreation, and so an hour passed pleasantly. Yet I realized that this was an occupation of which I would soon tire, for it was not the amusement of teaching a child that I craved, but the companionship of a woman of intelligence.

As we turned the last page I arose to take my departure. " If I leave the book with you," I said, " will you read it all, very carefully? And then when I come again I will explain those things you can not understand."

" But it is so big, I couldn't read it in a day," replied Bertha, as she looked at me appealingly.

I steeled myself against that appeal. I wanted very much to get my mind back on my chemistry, and I wanted also to give her time to read and ponder over the wonders of the great unknown world. Moreover, I no longer felt so grievously concerned, for the calamity which had overshadowed her had been for the while removed. And I had, too, my own struggle to cherish her innocence, and that without the usual help extended by conventional society. So I made brave resolutions and explained the urgency of my work and insisted that I could not see her for five days.

Hungrily she pleaded for a quicker return; and I stubbornly resisted the temptation. "No," I insisted, " not tomorrow, nor the next day, but I will come back in three days at the same hour that I came tonight."

Then taking her in my arms, I kissed her in feverish haste and tore myself from the enthralling lure of her presence.

5

When I reached the café the following evening to keep my appointment with Zimmern, the waiter directed me to one of the small enclosed booths. As I entered, closing the door after me, I found myself confronting a young woman.

"Are you Col. Armstadt?" she asked with a clear, vibrant voice. She smiled cordially as she gave me her hand. "I am Marguerite. Dr. Zimmern has gone to bring Col. Hellar, and he asked me to entertain you until his return."

The friendly candour of this greeting swept away the grey walls of Berlin, and I seemed again face to face with a woman of my own people. She was a young woman of distinctive personality. Her features, though delicately moulded, bespoke intelligence and strength of character that I had not hitherto seen in the women of Berlin. Framing her face was a luxuriant mass of wavy brown hair, which fell loosely about her shoulders. Her slender figure was draped in a cape of deep blue cellulose velvet.

" Dr. Zimmern tells me," I said as I seated myself across the table from her, " that you are a dear friend of his."

A swift light gleamed in her deep brown eyes. " A very dear friend," she said feelingly, and then a shadow flitted across her face as she added, " Without him life for me would be unbearable here."

" And how long, if I may ask, have you been here? "

" About four years. Four years and six days, to be exact. I can keep count you know," and she smiled whimsically, " for I came on the day of my birth, the day I was sixteen."

" That is the same for all, is it not? "

" No one can come here before she is sixteen," replied Marguerite, " and all must come before they are eighteen."

" But why did you come at the first opportunity? " I asked, as I mentally compared her confession with that of Bertha who had so courageously postponed as long as she could the day of surrender to this life of shamefully commercialized love.

" And why should I not come? " returned Marguerite. " I had a chance to come, and I accepted it. Do you think life in the school for girls of forbidden birth is an enjoyable one? "

I wanted to press home the point of my argument, to proclaim my pride in Bertha's more heroic struggle with the system, for this girl with whom I now conversed was obviously a woman of superior intelligence, and it angered me to know that she had so easily surrendered to the life for which German society had ordained her. But I restrained my speech, for I realized that in criticizing her way of life I would be criticizing her obvious relation to Zimmern, and like all men I found myself inclined to be indulgent with the personal life of a man who was my friend. Moreover, I perceived the presumptuousness of assuming a superior air towards an established and accepted institution. Yet, strive as I might to be tolerant, I felt a growing antagonism towards this attractive and cultured girl who had surrendered without a struggle to a life that to me was a career of shame — and who seemed quite content with her surrender.

" Do you like it here? " I asked, knowing that my question was stupid, but anxious to avoid a painful gap in what was becoming, for me, a difficult conversation.

Marguerite looked at me with a queer penetrating gaze. " Do I like it here? " she repeated. " Why should you ask, and how can I answer? Can I like it or not like it, when there was no choice for me? Can I push out the walls of Berlin? "— and she thrust mockingly into the air with a delicately chiselled hand —"It is a prison. All life is a prison."

"Yes," I said, "it is a prison, but life on this level is more joyful than on many others."

Her lip curled in delicate scorn. "For you men — of course — and I suppose it is for these women too — perhaps that is why I hate it so, because they do enjoy it, they do accept it. They sell their love for food and raiment, and not one in all these millions seems to mind it."

"In that," I remarked, "perhaps you are mistaken. I have not come here often as most men do, but I have found one other who, like you, rebels at the system — who in fact, was starving because she would not sell her love."

Marguerite flashed on me a look of pitying suspicion as she asked: "Have you gone to the Place of Records to look up this rebel against the sale of love?"

A fire of resentment blazed up in me at this question. I did not know just what she meant by the Place of Records, but I felt that this woman who spoke cynically of rebellion against the sale of love, and yet who had obviously sold her love to an old man, was in no position to discredit a weaker woman's nobler fight.

"What right," I asked coldly, "have you to criticize another whom you do not know?"

"I am sorry," replied Marguerite, "if I seem to quarrel with you when I was left here to entertain you, but I could not help it — it angers me to have

you men be so fond of being deceived, such easy prey
to this threadbare story of the girl who claims she
never came here until forced to do so. But men
love to believe it. The girls learn to use the story
because it pays."

A surge of conflicting emotion swept through me
as I recalled the child-like innocence of Bertha and
compared it with the critical scepticism of this superior woman. "It only goes to show," I thought,
"what such a system can do to destroy a woman's
faith in the very existence of innocence and virtue."

Marguerite did not speak; her silence seemed to
say: "You do not understand, nor can I explain
— I am simply here and so are you, and we have
our secrets which cannot be committed to words."

With idle fingers she drummed lightly on the
table. I watched those slender fingers and the
rhythmic play of the delicate muscles of the bare
white arm that protruded from the rich folds of the
blue velvet cape. Then my gaze lifted to her face.
Her downcast eyes were shielded by long curving
lashes; high arched silken brows showed dark
against a skin as fresh and free from chemist's pig-
ment as the petal of a rose. In exultant rapture
my heart within me cried that here was something
fine of fibre, a fineness which ran true to the depths
of her soul.

In my discovery of Bertha's innocence and in my
faith in her purity and courage I had hoped to find
relief from the spiritual loneliness that had grown
upon me during my sojourn in this materialistic city.

But that faith was shaken, as the impression Bertha
had made upon my over-sensitized emotions, now
dimmed by a brighter light, flickered pale on the
screen of memory. The mere curiosity and pity
I had felt for a chance victim singled out among
thousands by the legend of innocence on a pretty
face could not stand against the force that now
drew me to this woman who seemed to be not of a
slavish race — even as Dr. Zimmern seemed a
man apart from the soulless product of the science
he directed. But as I acknowledged this new mag-
net tugging at the needle of my floundering heart,
I also realized that my friendship for the lovable
and courageous Zimmern reared an unassailable
barrier to shut me into outer darkness.

The thought proved the harbinger of the reality,
for Dr. Zimmern himself now entered. He was
accompanied by Col. Hellar of the Information
Staff, a man of about Zimmern's age. Col. Hellar
bore himself with a gracious dignity; his face was
sad, yet there gleamed from his eye a kindly humour.

Marguerite, after exchanging a few pleasantries
with Col. Hellar and myself, tenderly kissed the old
doctor on the forehead, and slipped out.

" You shall see much of her," said Zimmern, " she
is the heart and fire of our little group, the force
that holds us together. But tonight I asked her not
to remain "— the old doctor's eyes twinkled with
merriment,— " for a young man cannot get acquainted with a beautiful woman and with ideas
at the same time."

6

" And now," said Zimmern, after we had finished
our dinner, " I want Col. Hellar to tell you more
of the workings of the Information Service."
" It is a very complex system," began Hellar.
" It is old. Its history goes back to the First
World War, when the military censorship began
by suppressing information thought to be dangerous
and circulating fictitious reports for patriotic purposes. Now all is much more elaborately organized; we provide that every child be taught only
the things that it is decided he needs to know, and
nothing more. Have you seen the bulletins and
picture screens in the quarters for the workers? "
" Yes," I replied, " but the lines were all in old
German type."
" And that," said Hellar, " is all that the workers and soldiers can read. The modern type could
be taught them in a few days, but we see to it that
they have no opportunity to learn it. As it is now,
should they find or steal a forbidden book, they
cannot read it."
" But is it not true," I asked, " that at one time
the German workers were most thoroughly educated? "
" It is true," said Hellar, " and because of that
universal education Germany was defeated in the
First World War. The English contaminated the
soldiers by flooding the trenches with democratic
literature dropped from airplanes. Then came the

Bolshevist régime in Russia with its passio.1 for revolutionary propaganda. The working men and soldiers read this disloyal literature and they forced the abdication of William the Great. It was because of this that his great grandson, when the House of Hohenzollern was restored to the throne, decided to curtail universal education.

"But while William III curtailed general education he increased the specialized education and established the Information Staff to supervise the dissemination of all knowledge."

"It is an atrocious system," broke in Zimmern, "but if we had not abolished the family, curtailed knowledge and bred soldiers and workers from special non-intellectual strains this sunless world of ours could not have endured."

"Quite so," said Hellar, "whether we approve of it or not certainly there was no other way to accomplish the end sought. By no other plan could German isolation have been maintained."

"But why was isolation deemed desirable?" I enquired.

"Because," said Zimmern, "it was that or extermination. Even now we who wish to put an end to this isolation, we few who want to see the world as our ancestors saw it, know that the price may be annihilation."

"So," repeated Hellar, "so annihilation for Germany, but better so — and yet I go on as Director of Information; Dr. Zimmern goes on as Chief Eugenist; and you go on seeking to increase the

food supply, and so we all go on as part of the dia-
bolic system, because as individuals we cannot destroy it, but must go on or be destroyed by
it. We have riches here and privileges. We
keep the labourers subdued below us, Royalty en-
throned above us, and the World State at bay
about us, all by this science and system which only
we few intellectuals understand and which we keep
going because we can not stop it without being destroyed by the effort."

"But we shall stop it," declared Zimmern, "we
must stop it — with Armstadt's help we can stop
it. You and I, Hellar, are mere cogs; if we break
others can take our places, but Armstadt has power.
What he knows no one else knows. He has power.
We have only weakness because others can take our
place. And because he has power let us help him
find a way."

"It seems to me," I said, "that the way must be
by education. More men must think as we do."

"But they can not think," replied Hellar, "they
have nothing to think with."

"But the books," I said, "there is power in
knowledge."

"But," said Hellar, "the labourer can not read
the forbidden book and the intellectual will not,
for if he did he would be afraid to talk about it,
and what a man can not talk about he rarely cares
to read. The love or hatred of knowledge is a matter of training. It was only last week that I was
visiting a boy's school in order to study the effect of

a new reader of which complaint had been made that it failed sufficiently to exalt the virtue of obedience. I was talking with the teacher while the boys assembled in the morning. We heard a great commotion and a mob of boys came in dragging one of their companions who had a bruised face and torn clothing. ' Master, he had a forbidden book,' they shouted, and the foremost held out the tattered volume as if it were loathsome poison. It proved to be a text on cellulose spinning. Where the culprit had found it we could not discover but he was sent to the school prison and the other boys were given favours for apprehending him."

"But how is it," I asked, " that books are not written by free-minded authors and secretly printed and circulated? "

At this question my companions smiled. "You chemists forget," said Hellar, " that it takes printing presses to make books. There is no press in all Berlin except in the shops of the Information Staff. Every paper, every book, and every picture originates and is printed there. Every news and book distributor must get his stock from us and knows that he must have only in his possession that which bears the imprint for his level. That is why we have no public libraries and no trade in second-hand books.

" In early life I favoured this system, but in time the foolishness of the thing came to perplex, then to annoy, and finally to disgust me. But I wanted the money and honour that promotion brought and so I have won to my position and power; with my right hand I uphold the system and with my left hand I seek to pull out the props on which it rests. For twenty years now I have nursed the secret traffic in books and risked my life many times thereby, yet my successes have been few and scattered. Every time the auditors check my stock and accounts I tremble in fear, for embezzling books is more dangerous than embezzling credit at the bank."

"But who," I asked, "write the books?"

"For the technical books it is not hard to find authors," explained Hellar, "for any man well schooled in his work can write of it. But the task of getting the more general books written is not so easy. For then it is not so much a question of the author knowing the things of which he writes but of knowing what the various groups are to be permitted to know.

"That writing is done exclusively by especially trained workers of the Information Service. I myself began as such a writer and studied long under the older masters. The school of scientific lying, I called it, but strange to say I used to enjoy such work and did it remarkably well. As recognition of my ability I was commissioned to write the book 'God's Anointed.' Through His Majesty's approval of my work I now owe my position on the Staff.

"His Majesty," continued Hellar, "was only twenty-six years of age when he came to the throne, but he decided at once that a new religious book should be written in which he would be proclaimed as ' God's Anointed ruler of the World.'

" I had never before spoken with the high members of the Royal House, and I was trembling with eagerness and fear as I was ushered into His Majesty's presence.   The Emperor sat at his great black table; before him was an old book.   He turned to me and said, ' Have you ever heard of the Christian Bible?'

" My Chief had informed me that the new book was to be based on the old Bible that the Christians had received from the Hebrews.   So I said, ' Yes, Your Majesty, I am familiar with many of its words.'

" He looked at me with a gloating suspicion. ' Ah, ha,' he said, ' then there is something amiss in the Information Service — you are in the third rank of your service and the Bible is permitted only to the first rank.'

" I saw that my statement unless modified would result in an embarrassing investigation.   ' I have never read the Christian Bible,' I said, ' but my mother must have read it for when as a child I visited her she quoted to me long passages from the Bible.'

" His Majesty smiled in a pleased fashion. ' That is it,' he said, ' women are essentially religious by nature, because they are trusting and obedient. It was a mistake to attempt to stamp out religion. It is the doctrine of obedience.   Therefore I shall revive religion, but it shall be a religion of obedience

to the House of Hohenzollern. The God of the
Hebrews declared them to be his chosen people.
But they proved a servile and mercenary race.
They traded their swords for shekels and became a
byword and a hissing among the nations — and they
were scattered to the four corners of the earth.   I
shall revive that God.   And this time he shall chose
more wisely, for the Germans shall be his people.
The idea is not mine.   William the Great had that
idea, but the revolution swept it away.   It shall be
revived.   We shall have a new Bible, based upon
the old one, a third dispensation, to replace the
work of Moses and Jesus.   And I too shall be a
lawgiver — I shall speak the word of God.' "

Hellar paused; a smile crept over his face.   Then
he laughed softly and to himself — but Dr. Zimmern only shook his head sadly.

" Yes, I wrote the book," continued Hellar.   " It
required four years, for His Majesty was very
critical, and did much revising.   I had a long argument with him over the question of retaining Hell.
I was bitterly opposed to it and represented to His
Majesty that no religion had ever thrived on fear of
punishment without a corresponding hope of re-
ward. ' If you are to have no Heaven,' I insisted,
' then you must have no Hell.'

" ' But we do not need Heaven,' argued His
Majesty, ' Heaven is superfluous.   It is an insult
to my reign.   Is it not enough that a man is a German, and may serve the House of Hohenzollern? '

" ' Then why,' I asked, ' do you need a Hell? '

I should have been shot for that but His Majesty did not see the implication. He replied coolly:

" ' We must have a Hell because there is one way that my subjects can escape me. It is a sin of our race that the Eugenics Office should have bred out — but they have failed. It is an inborn sin for it is chiefly committed by our children before they come to comprehend the glory of being German. How else, if you do not have a Hell in your religion, can you check suicide ? '

" Of course there was logic in his contention and so I gave in and made the Children's Hell. It is a gruesome doctrine, that a child who kills himself does not really die. It is the one thing in the whole book that makes me feel most intellectually unclean for writing it. But I wrote it and when the book was finished and His Majesty had signed the manuscript, for the first time in over a century we printed a bible on a German press. The press where the first run was made we named ' Old Gutenberg.' "

"Gutenberg invented the printing press," explained Zimmern, fearing I might not comprehend.

" Yes," said Hellar with a curling lip, " and Gutenberg was a German, and so am I. He printed a Bible which he believed, and I wrote one which I do not believe."

" But I am glad," concluded Hellar as he arose, " that I do not believe Gutenberg's Bible either, for I should very much dislike to think of meeting him in Paradise."

7

After taking leave of my companions I walked on alone, oblivious to the gay throng, for I had many things on which to ponder. In these two men I felt that I had found heroic figures. Their fund of knowledge, which they prized so highly, seemed to me pitifully circumscribed and limited, their revolutionary plans hopelessly vague and futile. But the intellectual stature of a man is measured in terms of the average of his race, and, thus viewed, Zimmern and Hellar were intellectual giants of heroic proportions.

As I walked through a street of shops, I paused before the display window of a bookstore of the level. Most of these books I had previously discovered were lurid-titled tales of licentious love. But among them I now saw a volume bearing the title " God's Anointed," and recalled that I had seen it before and assumed it to be but another like its fellows.

Entering the store I secured a copy and, impatient to inspect my purchase, I bent my steps to my favourite retreat in the nearby Hall of Flowers. In a secluded niche near the misty fountain I began a hasty perusal of this imperially inspired word of God who had anointed the Hohenzollerns masters of the earth. Hellar's description had prepared me for a preposterous and absurd work, but I had not anticipated anything quite so audacious could be presented to a race of civilized men, much less that they could have accepted it in good faith as the Germans evidently did.

" God's Anointed," as Hellar had scoffingly inferred, not only proclaimed the Germans as the chosen race, but also proclaimed an actual divinity of the blood of the House of Hohenzollern. That William II did have some such notions in his egomania I believe is recorded in authentic history. But the way Eitel I had adapted that faith to the rather depressing facts of the failure of world conquest would have been extremely comical to me, had I not seen ample evidence of the colossal effect of such a faith working in the credulous child-mind of a people so utterly devoid of any saving sense of humour.

Not unfamiliar with the history of the temporal reign of the Popes of the middle ages, I could readily comprehend the practical efficiency of such a mixture of religious faith with the affairs of earth. For the God of the German theology exacted no spiritual worship of his people, but only a very temporal service to the deity's earthly incarnation in the form of the House of Hohenzollern.

The greatest virtue, according to this mundane theology, was obedience, and this doctrine was closely interwoven with the caste system of German society. The virtue of obedience required the German to renounce discontent with his station, and to accept not only the material status into which he was born, with science aforethought, but the intellectual limits and horizons of that status. The old Christian doctrine of heresy was broadened to encompass the entire mental life. To think forbidden thoughts, to search after forbidden knowledge, that was at once treason against the Royal House and rebellion against the divine plan. German theology, confounding divine and human laws, permitted no dual overlapping spheres of mundane and celestial rule as had all previous religious and social orders since Christ had commanded his disciples to " Render unto Caesar —" There could be no conscientious objection to German law on religious grounds; no problem of church and state, for the church was the state.

In this book that masqueraded as the word of God, I looked in vain for some revelation of future life. But it was essentially a one-world theology; the most immortal thing was the Royal House for which the worker was asked to slave, the soldier to die that Germany might be ruled by the Hohenzollerns and that the Hohenzollerns might sometime rule the world.

As the freedom of conscience and the institution of marriage had been discarded so this German faith had scrapped the immortality of the soul, save for the single incongruous doctrine that a child taking his own life does not die but lives on in ceaseless torment in a ghoulish Children's Hell.

As I closed the cursed volume my mind called up a picture of Teutonic hordes pouring from the forests of the North and blotting out what Greece and Rome had builded. From thence my roving

fancy tripped over the centuries and lived again with
men who cannot die. I stood with Luther at the
Diet of Worms. With Kant I sounded the deeps
of philosophy. I sailed with Humboldt athwart
uncharted seas. I fought with Goethe for the re-
demption of a soul sold to the Devil. And with
Schubert and Heine I sang:

> *Du bist wie eine Blume,*
> *So hold und schoen und rein,*
>
> . . . . . .
>
> *Betend dass Gott dich erhalte,*
> *So rein und schoen und hold.*

But what a cankerous end was here. This people which the world had once loved and honoured
was now bred a beast of burden, a domesticated
race, saddled and trained to bear upon its back the
House of Hohenzollern as the ass bore Balaam.
But the German ass wore the blinders that science
had made — and saw no angel.

8

As I sat musing thus and gazing into the spray
of the fountain I glimpsed a grey clad figure, standing in the shadows of a viney bower. Although I
could not distinguish her face through the leafy
tracery I knew that it was Bertha, and my heart
thrilled to think that she had returned to the site
of our meeting. Thoroughly ashamed of the faithless doubts that I had so recently entertained of her
innocence and sincerity, I arose and hastened toward

her. But in making the detour about the pool I lost sight of the grey figure, for she was standing well back in the arbour. As I approached the place where I had seen her I came upon two lovers standing with arms entwined in the path at the pool's edge. Not wishing to disturb them, I turned back through one of the arbours and approached by another path. As I slipped noiselessly along in my felt-soled shoes I heard Bertha's voice, and quite near, through the leafy tracery, I glimpsed the grey of her gown.

" Why with your beauty," came the answering voice of a man, " did you not find a lover from the Royal Level? "

" Because," Bertha's voice replied, " I would not accept them. I could not love them. I could not give myself without love."

" But surely," insisted the man, " you have found a lover here? "

" But I have not," protested the innocent voice, " because I have sought none."

" Now long have you been here? " bluntly asked the man.

" Thirty days," replied the girl.

" Then you must have found a lover, your début fund would all be gone."

" But," cried Bertha, in a tearful voice, " I only· eat one meal a day — do you not see how thin I am? "

" Now that's clever," rejoined the man, " come, I'll accept it for what it is worth, and look you up afterwards," and he laughingly led her away, leaving me undiscovered in the neighbouring arbour to pass judgment on my own simplicity.

As I walked toward the elevator, I was painfully conscious of two ideas. One was that Marguerite had been quite correct with her information about the free women who found it profitable to play the rôle of maidenly innocence. The other was that Dr. Zimmern's precious geography was in the hands of the artful, child-eyed hypocrite who had so cleverly beguiled me with her rôle of heroic virtue. Clearly, I was trapped, and to judge better with what I had to deal I decided to go at once to the Place of Records, of which I had twice heard.

The Place of Records proved to be a public directory of the financial status of the free women. Since the physical plagues that are propagated by promiscuous love had been completely exterminated, and since there were no moral standards to preserve, there was no need of other restrictions on the lives of the women than an economic one.

The rules of the level were prominently posted. As all consequential money exchanges were made through bank checks, the keeping of the records was an easy matter. These rules I found forbade any woman to cash checks in excess of one thousand marks a month, or in excess of two hundred marks from any one man. That was simple enough, and I smiled as I recalled that I had gone the legal limit in my first adventure.

Following the example of other men, I stepped to

the window and gave the name: " Bertha 34 R 6."
A clerk brought me a book opened to the page of her
record.   At the top of the page was entered this
statement, " Bred for an actress but rejected for
both professional work and maternity because found
devoid of sympathetic emotions." I laughed as I
read this, but when on the next line I saw from the
date of her entrance to the level that Bertha's
thirty days was in reality nearly three years, my
mirth turned to anger. I looked down the list of
entries and found that for some time she had been
cashing each month the maximum figure of a
thousand marks. Evidently her little scheme of
pensive posing in the Hall of Flowers was working nicely.   In the current month, hardly half gone,
she already had to her credit seven hundred marks;
and last on the list was my own contribution, freshly
entered.

" She has three hundred marks yet," commented
the clerk.

" Yes, I see,"— and I turned to go. But I
paused and stepped again to the window. " There
is another girl I would like to look up," I said, " but
I have only her name and no number."

" Do you know the date of her arrival? " asked
the clerk.

" Yes, she has been here four years and six days.
The name is Marguerite."

The clerk walked over to a card file and after
some searching brought back a slip with half a
dozen numbers. " Try these," he said, and he

brought me the volumes. The second record I inspected read: " Marguerite, 78 K 4, Love-child."
On the page below was a single entry for each month
of two hundred marks and every entry from the
first was in the name of Ludwig Zimmern.

9

I kept my appointment with Bertha, but found
it difficult to hide my anger as she greeted me.
Wishing to get the interview over, I asked abruptly,
" Have you read the book I left? "

" Not all of it," she replied, " I found it rather
dull."

" Then perhaps I had better take it with me."

" But I think I shall keep it awhile," she demurred.

" No," I insisted, as I looked about and failed
to see the geography, " I wish you would get it for
me. I want to take it back, in fact it was a bor-
rowed book."

" Most likely," she smiled archly, " but since you
are not a staff officer, and had no right to have that
book, you might as well know that you will get it
when I please to give it to you."

Seeing that she was thoroughly aware of my
predicament, I grew frightened and my anger
slipped from its moorings. " See here," I cried,
" your little story of innocence and virtue is very
clever, but I've looked you up and — "

" And what —," she asked, while through her

child-like mask the subtle trickery of her nature mocked me with a look of triumph — " and what do you propose to do about it? "

I realized the futility of my rage. " I shall do nothing. I ask only that you return the book."

" But books are so valuable," taunted Bertha. Dejectedly I sank to the couch. She came over and sat on a cushion at my feet. " Really Karl," she purred, " you should not be angry. If I insist on keeping your book it is merely to be sure that you will not forget me. I rather like you; you are so queer and talk such odd things. Did you learn your strange ways of making love from the book about the inferior races in the world outside the walls? I really tried to read some of it, but I could not understand half the words."

I rose and strode about the room. " Will you get me the book? " I demanded.

" And lose you? "

" Well, what of it? You can get plenty more fools like me."

" Yes, but I would have to stand and stare into that fountain for hours at a time. It is very tiresome."

" Just what do you want? " I asked, trying to speak calmly.

" Why you," she said, placing her slender white hands upon my arm, and holding up an inviting face.

But anger at my own gullibility had killed her

power to draw me, and I shook her off. " I want that book," I said coldly, " what are your terms? " And I drew my check book from my pocket.

" How many blanks have you there? " she asked with a greedy light in her eyes — " but never mind to count them. Make them all out to me at two hundred marks, and date each one a month ahead."

Realizing that any further exhibition of fear or anger would put me more within her power, I sat down and began to write the checks. The fund I was making over to her was quite useless to me but when I had made out twenty checks I stopped. " Now," I said, " this is enough. You take these or nothing." Tearing out the written checks I held them toward her.

As she reached out her hand I drew them back — " Go get the book," I demanded.

" But you are unfair," said Bertha, " you are the stronger. You can take the book from me. I cannot take the checks from you."

" That is so," I admitted, and handed the checks to her. She looked at them carefully and slipped them into her bosom, and then, reaching under the pile of silken pillows, she pulled forth the geography.

I seized it and turned toward the door, but she caught my arm. " Don't," she pleaded, " don't go. Don't be angry with me. Why should you dislike me? I've only played my part as you men make it for us — but I do not want your money for nothing. You liked me when you thought me innocent. Why hate me when you find that I am clever?"

Again those slender arms stole around my neck, and the entrancing face was raised to mine. But the vision of a finer, nobler face rose before me, and I pushed away the clinging arms. "I'm sorry," I said, "I am going now — going back to my work and forget you. It is not your fault. You are only what Germany has made you — but," I added with a smile, "if you must go to the Hall of Flowers, please do not wear that grey gown."

She stood very still as I edged toward the door, and the look of baffled child-like innocence crept back into her eyes, a real innocence this time of things she did not know, and could not understand.

CHAPTER VII

THE SUN SHINES UPON A KING AND A GIRL READS OF THE FALL OF BABYLON

I

EMBITTERED by this unhappy ending of my romance, I turned to my work with savage zeal, determined not again to be diverted by a personal effort to save the Germans from their sins. But this application to my test-tubes was presently interrupted by a German holiday which was known as The Day of the Sun.

From the conversation of my assistants I gathered that this was an annual occasion of particular importance. It was, in fact, His Majesty's birthday, and was celebrated by permitting the favoured classes to see the ruler himself at the Place in the Sun. For this Royal exhibition I received a blue ticket of which my assistants were curiously envious. They inspected the number of it and the hour of my admittance to the Royal Level. "It is the first appearance of the day," they said. "His Majesty will be fresh to speak; you will be near; you will be able to see His Face without the aid of a glass; you will be able to hear His Voice, and not merely the reproducing horns."

In the morning our news bulletin was wholly devoted to announcements and patriotic exuberances. Across the sheet was flamed a headline stating that the meteorologist of the Roof Observatory reported that the sun would shine in full brilliancy upon the throne. This seemed very puzzling to me. For the Place in the Sun was clearly located on the Royal Level and some hundred metres beneath the roof of the city.

I went, at the hour announced on my ticket, to the indicated elevator; and, with an eager crowd of fellow scientists, stepped forth into a vast open space where the vaulted ceiling was supported by massive fluted columns that rose to twice the height of the ordinary spacing of the levels of the city.

An enormous crowd of men of the higher ranks was gathering. Closely packed and standing, the multitude extended to the sides and the rear of my position for many hundred metres until it seemed quite lost under the glowing lights in the distance. Before us a huge curtain hung. Emblazoned on its dull crimson background of subdued socialism was a gigantic black eagle, the leering emblem of autocracy. Above and extending back over us, appeared in the ceiling a deep and unlighted crevice.

As the crowd seemed complete the men about me consulted their watches and then suddenly grew quiet in expectancy. The lights blinked twice and went out, and we were bathed in a hush of darkness. The heavy curtain rustled like the mantle of Jove while from somewhere above I heard the shutters of the windows of heaven move heavily on their rollers. A flashing brilliant beam of light shot through the blackness and fell in wondrous splendour upon a dazzling metallic dais, whereon rested the gilded throne of the House of Hohenzollern.

Seated upon the throne was a man — a very little man he seemed amidst such vast and vivid surroundings. He was robed in a cape of dazzling white, and on his head he wore a helmet of burnished platinum. Before the throne and slightly to one side stood the round form of a paper globe.

His Majesty rose, stepped a few paces forward; and, as he with solemn deliberation raised his hand into the shaft of burning light, from the throng there came a frenzied shouting, which soon changed into a sort of chanting and then into a throaty song.

His Majesty lowered his hand; the song ceased; a great stillness hung over the multitude. Eitel I, Emperor of the Germans, now raised his face and stared for a moment unblinkingly into the beam of sunlight, then he lowered his gaze toward the sea of upturned faces.

" My people," he said, in a voice which for all his pompous effort, fell rather flat in the immensity, " you are assembled here in the Place of the Sun to do honour to God's anointed ruler of the world."

From ten thousand throats came forth another raucous shout.

" Two and a half centuries ago," now spoke His Majesty, " God appointed the German race, under

William the Great, of the House of Hohenzollern, to be the rulers of the world.

"For nineteen hundred years, God in his infinite patience, had awaited the outcome of the test of the Nazarene's doctrine of servile humility and effeminate peace. But the Christian nations of the earth were weighed in the balance of Divine wrath and found wanting. Wallowing in hypocrisy and ignorance, wanting in courage and valour; behind a pretence of altruism they cloaked their selfish greed for gold.

"Of all the people of the earth our race alone possessed the two keys to power, the mastery of science and the mastery of the sword. So the Germans were called of God to instil fear and reverence into the hearts of the inferior races. That was the purpose of the First World War under my noble ancestor, William II.

"But the envious nations, desperate in their greed, banded together to defy our old German God, and destroy His chosen people. But this was only a divine trial of our worth, for the plans of God are for eternity. His days to us are centuries. And we did well to patiently abide the complete unfoldment of the Divine plan.

"Before two generations had passed our German ancestors cast off the yoke of enslavement and routed the oppressors in the Second World War. Lest His chosen race be contaminated by the swinish herds of the mongrel nations God called upon His people to relinquish for a time the fruits of conquest, that they might be further purged by science and become a pure-bred race of super-men.

"That purification has been accomplished for every German is bred and trained by science as ordained by God. There are no longer any mongrels among the men of Germany, for every one of you is created for his special purpose and every German is fitted for his particular place as a member of the super-race.

"The time now draws near when the final purpose of our good old German God is to be fulfilled. The day of this fulfilment is known unto me. The sun which shines upon this throne is but a symbol of that which has been denied you while all these things were being made ready. But now the day draws near when you shall, under my leadership, rule over the world and the mongrel peoples. And to each of you shall be given a place in the sun."

The voice had ceased. A great stillness hung over the multitude. Eitel I, Emperor of the Germans, threw back his cape and drew his sword. With a sweeping flourish he slashed the paper globe in twain.

From the myriad throated throng came a reverberating shout that rolled and echoed through the vaulted catacomb. The crimson curtain dropped. The shutters were thrown athwart the reflected beam of sunlight. The lights of man again glowed pale amidst the maze of columns.

Singing and marching, the men filed toward the elevators. The guards urged haste to clear the way, for the God of the Germans could not stay the march of the sun across the roof of Berlin, and a score of paper globes must yet be slashed for other shouting multitudes before the sun's last gleam be twisted down to shine upon a king.

2

Although the working hours of the day were scarcely one-fourth gone, it was impossible for me to return to my laboratory for the lighting current was shut off for the day. I therefore decided to utilize the occasion by returning the geography which I had rescued from Bertha.

Dr. Zimmern's invitation to make use of his library had been cordial enough, but its location in Marguerite's apartment had made me a little reticent about going there except in the Doctor's company. Yet I did not wish to admit to Zimmern my sensitiveness in the matter — and the geography had been kept overlong.

This occasion being a holiday, I found the resorts on the Level of Free Women crowded with merrymakers. But I sought the quieter side streets and made my way towards Marguerite's apartment.

" I thought you would be celebrating today," she said as I entered.

" I feel that I can utilize the time better by reading," I replied. " There is so much I want to learn, and, thanks to Dr. Zimmern, I now have the opportunity."

" But surely you are to see the Emperor in the

Place in the Sun," said Marguerite when she had returned the geography to the secret shelf.

"I have already seen him," I replied, "my ticket was for the first performance."

"It must be a magnificent sight," she sighed. "I should so love to see the sunlight. The pictures show us His Majesty's likeness, but what is a picture of sunlight?"

"But you speak only of a reflected beam; how would you like to see real sunshine?"

"Oh, on the roof of Berlin? But that is only for Royalty and the roof guards. I've tried to imagine that, but I know that I fail as a blind man must fail to imagine colour."

"Close your eyes," I said playfully, "and try very hard."

Solemnly Marguerite closed her eyes.

For a moment I smiled, and then the smile relaxed, for I felt as one who scoffs at prayer.

"And did you see the sunlight?" I asked, as she opened her eyes and gazed at me with dilated pupils.

"No," she answered hoarsely, "I only saw manlight as far as the walls of Berlin, and beyond that it was all empty blackness — and it frightens me."

"The fear of darkness," I said, "is the fear of ignorance."

"You try," and she reached over with a soft touch of her finger tips on my closing eyelids. "Now keep them closed and tell me what you see. Tell me it is not all black."

" I see light," I said, " white light, on a billowy
sea of clouds, as from a flying plane. . . . And now
I see the sun — it is sinking behind a rugged line of
snowy peaks and the light is dimming. . . . It is
gone now, but it is not dark, for moonlight, pale and
silvery, is shimmering on a choppy sea. . . . Now it
is the darkest hour, but it is never black, only a dark,
dark grey, for the roof of the world is pricked with
a million points of light. . . . The grey of the east
is shot with the rose of dawn. . . . The rose bright-
ens to scarlet and the curve of the sun appears —
red like the blood of war. . . . And now the sky is
crystal blue and the grey sands of the desert have
turned to glittering gold."

I had ceased my poetic visioning and was looking
into Marguerite's face. The light of worship I
saw in her eyes filled me with a strange trembling
and holy awe.

" And I saw only blackness," she faltered. " Is
it that I am born blind and you with vision? "

" Perhaps what you call vision is only memory,"
I said — but, as I realized where my words were
leading, I hastened to add —" Memory, from another life. Have you ever heard of such a thing
as the reincarnation of the soul? "

" That means," she said hesitatingly, " that there
is something in us that does not die — immortality,
is it not? "

" Well, it is something like that," I answered
huskily, as I wondered what she might know or
dream of that which lay beyond the ken of the gross

materialism of her race. "Immortality is a very beautiful idea," I went on, " and science has destroyed much that is beautiful. But it is a pity that Col. Hellar had to eliminate the idea of immortality from the German Bible. Surely such a book makes no pretence of being scientific."

"So Col. Hellar has told you that he wrote ' God's Anointed '? " exclaimed Marguerite with eager interest.

" Yes, he told me of that and I re-read the book with an entirely different viewpoint since I came to understand the spirit in which it was written."

"Ah — I see." Marguerite rose and stepped toward the library. " We have a book here," she called, " that you have not read, and one that you cannot buy. It will show you the source of Col. Hellar's inspiration."

She brought out a battered volume. " This book," she stated, " has given the inspectors more trouble than any other book in existence. Though they have searched for thirty years, they say there are more copies of it still at large than of all other forbidden books combined."

I gazed at the volume she handed me — I was holding a copy of the Christian Bible translated six centuries previous by Martin Luther. It was indeed the very text from which as a boy I had acquired much of my reading knowledge of the language. But I decided that I had best not reveal to Marguerite my familiarity with it, and so I sat

down and turned the pages with assumed perplexity.
" It is a very odd book," I remarked presently.
" Have you read it? "

" Oh, yes," exclaimed Marguerite. " I often
read it; I think it is more interesting than all these
modern books, but perhaps that is because I cannot
understand it; I love mysterious things."

" There is too much of it for a man as busy as
I am to hope to read," I remarked, after turning a
few more pages, " and so I had better not begin.
Will you not choose something and read it aloud to
me? "

Marguerite declined at first; but, when I insisted,
she took the tattered Bible and turned slowly through
its pages.

And when she read, it was the story of a king
who revelled with his lords, and of a hand that
wrote upon a wall.

Her voice was low, and possessed a rhythm and
cadence that transmuted the guttural German tongue
into musical poetry.

Again she read, of a man who, though shorn of
his strength by the wiles of a woman and blinded
by his enemies, yet pushed asunder the pillars of a
city.

At random she read other tales, of rulers and of
slaves, of harlots and of queens — the wisdom of
prophets — the songs of kings.

Together we pondered the meanings of these
strange things, and exulted in the beauty of that

which was meaningless.   And so the hours passed;
the day drew near its close and Marguerite read
from the last pages of the book, of a voice that cried
mightily —" Babylon the great is fallen, is fallen,
and is become the habitation of devils and the hold
of every foul spirit."

CHAPTER VIII

I

MY first call upon Marguerite had been followed by other visits when we had talked
of books and read together. On these
occasions I had carefully suppressed my desire to
speak of more personal things. But, constantly re-
minded by my own troubled conscience, I grew fearful lest the old doctor should discover that the books
were the lesser part of the attraction that drew me
to Marguerite's apartment, and my fear was increased as I realized that my calls on Zimmern had
abruptly ceased.

Thinking to make amends I went one evening to
the doctor's apartment.

"I was going out shortly," said Zimmern, as he
greeted me. "I have a dinner engagement with
Hellar on the Free Level. But I still have a little
time; if it pleases you we might walk along to our
library."

I promptly accepted the invitation, hoping that
it would enable me better to establish my relation
to Marguerite and Zimmern in a safe triangle of
mutual friendship. As we walked, Zimmern, as if

he read my thoughts, turned the conversation to the very subject that was uppermost in my mind.

"I am glad, Armstadt," he said with a gracious smile, "that you and Marguerite seem to enjoy each other's friendship. I had often wished there were younger men in our group, since her duties as care-taker of our books quite forbids her cultivating the acquaintance of any men outside our chosen few. Marguerite is very patient with the dull talk of us old men, but life is not all books, and there is much that youth may share."

For these words of Zimmern's I was quite unpre-pared. He seemed to be inviting me to make love to Marguerite, and I wondered to what extent the prevailing social ethics might have destroyed the finer sensibilities that forbid the sharing of a wom-an's love.

When we reached the apartment Marguerite greeted us with a perfect democracy of manner. But my reassurance of the moment was presently disturbed when she turned to Zimmern and said: "Now that you are here, I am going for a bit of a walk; I have not been out for two whole days."

"Very well," the doctor replied. "I cannot re-main long as I have an engagement with Hellar, but perhaps Armstadt will remain until you return."

"Then I shall have him all to myself," declared Marguerite with quiet seriousness.

Though I glanced from the old doctor to the young woman in questioning amazement, neither seemed in the least embarrassed or aware that anything had been said out of keeping with the customary propriety of life.

Marguerite, throwing the blue velvet cape about her bare white shoulders, paused to give the old doctor an affectionate kiss, and with a smile for me was gone.

For a few moments the doctor sat musing; but when he turned to me it was to say: " I hope that you are making good use of our precious accumulation of knowledge."

In reply I assured him of my hearty appreciation of the library.

" You can see now," continued Zimmern, " how utterly the mind of the race has been enslaved, how all the vast store of knowledge, that as a whole makes life possible, is parcelled out for each. Not one of us is supposed to know of those vital things outside our own narrow field. That knowledge is forbidden us lest we should understand the workings of our social system and question the wisdom of it all. And so, while each is wiser in his own little cell than were the men of the old order, yet on all things else we are little children, accepting what we are taught, doing what we are told, with no mind, no souls of our own. Scientists have ceased to be men, and have become thinking machines, specialized for their particular tasks."

" That is true," I said, " but what are we to do about it? You have by these forbidden books acquired a realization of the enslavement of the race — but the others, all these millions of professional men, are they not hopelessly rendered impotent by the systematic suppression of knowledge? "

" The millions, yes," replied Zimmern, " but there are the chosen few; we who have seen the light must find a way for the liberation of all."

" Do you mean," I asked eagerly, " that you are planning some secret rebellion — that you hope for some possible rising of the people to overthrow the system? "

Zimmern looked at me in astonishment. " The people," he said, " cannot rise. In the old order such a thing was possible — revolutions they called them — the people led by heroes conceived passions for liberty. But such powers of mental reaction no longer exist in German minds. We have bred and trained it out of them. One might as well have expected the four-footed beasts of burden in the old agricultural days to rebel against their masters."

" But," I protested, " if the people could be enlightened? "

" How," exclaimed Zimmern impatiently, " can you enlighten them? You are young, Armstadt, very young to talk of such things — even if a rebellion was a possibility what would be the gain? Rebellion means disorder — once the ventilating machinery of the city and the food processes were disturbed we should all perish in this trap — we should all die of suffocation and starvation."

" Then why," I asked, " do you talk of this thing? If rebellion is impossible and would, if possible, destroy us all, then is there any hope? "

Zimmern paced the floor for a time in silence and then, facing me squarely, he said, " I have confessed to you my dissatisfaction with the existing state. In doing this I placed myself in great danger, but I risked that and now I shall risk more.   I ask you now, Are you with us to the end? "

" Yes," I replied very gravely, " I am with you although I cannot fully understand on what you base your hope."

" Our hope," replied Zimmern, " is out there in the world from whence come those flying men who rain bombs on the roof of Berlin and for ever keep us patching it.   We must get word to them.   We must throw ourselves upon the humanity of our enemies and ask them to save us."

" But," I questioned, in my excitement, " what can Germany expect of the enemy?   She has made war against the world for centuries — will that world permit Germany to live could they find a way to destroy her? "

" As a nation, no, but as men, yes.   Men do not kill men as individuals, they only make war against a nation of men.   As long as Germany is capable of making war against the world so long will the world attempt to destroy her.   You, Colonel Armstadt, hold in your protium secret the power of Germany to continue the war against the world.   Because you were about to gain that power I risked my own life to aid you in getting a wider knowledge.   Because you now hold that power I risk it again by asking you to use it to destroy Germany and save the Germans. The men who are with me in this cause, and for whom I speak, are but a few. The millions materially alive, are spiritually dead. The world alone can give them life again as men. Even though a few million more be destroyed in the giving have not millions already been destroyed? What if you do save Germany now — what does it mean merely that we breed millions more like we now have, soulless creatures born to die like worms in the ground, brains working automatically, stamping out one sort of idea, like machines that stamp out buttons — or mere mouths shouting like phonographs before this gaudy show of royalty?"

" But," I said, " you speak for the few emancipated minds; what of all these men who accept the system — you call them slaves, yet are they not content with their slavery, do they want to be men of the world or continue here in their bondage and die fighting to keep up their own system of enslavement?"

" It makes no difference what they want," replied Zimmern, in a voice that trembled with emotion; " we bred them as slaves to the *kultur* of Germany, the thing to do is to stop the breeding."

" But how," I asked, " can men who have been beaten into the mould of the ox ever be restored to their humanity?"

" The old ones cannot," sighed Zimmern; " it was always so; when a people has once fallen into evil ways the old generation can never be wholly redeemed, but youth can always be saved — youth is plastic."

"But the German race," I said, "has not only been mis-educated, it has been mis-bred. Can you undo inheritance? Can this race with its vast horde of workers bred for a maximum of muscle and a minimum of brains ever escape from that stupidity that has been bred into the blood?"

"You have been trained as a chemist," said Zimmern, "you despair of the future because you do not understand the laws of inheritance. A specialized type of man or animal is produced from the selection of the extreme individuals. That you know. But what you do not know is that the type once established does not persist of its own accord. It can only be maintained by the rigid continuance of the selection. The average stature of man did not change a centimetre in a thousand years, till we came in with our meddlesome eugenics. Leave off our scientific meddling and the race will quickly revert to the normal type.

"That applies to the physical changes; in the mental powers the restoration will be even more rapid, because we have made less change in the psychic elements of the germ plasm. The inborn capacity of the human brain is hard to alter. Men are created more nearly equal than even the writers of democratic constitutions have ever known. If the World State will once help us to free ourselves from these shackles of rigid caste and cultured ignorance, this folly of scientific meddling with the blood and brains of man, there is yet hope for this race, for we have changed far less than we pretend, in the marrow we are human still."

The old man sank back in his chair. The fire in his soul had burned out. His hand fumbled for his watch. " I must leave you now," he said; " Marguerite should be back shortly. From her you need conceal nothing. She is the soul of our hopes and our dreams. She keeps our books safe and our hearts fine. Without her I fear we should all have given up long ago."

With a trembling handclasp he left me alone in Marguerite's apartment. And alone too with my conflicting and troubled emotions. He was a lovable soul, ripe with the wisdom of age, yet youthful in his hopes to redeem his people from the curse of this unholy blend of socialism and autocracy that had prostituted science and made a black Utopian nightmare of man's millennial dream.

Vaguely I wondered how many of the three hundred millions of German souls — for I could not accept the soulless theory of Zimmern — were yet capable of a realization of their humanity. To this query there could be no answer, but of one conclusion I was certain, it was not my place to ask what these people wanted, for their power to decide was destroyed by the infernal process of their making — but here at least, my democratic training easily gave the answer that Dr. Zimmern had achieved by sheer genius, and my answer was that for men whose desire for liberty has been destroyed, liberty must be thrust upon them.

But it remained for me to work out a plan for so difficult a salvation. Of this I was now assured that I need no longer work alone, for as I had long suspected, Dr. Zimmern and his little group of rebellious souls were with me. But what could so few do amidst all the millions? My answer, like Zimmern's, was that the salvation of Germany lay in the enemies' hands — and I alone was of that enemy. Yet never again could I pray for the destruction of the city at the hands of the outraged god — Humanity. And I thought of Sodom and Gomorrah which the God of Abraham had agreed to spare if there be found ten righteous men therein.

2

From these far-reaching thoughts my mind was drawn sharply back to the fact of my presence in Marguerite's apartment and the realization that she would shortly return to find me there alone. I resented the fact that the old doctor and the young woman could conspire to place me in such a situation. I resented the fact that a girl like Marguerite could be bound to a man three times her age, and yet seem to accept it with perfect grace. But I resented most of all the fact that both sne and Zimmern appeared to invite me to share in a triangle of love, open and unashamed.

My bitter brooding was disturbed by the sound of a key turning in the lock, and Marguerite, fresh and charming from the exhilaration of her walk, came into the room.

" I am so glad you remained," she said. " I hope no one else comes and we can have the evening to ourselves."

" It seems," I answered with a touch of bitterness, " that Dr. Zimmern considers me quite a safe playmate for you."

At my words Marguerite blushed prettily. " I know you do not quite understand," she said, " but you see I am rather peculiarly situated. I cannot go out much, and I can have no girl friends here, and no men either except those who are in this little group who know of our books. And they, you see, are all rather old, mostly staff officers like the doctor himself, and Col. Hellar. You rank quite as well as some of the others, but you are ever so much younger. That is why the doctor thinks you are so wonderful — I mean because you have risen so high at so early an age — but perhaps I think you are rather wonderful just because you are young. Is it not natural for young people to want friends of their own age? "

" It is," I replied with ill-concealed sarcasm.

" Why do you speak like that? " asked Marguerite in pained surprise.

" Because a burnt child dreads the fire."

" I do not understand," she said, a puzzled look in her eyes. " How could a child be burned by a fire since it could never approach one. They only have fires in the smelting furnaces, and children could never go near them."

Despite my bitter mood I smiled as I said: "It is just a figure of speech that I got out of an old book. It means that when one is hurt by something he does not want to be hurt in the same way again. You remember what you said to me in the café about looking up the girl who played the innocent rôle? I did look her up, and you were right about it. She has been here three years and has a score of lovers."

"And you dropped her?"

"Of course I dropped her."

"And you have not found another?"

"No, and I do not want another, and I had not made love to this girl either, as you think I had; perhaps I would have done so, but thanks to you I was warned in time. I may be even younger than you think I am, young at least in experience with the free women of Berlin. This is the second apartment I have ever been in on this level."

"Why do you tell me this?" questioned Marguerite.

"Because," I said doggedly, "because I suppose that I want you to know that I have spent most of my time in a laboratory. I also want you to know that I do not like the artful deceit that you all seem to cultivate."

"And do you think I am trying to deceive you?" cried Marguerite reproachfully.

" Your words may be true," I said, " but the situation you place me in is a false one.   Dr. Zimmern brings me here that I may read your books.   He leaves me alone here with you and urges me to come as often as I choose.   All that is hard enough, but to make it harder for me, you tell me that you particularly want my company because you have no other young friends.   In fact you practically ask me to make love to you and yet you know why I cannot."

In the excitement of my warring emotions I had risen and was pacing the floor, and now as I reached the climax of my bitter speech, Marguerite, with a choking sob, fled from the room.

Angered at the situation and humiliated by what I had said, I was on the point of leaving at once. But a moment of reflection caused me to turn back. I had forced a quarrel upon Marguerite and the cause for my anger she perhaps did not comprehend. If I left now it would be impossible to return, and if I did not come back, there would be explanations to make to Zimmern and perhaps an ending of my association with him and his group, which was not only the sole source of my intellectual life outside my work, but which I had begun to hope might lead to some enterprise of moment and possibly to my escape from Berlin.

So calming my anger, I turned to the library and doggedly pulled down a book and began scanning its contents.   I had been so occupied for some time, when there was a ring at the bell.   I peered out into the reception-room in time to see Marguerite come from another door. Her eyes revealed the fact that she had been crying. Quickly she closed the door of the little library, shutting me in with the books. A moment later she came in with a grey-haired man, a staff officer of the electrical works. She introduced us coolly and then helped the old man find a book he wanted to take out, and which she entered on her records.

After the visitor had gone Marguerite again slipped out of the room and for a time I despaired of a chance to speak to her before I felt I must depart. Another hour passed and then she stole into the library and seated herself very quietly on a little dressing chair and watched me as I proceeded with my reading.

I asked her some questions about one of the volumes and she replied with a meek and forgiving voice that made me despise myself heartily. Other questions and answers followed and soon we were talking again of books as if we had no overwhelming sense of the personal presence of each other.

The hours passed; by all my sense of propriety I should have been long departed, but still we talked of books without once referring to my heated words of the earlier evening.

She had stood enticingly near me as we pulled down the volumes. My heart beat wildly as she sat by my side, while I mechanically turned the pages. The brush of her garments against my sleeve quite maddened me. I had not dared to look into her eyes, as I talked meaningless, bookish words.

Summoning all my self-control, I now faced her. " Marguerite," I said hoarsely, " look at me."

She lifted her eyes and met my gaze unflinchingly, the moisture of fresh tears gleaming beneath her lashes.

" Forgive me," I entreated.

" For what? " she asked simply, smiling a little through her tears.

" For being a fool," I declared fiercely, " for be- lieving your cordiality toward me as Dr. Zimmern's friend to mean more than — than it should mean."

" But I do not understand," she said. " Should I not have told you that I liked you because you were young? Of course if you don't want me to — to —" She paused abruptly, her face suffused with a delicate crimson.

I stepped toward her and reached out my arms. But she drew back and slipped quickly around the table. " No," she cried, " no, you have said that you did not want me."

" But I do," I cried. " I do want you."

" Then why did you say those things to me? " she asked haughtily.

I gazed at her across the narrow table. Was it possible that such a woman had no understanding of ideals of honour in love? Could it be that she had no appreciation of the fight I had waged, and so nearly lost, to respect the trust and confidence that the old doctor had placed in me. With these thoughts the ardour of my passion cooled and a

feeling of pity swept over me, as I sensed the tragedy of so fine a woman ethically impoverished by
false training and environment.   Had she known
honour, and yet discarded it, I too should have been
unable to resist the impulse of youth to deny to age
its less imperious claims.

But either she chose artfully to ignore my struggle or she was truly unaware of it.   In either case
she would not share the responsibility for the breach
of faith.   I was puzzled and confounded.

It was Marguerite who broke the bewildering silence.   "I wish you would go now," she said
coolly; "I am afraid I misunderstood."

"And shall I come again?" I asked awkwardly.
She looked up at me and smiled bravely.   "Yes,"
she said, "if — you are sure you wish to."

A resurge of passionate longing to take her in my
arms swept over me, but she held out her hand with
such rare and dignified grace that I could only take
the slender fingers and press them hungrily to my
fevered lips and so bid her a wordless adieu.

3

But despite wild longing to see her again, I did
not return to Marguerite's apartment for many
weeks.   A crisis in my work at the laboratory denied me even a single hour of leisure outside brief
snatches of food and sleep.

I had previously reported to the Chemical Staff
that I had found means to increase materially the
extraction percentage of the precious element pro-

tium from the crude imported ore. I had now received word that I should prepare to make a trial demonstration before the Staff.

Already I had revealed certain results of my progress to Herr von Uhl, as this had been necessary in order to get further grants of the rare material and of expensive equipment needed for the research, but in these smaller demonstrations, I had not been called upon to disclose my method. Now the Staff, hopeful that I had made the great discovery, insisted that I prepare at once to make a large scale demonstration and reveal the method that it might immediately be adopted for the wholesale extraction in the industrial works.

If I now gave away the full secret of my process, I would receive compensation that would indeed seem lavish for a man whose mental horizon was bounded by these enclosing walls; yet to me for whom these walls would always be a prison, credit at the banks of Berlin and the baubles of decoration and rank and social honour would be sounding brass. But I wanted power; and, with the secret of protium extraction in my possession, I would have control of life or death over three hundred million men. Why should I sacrifice such power for useless credit and empty honour? If Eitel I of the House of Hohenzollern would lengthen the days of his rule, let him deal with me and meet whatever terms I chose to name, for in my chemical retorts I had brewed a secret before which vaunted efficiency and hypocritical divinity could be made to bend a hungry belly and beg for food!

It was a laudable and rather thrilling ambition, and yet I was not clear as to just what terms I would dictate, nor how I could enforce the dictation. To ask for an audience with the Emperor now, and to take any such preposterous stand would merely be to get myself locked up for a lunatic. But I reasoned that if I could make the demonstration so that it would be accepted as genuine and yet not give away my secret, the situation would be in my hands. Yet I was expected to reveal the process step by step as the demonstration proceeded. There was but one way out and that was to make a genuine demonstration, but with falsely written formulas.

To plan and prepare such a demonstration required more genuine invention than had the discovery of the process, but I set about the task with feverish enthusiasm. I kept my assistants busy with the preparation of the apparatus and the more simple work which there was no need to disguise, while night after night I worked alone, altering and disguising the secret steps on which my great discovery hinged. As these preparations were nearing completion I sent for Dr. Zimmern and Col. Hellar to meet me at my apartment.

" Comrades," I said, " you have endangered your own lives by confiding in me your secret desires to overthrow the rule of the House of Hohenzollern as it was overthrown once before. You have done this because you believed that I would have power that others do not have."

The two old men nodded in grave assent.

" And you have been quite fortunate in your choice," I concluded, " for not only have I pledged myself to your ends, but I shall soon possess the coveted power. In a few days I shall demonstrate my process on a large scale before the Chemical Staff. But I shall do this thing without revealing the method. The formulas I shall give them will be meaningless. As long as I am in charge in my own laboratory the process will be a success; when it is tried elsewhere it will fail, until I choose to make further revelations.

" So you see, for a time, unless I be killed or tortured into confession, I shall have great power. How then may I use that power to help you in the cause to which we are pledged? "

The older men seemed greatly impressed with my declaration and danced about me and cried with joy. When they had regained their composure Zimmern said: " There is but one thing you can do for us and that is to find some way to get word of the protium mines to the authorities of the World State. Berlin will then be at their mercy, but whatever happens can be no worse than the continuance of things as they are."

" But how," I said, " can a message be sent from Berlin to the outer world? "

" There is only one way," replied Hellar, " and that is by the submarines that go out for this ore.

The Submarine Staff are members of the Royal House. So, indeed, are the captains. We have tried for years to gain the confidence of some of these men, but without avail. Perhaps through your work on the protium ore you can succeed where we have failed."

"And how," I asked eagerly, "do the ore-bringing vessels get from Berlin to the sea?"

My visitors glanced at each other significantly. "Do you not know that?" exclaimed Zimmern. "We had supposed you would have been told when you were assigned to the protium research."

By way of answer I explained that I knew the source of the ore but not the route of its coming.

"All such knowledge is suppressed in books," commented Hellar; "we older men know of this by word of mouth from the days when the submarine tunnel was completed to the sea, but you are younger. Unless this was told you at the time you were assigned the work it is not to be expected that you would know."

I questioned Hellar and Zimmern closely but found that all they knew was that a submarine tunnel did exist leading from Berlin somewhere into the open sea; but its exact location they did not know. Again I pressed my question as to what I could do with the power of my secret and they could only repeat that they staked their hopes on getting word to the outer world by way of submarines.

Much as I might admire the strength of character that would lead men to rebel against the only

life they knew beçause they sensed that it was hopeless, I now found myself a little exasperated at the
vagueness of their plans. Yet I had none better.
To defy the Emperor would merely be to risk my
life and the possible loss of my knowledge to the
world. Perhaps after all the older heads were
wiser than my own rebellious spirit; and so, without
making any more definite plans, I ended the interview with a promise to let them know of the outcome of the demonstration.

Returning once more to my work I finished my
preparations and sent word to the Chemical Staff
that all was ready. They came with solemn faces.
The laboratory was locked and guards were posted.
The place was examined thoroughly, the apparatus
was studied in detail. All my ingredients were
tested for the presence of extracted protium, lest I
be trying to " salt the mine." But happily for me
they accepted my statement as to their chemical nature in other respects. Then when all had been
approved the test lot of ore was run. It took us
thirty hours to run the extraction and sample and
weigh and test the product. But everything went
through exactly as I had planned.

With solemn faces the Chemical Staff unanimously
declared that the problem had been solved and marvelled that the solution should come from the brain
of so young a man. And so I received their adula-
tion and worship, for I could not give credit to the
chemists of the world outside to whom I was really
indebted for my seeming miraculous genius. Tell-

ing me to take my rest and prepare myself for an
audience with His Majesty three days later, the
Chemical Staff departed, carrying, with guarded secrecy, my false formulas.

4

Exultant and happy I left the laboratory. I had
not slept for forty hours and scarcely half my regular allotment for many weeks. And yet I was not
sleepy now but awake and excited. I had won a
great victory, and I wanted to rejoice and share my
conquest with sympathetic ears. I could go to Zimmern, but instead I turned my steps toward the elevator and, alighting on the Level of the Free
Women, I went straightway to Marguerite's apartment.

Despite my feeling of exhilaration, my face must
have revealed something of my real state of exhaus-
tion, for Marguerite cried in alarm at the sight of
me.

" A little tired," I replied, in answer to her solicitous questions; " I have just finished my demonstration before the Chemical Staff."

" And you won? " cried Marguerite in a burst of
joy. " You deceived them just as the doctor said
you would. And they know you have solved the
protium problem and they do not know how you
did it? "

" That is correct," I said, sinking back into the
cushions of the divan. " I have done all that. I
came here first to tell you. You see I could not

come before, all these weeks, I have had no time for sleep or anything. I would have telephoned or written but I feared it would not be safe. Did you think I was not coming again? "

" I missed you at first,— I mean at first I thought you were staying away because you did not want to see me, and then Dr. Zimmern told me what you were doing, and I understood — and waited, for I somehow knew you would come as soon as you could."

" Yes, of course you knew. Of course, I had to come — Marguerite —" But Marguerite faded before my vision. I reached out my hand for her — and it seemed to wave in empty space. . . .

5

When I awoke, I was lying on a couch and a screen bedecked with cupids was standing before me. At first I thought I was alone and then I realized that I was in Marguerite's apartment and that Marguerite herself was seated on a low stool beside the couch and gazing at me out of dreamy eyes.

" How did I get here? " I asked.

" You fell asleep while you were talking, and then some one came for books, and when the bell rang I hid you with the screen."

" How long have I slept? "

" For many hours," she answered.

" I ought not to have come," I said, but despite my remark I made no haste to go, but reached out and ran my fingers through her massy hair. And then I slowly drew her toward me until her luxuriant locks were tumbled about my neck and face and her head was pillowed on my breast.

" I am so happy," she whispered.   " I am so glad you came first to me."

For a moment my reason was drugged by the opiate of her touch; and then, as the realization of the circumstances re-formed in my brain, the feeling of guilt arose and routed the dreamy bliss.   Yet I could only blame myself, for there was no guile in her act or word, nor could I believe there was guile in her heart.   Gently I pushed her away and arose, stating that I must leave at once.

It was plainly evident that Marguerite did not share my sense of embarrassment, that she was aware of no breach of ethics.   But her ease only served to impress upon me the greater burden of my responsibility and emphasize the breach of honour of which I was guilty in permitting this expression of my love to a woman whom circumstances had bound to Zimmern.

Pleading need for rest and for time to plan my interview with His Majesty, I hastened away, feeling that I dare not trust myself alone with her again.

6

I returned to my own apartment, and when another day had passed, food and sleep had fully restored me to a normal state.   I then recalled my promise to inform Hellar and Zimmern of the outcome of my demonstration.   I called at Zimmern's quarters but he was not at home.   Hence I went to call on Hellar, to ask of Zimmern's whereabouts.

" I have an appointment to meet him tonight," said Hellar, " on the Level of Free Women.   Will you not come along? "

I could not well do otherwise than accept, and Hellar led me again to the apartment from which I had fled twenty-four hours before.   There we found Zimmern, who received me with his usual graciousness.

" I have already heard from Marguerite," said Zimmern, " of your success."

I glanced apprehensively at the girl but she was in no wise disturbed, and proceeded to relate for Hellar's information the story of my coming to her exhausted from my work and of my falling asleep in her apartment.   All of them seemed to think it amusing, but there was no evidence that any one considered it the least improper.   Their matter-of-fact attitude puzzled and annoyed me; they seemed to treat the incident as if it had been the experience of a couple of children.

This angered me, for it seemed proof that they considered Marguerite's love as the common property of any and all.

" Could it be," I asked myself, " that jealousy has been bred and trained out of this race?   Is it possible they have killed the instinct that demands private and individual property in love? "   Even as I pondered the problem it seemed answered, for as I sat and talked with Zimmern and Hellar of my chemical demonstration and the coming interview with His Majesty, Marguerite came and seated herself on the arm of my chair and pillowed her head on my shoulder. Troubled and embarrassed, yet not having the courage to repulse her caresses, I stared at Zimmern, who smiled on us with indulgence. In fact it seemed that he actually enjoyed the scene. My anger flamed up against him, but for Marguerite I had only pity, for her action seemed so natural and unaffected that I could not believe that she was making sport of me, and could only conclude that she had been so bred in the spirit of the place that she knew nothing else.

My talk with the men ended as had the last one, without arriving at any particular plan of action, and when Hellar arose first to go, I took the opportunity to escape from what to me was an intolerable situation.

7

I separated from Hellar and for an hour or more I wandered on the level. Then resolving to end the strain of my enigmatical position I turned again toward Marguerite's apartment. She answered my ring. I entered and found her alone.

" Marguerite," I began, " I cannot stand this intolerable situation. I cannot share the love of a woman with another man — I cannot steal a woman's love from a man who is my friend —"

At this outburst Marguerite only stared at me in

puzzled amazement. "Then you do not want me to love you," she stammered.

"God knows," I cried, "how I do want you to love me, but it must not be while Dr. Zimmern is alive and you —"

"So," said a voice — and glancing up I saw Zimmern himself framed in the doorway of the book room. The old doctor looked from me to Marguerite, while a smile beamed on his courtly countenance.

"Sit down and calm yourself, Armstadt," said Zimmern. "It is time I spoke to you of Marguerite and of the relation I bear to her. As you know, I brought her to this level from the school for girls of forbidden birth. But what you do not know is that she was born on the Royal Level.

"I knew Marguerite's mother. She was Princess Fedora, a third cousin of the Empress. I was her physician, for I have not always been in the Eugenic Service. But Marguerite was born out of wedlock, and the mother declined to name the father of her child. Because of that the child was consigned to the school for forbidden love-children, which meant that she would be fated for the life of a free woman and become the property of such men as had the price to pay.

"When her child was taken away from her, the mother killed herself; and because I declined to testify as to what I knew of the case I lost my commission as a physician of Royalty. But still having the freedom of the school levels, I was permitted to keep track of Marguerite. As soon as she reached the age of her freedom I brought her here, and by the aid of her splendid birth and the companionship of thinking men she has become the woman you now find her."

In my jealousy I had listened to the first words of the old doctor with but little comprehension. But as he talked on so calmly and kindly an eager hope leaped up within me. Was it possible that it had been I who had misunderstood — and that Zimmern's love for Marguerite was of another sort than mine?

Tensely I awaited his further words, but I did not dare to look at Marguerite, who had taken her place beside him.

" I brought her here," Zimmern continued, " for there was no other place where she could go except into the keeping of some man. I have given her the work of guarding our books, and for that I could have well afforded to pay for her living.

" You find in Marguerite a woman of intelligence, and there are few enough like her. And she finds in you a man of rare gifts, and you are both young, so it is not strange that you two should love each other. All this I considered before I brought you here to meet her. I was happy when Marguerite told me that it was so. But your happiness is marred, because you, Armstadt, think that I am in the way; you have believed that I bear the relation to Marguerite that the fact of my paying for her presence on this level would imply.

" It speaks well of your honour," the doctor went on, " that you have felt as you did.   I should have explained sooner, but I did not wish to speak of this until it was necessary to Marguerite's happiness. But now that I have spoken there is nothing to stand in the way of your happiness, for Marguerite is as worthy of your love as if she had but made her début on the Royal Level to which she was born. As for what is to be between you, I can only leave it to the best that is in yourselves, and whatever that may be has my blessing."

As I listened to the doctor's words entranced with rapture, the vision of Marguerite floated hazily before my eyes as if she were an ethereal essence that might, at any moment, be snatched away.   But as the doctor's words ceased my eyes met Marguerite's and all else seemed to fade but the love light that shone from out their liquid depths.

Forgetting utterly the presence of the man whose words had set us free, our hearts reached out with hungry arms to claim their own.

For us, time lost her reckoning amidst our tears and kisses, and when my brain at last made known to me the existence of other souls than ours, I looked up and found that we were alone.   A saucy little clock ticked rhythmically on a mantel.   I felt an absurd desire to smash it, for the impudent thing had been running all the while.

CHAPTER IX

IN WHICH I SALUTE THE STATUE OF GOD AND A
PSYCHIC EXPERT EXPLORES MY BRAIN AND
FINDS NOTHING

I

THE Chemical Staff called for me at my laboratory to conduct me to the presence of the Emperor. At the elevator we were met by an electric vehicle manned fore and aft by pompous guards. Through the wide, high streets we rolled noiselessly past the decorated facades of the spacious apartments that housed the seventeen thousand members of the House of Hohenzollern.

At times the ample streets broadened into still more roomy avenues where potted trees alternated with the frescoed columns, and beyond which were luxurious gardens and vast statuary halls. On the Level of Free Women the life was one of crowded revelry, of the bauble and delights of carnival, but on the Royal Level there was an atmosphere of luxurious leisure, with vast spaces given over to the privacy of aristocratic idleness.

An occasional vehicle rolled swiftly past us on the glassy smoothness of the pavement; more rarely lonely couples strolled among the potted trees or sat in dreamy indolence beside the fountains. There was no crowding, no mass of humanity, no narrow halls, no congested apartments. All structure here was on a scale of magnificent size and distances, while by comparison the men and women appeared dwarfed, but withal distinctive in their costumes and regal in their leisurely idleness.

After some kilometres of travel we came to His Majesty's palace, which stood detached from all other enclosed structures and was surrounded on all sides by ever-necessary columns that seemed like a forest of tree trunks spaced and distanced in geometrical design.

As we approached the massive doorway of the palace, our party paused, and stood stiffly erect. Before us were two colossal statues of glistening white crystal. My fellow scientists faced one of the figures, which I recognized as that of William II, and I, a little tardily, saluted with them. And now we turned sharply on our heels and saluted the second figure of these twin German heroes. For German it was unmistakably in every feature, save for the one oddity that the Teutonic face wore a flowing beard not unlike that of Michael Angelo's Moses. As we moved forward my eye swept in the lettering on the pedestal,*" Unser Alte Deutche Gott,"* and I was aware that I had acknowledged my allegience to the supreme war lord — I had saluted the Statue of God.

Entering the palace we were conducted through a long hall-way hung with floral tapestries. We passed through several great metal doors guarded by stalwart leaden-faced men and came at last into the imperial audience room, where His Majesty, Eitel I, satellited by his ministers, sat stiff and upright at the head of the council table.

Though he had seemed a small man when I had seen him in the dazzling beam of the reflected sunlight, I now perceived that he was of more than average stature. He wore no crown and no helmet, but only a crop of stiff iron grey hair brushed boldly upright. His face was stern, his nose beak-like, and his small eyes grey and piercing. Over the high back of his chair was thrown his cape, and he was clad in a jacket of white cellulose velvet buttoned to the throat with large platinum buttons.

Formally presented by one of the secretaries we made our stiff bows and were seated at the table facing His Majesty across the unlittered surface of black glass.

The Emperor nodded to the Chief of the Chemical Staff who arose and read the report of my solution of the protium problem. He ended by advising that the process should immediately replace the one then in use in the extraction of the ore in the industrial works and that I was recommended for promotion to the place to be vacated by the retiring member of the Chemical Staff and should be given full charge of the protium industry.

Emperor Eitel listened with solemn nods of approval. When the reading was finished he arose and proclaimed the retirement with honour, and because of his advanced age, of Herr von Uhl. The old chemist now stepped forward and the Emperor removed from von Uhl's breast the insignia of active Staff service and replaced it with the insignia of honourable retirement.

In my turn I also stood before His Majesty, who when he had pinned upon my breast the Staff insignia said: " I hereby commission you as Member of the Chemical Staff and Director of the Protium Works. Against the fortune, to be accredited to you and your descendants, you are authorized to draw from the Imperial Bank a million marks a year. That you shall more graciously befit this fortune I confer upon you the title of ' von ' and the social privilege of the Royal Level."

When the formal ceremonies were ended I again arose and addressed the Emperor. " Your Majesty," I said, as I looked unflinchingly at his iron visage, " I beg leave to make a personal petition."

" State it," commanded the Emperor.

" I wish to ask that you restore to the Royal Level a girl who is now in the Level of the Free Women, and known there as Marguerite 78 K 4, but who was born on the Royal Level as a daughter of Princess Fedora of the House of Hohenzollern."

A hush of consternation fell upon those about the table.

" Your petition," said the Emperor, " cannot be granted."

" Then," I said, speaking with studied emphasis, " I cannot proceed with the work of extracting protium."

An angry cloud gathered on the face of Eitel I.

"Herr von Armstadt," he said, "the title and awards which have just been conferred upon you are irrevocable. But if you decline to perform the duties of your office those duties can be performed by others."

"But others cannot perform them," I replied. "The demonstration I conducted was genuine, but the formulas I have given were not genuine. The true formulas for my method of extracting protium are locked within my brain and I will reveal them only when the petition I ask has been granted."

At these words the Emperor pounded on the table with a heavy fist. "What does this mean?" he demanded of the Chemical Staff.

"It is a lie," shouted the Chief of the Staff. "We have the formulas and they are correct, for we saw the demonstration conducted with the ingredients stated in the formulas which Armstadt gave us."

"Very well," I cried; "go try your formulas; go repeat the demonstration, if you can."

The Emperor, glaring his rage, punched savagely at a signal button on the arm of his chair.

Two palace guards answered the summons. "Arrest this man," shouted His Majesty, "and keep him in close confinement; permit him to see no one."

Without further ado I was led off by the guards, while the Emperor shouted imprecations at the Chemical Staff.

2

The place to which I was conducted was a suite of rooms in a remote corner of the Royal Palace. There was a large bedroom and bath, and a luxurious study or lounging room. Here I found a case of books, which proved to be novels bearing the imprint of the Royal Level.

Despite the comfortable surroundings, it was evident that I was securely imprisoned, for the door was of metal, the ventilating gratings were long narrow slits, and the walls were of heavy concrete — and there being no windows, no bars were needed.

Any living apartment in the city would have served equally well the jailor's purpose; for it were only necessary to turn a key from without to make of it a cell in this gigantic prison of Berlin.

The regular appearance of my meals by mechanical carrier was the only way I had to reckon the passing of time, for it had chanced that I had forgotten my watch when dressing for the audience with His Majesty. I wrestled with unmeasured time by perusing the novels which gave me fragmentary pictures of the social life on the Royal Level.

As I turned over the situation in my mind I reassured myself that the secrecy of my formulas was impregnable. The discovery of the process had been rendered possible by knowledge I had brought with me from the outer world. The re-agents that I had used were synthetic substances, the very existence of which was unknown to the Germans.   I had previously prepared these compounds and had used and completely destroyed them in making the demonstration, while I had taken pains to remove all traces of their preparation.   Hence I had little to fear of the Chemical Staff duplicating my work, though doubtless they were making desperate efforts to do so, and my imprisonment was very evidently for the purpose of permitting them to make that effort.

On that score I felt that I had played my cards well, but there were other thoughts that troubled me, chief of which was a fear that some investigation might be set on foot in regard to Marguerite and that her guardianship of the library of forbidden books might be discovered.   With this worry to torment me, the hours dragged slowly enough.

I had been some five days in this solitary confinement when the door opened and a man entered. He wore the uniform of a physician and introduced himself as Dr. Boehm, explaining that he had been sent by His Majesty to look after my health.   The idea rather amused me; at least, I thought, the Emperor had decided that the secrets of my brain were well worth preservation, and I reasoned that this was evidence that the Chemical Staff had made an effort to duplicate my work and had reported their failure to do so.

The doctor made what seemed to me a rather perfunctory physical examination, which included a very minute inspection of my eyes.   Then he put me through a series of psychological test queries. When he had finished he sighed deeply and said: " I am sorry to find that you are suffering from a disturbed balance of the altruistic and the egotistic cortical impulses; it is doubtless due to the intensive demands made upon the creative potential before you were completely recovered from the sub-normal psychosis due to the gas attack in the potash mines."

This diagnosis impressed me as a palpable fraud, but I became genuinely alarmed at the mention of the affair at the potash mines.   I was somewhat re-assured at the thought that this reference was prob-ably a part of the record of Karl Armstadt, which was doubtless on file at the medical headquarters, and had been looked up by Dr. Boehm who was in need of making out a plausible case for some pur-pose — perhaps that of confining me permanently on the grounds of insanity.   Whatever might be the move on foot it was clearly essential for me to keep myself cool and well in hand.

The doctor, after eyeing me calmly for a few mo-ments, said: " It will be necessary for me to go out for a time and secure apparatus for a more searching examination.   Meanwhile be assured you will not be further neglected.   In fact, I shall ar-range for the time to share your apartment with you, as loneliness will aggravate your derangement."

In a few hours the doctor returned.   He brought with him a complicated-looking apparatus and was followed by two attendants carrying a bed.

The doctor pushed the apparatus into the corner,

and, after seeing his bed installed in my sleeping chamber, dismissed the attendants and sat down and began to entertain me with accounts of various cases of mental derangement that had come under his care. So far as I could determine his object, if he had any other than killing time, it was to impress me with the importance of submitting graciously to his care.

Tiring of these stories of the doctor's professional successes with meek and trusting patients, I took the management of the conversation into my own hands.

" Since you are a psychic expert, Dr. Boehm, perhaps you can explain to me the mental processes that cause a man to prize a large bank credit when there is positively no legal way in which he can expend the credit."

The doctor looked at me quizzically. " How do you mean," he asked, " that there is no legal way in which he can expend the credit? "

" Well, take my own case. The Emperor has bestowed upon me a credit of a million marks a year. But I risked losing it by demanding that a young woman of the Free Level be restored to the Royal Level where she was born."

" Of this I am aware," replied the psychic physician. " That is why His Majesty became alarmed lest your mental equilibrium be disturbed. It seems to indicate an atavistic reversion to a condition of romantic altruism, but as your pedigree is normal, I deem it merely a temporary loss of balance."

" But why," I asked, " do you consider it abnormal at all? Is there evidence of any great degree of unselfishness in a man desiring the bestowal of happiness upon a particular woman in preference to bank credit which he cannot expend? What should I do with a million marks a year when I have been unable to expend the ten thousand a year I have had?"

"Ah," exclaimed the doctor, the light of a brilliant discovery breaking over his countenance. "Perhaps this in a measure explains your case. You have evidently been so absorbed in your work that you have not sufficiently developed your appetite for personal enjoyment."

"Perhaps I have not. But just how should I expend more funds; food, clothing, living quarters are all provided me, there is nothing but a few tawdry amusements that one can buy, nor is there any one to give the money to — even if a man had children they cannot inherit his wealth. Just what is money for, anyway?"

The doctor nodded his head and smiled in satisfaction. "You ask interesting questions," he said. "I shall try to answer them. Money or bank credit is merely a symbol of wealth. In ancient times wealth was represented by the private ownership of physical property, which was the basis of capitalistic or competitive society. Racial progress was then achieved by the mating of the men of superior brain with the most beautiful women. Women do not appreciate the mental power of man in its direct expression, or even its social use; they can only comprehend that power when it is translated into wealth. After the destruction of private property women refused to accept as mates the men of intellectual power, but preferred instead men of physical strength and personal beauty.

" At first this was considered to be a proof of the superiority of the proletariat. For, with all men economically equal, the beautiful women turned from the anemic intellectual and the sons of aristocracy, to the strong arms of labour. Believing themselves to be the source of all wealth, and by that right vested with sole political power, and now finding themselves preferred by the beautiful women, the labourer would soon have eliminated all other classes from human society. Had unbridled socialism with its free mating continued, we should have become merely a horde of handsome savages.

" Such would have been the destiny of our race had not William III foreseen the outcome and restored war, the blessings of which had been all but lost to the world. The progress of peace depended upon the competition of capitalism, but in peace progress is incidental. In war it is essential. Because war requires invention, it saved the intellectual classes, and because war requires authority it made possible the restoration of our Royal House. Labour, the tyrant of peace, became again the slave of war, and under the plea of patriotic necessity eugenics was established, which again restored the beautiful women to the superior men. And thus by Imperial Socialism the race was preserved from deterioriation."

"But surely," I said, "eugenics has more than remedied this defect of socialism, for the selection of men of superior mentality is much more rigid than it could have been under the capricious matings of capitalistic society. Why then this need of wealth?"

"Eugenics," replied Boehm, "breeds superior children, but eugenic mating is a cold scientific thing which fails to fan the flame of man's ambition to do creative work. That is why we have the Level of Free Women and have not bred the virility out of the intellectual group. That is also the reason we have retained the Free Level on a competitive commercial basis, and have given the intellectual man the bank credit, a symbol of wealth, that he may use it, as men have always used wealth, for the purpose of increasing his importance in the eyes of woman. This function of wealth is psychically necessary to the creative impulse, for the power of sexual conquest and the stimulus to creative thought are but different expressions of the same instinct. Wealth, or its symbol, is a medium of translating the one into the other. For example, take your discovery; it is important to you and to the state. Your fellow scientists appreciate it, His Majesty appreciates it, but women cannot appreciate it. But give it a money value and women appreciate it immediately. They know that the unlimited bank credit will give you the power to keep as many women on your list as you choose, and this means that you can select freely those you wish. So the most attractive women will compete for your preferment. We bow before the Emperor, we salute the Statue of God, but we make out our checks to buy baubles for women, and it is that which keeps the wheels of progress turning."

" So," I said, " this is your philosophy of wealth. I see, and yet I do not see. The legal limit a man may contribute to a woman is but twenty-four hundred marks a year, what then does he want with a million? "

But there is no legal limit," replied the Doctor, " to the number of women a man may have on his list. His relation to them may be the most casual, but the pursuit is stimulating to the creative imagination. But you forget, Herr von Armstadt, that with the compensation that was to be yours goes also the social privilege of the Royal Level. Evidently you have been so absorbed in your research that you had no time to think of the magnificent rewards for which you were working."

" Then perhaps you will explain them to me."

" With pleasure," said Dr. Boehm; " your social privilege on the Royal Level includes the right to marry and that means that you should have children for whom inheritance is permitted. How else did you suppose the ever-increasing numbers of the House of Hohenzollern should have maintained their wealth? "

" The question has never occurred to me," I answered, " but if it had, I should have supposed that their expenses were provided by appropriations from the state treasury."

Dr. Boehm chuckled. " Then they should all be dependents on the state like cripples and imbeciles. It would be a rather poor way to derive the pride of aristocracy. That can only come from inherited wealth: the principle is old, very old. The nobleman must never needs work to live. Then, if he wishes to give service to the state, he may give it without pay, and thus feel his nobility. You cannot aspire to full social equality with the Royal House both because you lack divinity of blood and because you receive your wealth for that which you have yourself given to the state. But because of your wealth you will find a wife of the Royal House, and she will bear you children who, receiving the divine blood of the Hohenzollerns from the mother and inherited wealth from the father, will thus be twice ennobled. To have such children is a rare privilege; not even Herr von Uhl with his thousands of descendants can feel such a pride of paternity.

" It is well, Herr von Armstadt, that you talked to me of these matters. Should you be restored to your full mental powers and be permitted to assume the rights of your new station, it would be most unfortunate if you should seem unappreciative of these ennobling privileges."

" Then, if I may, I shall ask you some further

questions. It seems that the inherited incomes of the Royal Level are from time to time reinforced by marriage from without. Does that not dilute the Royal blood?"

"That question," replied Dr. Boehm, "more properly should be addressed to a eugenist, but I shall try to give you the answer. The blood of the House of Hohenzollern is of a very high order for it is the blood of divinity in human veins. Yet since there is no eugenic control, no selection, the quality of that blood would deteriorate from inbreeding, were there no fresh infusion. Then where better could such blood come than from the men of genius? No man is given the full social privilege of the Royal Level except he who has made some great contribution to the state. This at once marks him as a genius and gives his wealth a noble origin."

"But how is it," I asked, "that this addition of men from without does not disturb the balance of the sexes?"

"It does disturb it somewhat," replied the doctor, "but not seriously, for genius is rare. There are only a few hundred men in each generation who are received into Royal Society. Of course that means some of the young men of the Royal Level cannot marry. But some men decline marriage of their own free will; if they are not possessed of much wealth they prefer to go unmarried rather than to accept an unattractive woman as a wife when they may have their choice of mistresses from the most beautiful virgins intended for the Free Level.

There is always an abundance of marriageable women on the Royal Level and with your wealth you will have your choice. Your credit, in fact, will be the largest that has been granted for over a decade."

" All that is very splendid," I answered. " I was not well informed on these matters. But why should His Majesty have been so incensed at my simple request for the restoration of the rights of the daughter of the Princess Fedora?"

" Your request was unusual; pardon if I may say, impudent; it seems to imply a lack of appreciation on your part of the honours freely conferred upon you — but I daresay His Majesty did not realize your ignorance of these things. You are very young and you have risen to your high station very quickly from an obscure position."

" And do you think," I asked, " that if you made these facts clear to him, he would relent and grant my request?"

Dr. Boehm looked at me with a penetrating gaze. " It is not my function," he said, " to intercede for you. I have only been commissioned to examine carefully the state of your mentality."

I smiled complacently at the psychic expert. " Now, doctor," I said, " you do not mean to tell me that you really think there is anything wrong with my mentality?"

A look of craftiness flashed from Boehm's eyes. " I have given you my diagnosis," he said, " but it may not be final. I have already communicated my first report to His Majesty and he has ordered me to remain with you for some days. If I should alter that opinion too quickly it would discredit me and gain you nothing. You had best be patient, and submit gracefully to further examination and treatment."

"And do you know," I asked, "what the chemical staff is doing about my formulas?"

"That is none of my affair," declared Boehm, emphatically.

There was a vigour in his declaration and a haste with which he began to talk of other matters that gave me a hint that the doctor knew more of the doings of the chemical staff than he cared to admit, but I thought it wise not to press the point.

3

The second day of Boehm's stay with me, he unmantled his apparatus and asked me to submit to a further examination. I had not the least conception of the purpose of this apparatus and with some misgivings I lay down on a couch while the psychic expert placed above my eyes a glass plate, on which, when he had turned on the current, there proceeded a slow rhythmic series of pale lights and shadows. At the doctor's command I fixed my gaze upon the lights, while he, in a monotonous voice, urged me to relax my mind and dismiss all active thought.

How long I stood for this infernal proceeding I do not know. But I recall a realization that I had lost grip on my thoughts and seemed to be floating off into a misty nowhere of unconsciousness. I struggled frantically to regain control of myself; and, for what seemed an eternity, I fought with a horrible nightmare unable to move a muscle or even close my eyelids to shut out that sickening sequence of creeping shadows. Then I saw the doctor's hand reaching slowly toward my face. It seemed to sway in its stealthy movement like the head of a serpent charming a bird, but in my helpless horror I could not ward it off.

At last the snaky fingers touched my eyelids as if to close them, and that touch, light though it was, served to snap the taut film of my helpless brain and I gave a blood-curdling yell and jumped up, knocking over the devilish apparatus and nearly upsetting the doctor.

"Calm yourself," said Boehm, as he attempted to push me again toward the couch. "There is nothing wrong, and you must surrender to the psychic equilibrator so that I can proceed with the examination."

"Examination be damned," I shouted fiercely; "you were trying to hypnotize me with that infernal machine."

Boehm did not reply but calmly proceeded to pick up the apparatus and restore it to its place in the corner, while I paced angrily about the room. He then seated himself and addressed me as I stood against the wall glaring at him. "You are labouring under hallucinations," he said. "I fear your case is even worse than I thought. But calm yourself. I shall attempt no further examination to-day."

I resumed a seat but refused to look at him. He did not talk further of my supposed mental state, but proceeded to entertain me with gossip of the Royal Level, and later discussed the novels in the bookcase.

It was difficult to keep up an open war with so charming a conversationalist, but I was thoroughly on my guard. I could now readily see through the whole fraud of my imputed mental derangement. I knew my mind was sound as a schoolboy's, and that this pretence of examination and treatment was only a blind. Evidently the Chemical Staff had failed to work the formulas I had given them and this psychic manipulator had been sent in here to filch the true formulas from my brain with his devilish art. I knew nothing of what progress the Germans might have made with hypnotism, but unless they had gone further than had the outer world, now that I was on my guard, I believed myself to be safe.

But there was yet one danger. I might be trapped in my sleep by an induced somnambulistic conversation. Happily I was fairly well posted on such things and believed that I could guard against that also. But the fear of the thing made me so nervous that I did not sleep all of the following night.

The doctor, evidently a keen observer, must have detected that fact from the sound of my breathing, for the lights were turned out and we slept in the pitchy blackness that only a windowless room can create.

"You did not sleep well," he remarked, as we breakfasted.

But I made light of his solicitous concern, and we passed another day in casual conversation.

As the sleeping period drew again near, the doctor said, "I will leave you tonight, for I fear my presence disturbs you because you misinterpret my purpose in observing you."

As the doctor departed, I noted that the mechanism of the hinges and the lock of the door were so perfect that they gave forth no sound. I was very drowsy and soon retired, but before I went to sleep I practised snapping off and on the light from the switch at the side of my bed. Then I repeated over and over to myself —"I will awake at the first sound of a voice."

This thought ingrained in my subconscious mind proved my salvation. I must have been sleeping some hours. I was dreaming of Marguerite. I saw her standing in an open meadow flooded with sunlight; and heard her voice as if from afar. I walked towards her and as the words grew more distinct I knew the voice was not Marguerite's. Then I awoke.

I did not stir but lay listening. The voice was speaking monotonously and the words I heard were the words of the protium formulas, the false ones I had given the Chemical Staff.

" But these formulas are not correct," purred the voice, " of course, they are not correct. I gave them to the Staff, but they will never know the real ones — Yes, the real ones — What are the real ones? Have I forgotten —? No, I shall never forget. I can repeat them now." Then the voice began again on one of the fake formulas. But when it reached the point where the true formula was different, it paused; evidently the Chemical Staff had found out where the difficulty lay. And so the voice had paused, hoping my sleeping mind would catch up the thread and supply the missing words. But instead my arm shot quickly to the switch. The solicitous Doctor Boehm, flooded with a blaze of light, glared blinkingly as I leaped from the bed.

" Oh, I was asleep all right," I said, " but I awoke the instant I heard you speak, just as I had assured myself that I would do before I fell asleep. Now what else have you in your bag of tricks? "

" I only came —" began the doctor.

" Yes, you only came," I shouted, " and you knew nothing about the work of the Chemical Staff on my formulas. Now see here, doctor, you had your try and you have failed. Your diagnosis of my mental condition is just as much a fraud as the formulas on which the Chemical Staff have been wasting their time — only it is not so clever. I fooled them and you have not fooled me. Waste no more time, but go back and report to His Majesty that your little tricks have failed."

" I shall do that," said Boehm. " I feared you

from the start; your mind is really an extraordinary one. But where," he said, " did you learn how to guard yourself so well against my methods? They are very secret. My art is not known even to physicians."

" It is known to me," I said, " so run along and get your report ready." The doctor shook my hand with an air of profound respect and took his leave. This time I balanced a chair overhanging the edge of a table so that the opening of the door would push it off, and I lay down and slept soundly.

4

I was left alone in my prison until late the next day. Then came a guard who conducted me before His Majesty. None of the Chemical Staff was present. In fact there was no one with the Emperor but a single secretary.

His Majesty smiled cordially. " It was fitting, Herr von Armstadt, for me to order your confinement for your demand was audacious; not that what you asked was a matter of importance, but you should have made the request in writing and privately and not before the Chemical Staff. For that breach of etiquette I had to humiliate you that Royal dignity might be preserved. As for the fact that you kept the formulas secret, none need know that but the Chemical Staff and they will have nothing further to say since you made fools of them." His Majesty laughed.

" As for the request you made, I have decided to grant it. Nor do I blame you for making it. The Princess Marguerite is a very beautiful girl. She is waiting now nearby. I should have sent for her sooner, but it was necessary to make an investigation regarding her birth. The unfortunate Princess Fedora never confessed the father. But I have arranged that, as you shall see."

The Emperor now pressed his signal button and a door opened and Marguerite was ushered into the room. I started in fear as I saw that she was accompanied by Dr. Zimmern. What calamity of discovery and punishment, I wondered, had my daring move brought to the secret rebel against the rule of the Hohenzollern?

Marguerite stepped swiftly toward me and gave me her hand. The look in her eyes I interpreted as a warning that I was not to recognize Zimmern. So I appeared the stranger while the secretary introduced us.

" Dr. Zimmern," said His Majesty, " was physician to Princess Fedora at the time of the birth of the Princess Marguerite. She confessed to him the father of her child. It was the Count Rudolph who died unmarried some years ago. There will be no questions raised. Our society will welcome his daughter, for both the Count Rudolph and the Princess Fedora were very popular."

During this speech, Dr. Zimmern sat rigid and stared into space. Then the secretary produced a document and read a confession to be signed by Zimmern, testifying to these statements of Marguerite's birth.

Zimmern, his features still unmoved, signed the paper and handed it again to the secretary.

His Majesty arose and held out his hand to Marguerite. " I welcome you," he said, " to the House of Hohenzollern. We shall do our best to atone for what you have suffered. And to you, Herr von Armstadt, I extend my thanks for bringing us so beautiful a woman. It is my hope that you will win her as a wife, for she will grace well the fortune that your great genius brings to us. But because you have loved her under unfortunate circumstances I must forbid your marriage for a period of two years. During that time you will both be free to make acquaintances in Royal Society. Nothing less than this would be fair to either of you, or to other women that may seek your fortune or to other men who may seek the beauty of your princess."

CHAPTER X

A GODDESS WHO IS SUFFERING FROM OBESITY AND A BRAVE MAN WHO IS AFRAID OF THE LAW OF AVERAGES

I

IT was not till we had reached Marguerite's apartment that Zimmern spoke. Then he and Marguerite both embraced me and cried with joy.

" Ah, Armstadt," said the old doctor, " you have done a wonderful thing, a wonderful thing, but why did you not warn us? "

" Yes," I stammered, " I know. You mean the books. It worried me, but, you see, I did not plan this thing. I did not know what I should do. It came to me like a flash as the Emperor was conferring the honours upon me. I had hoped to use my power to make him do my bidding, and yet we had contrived no way to use that power in furtherance of our great plans to free a race; but I could at least use it to free a woman. Let us hope that it augurs progress to the ultimate goal."

" It was very noble, but it was dangerous," replied Zimmern. " It was only through a coincidence that we were saved. Herr von Uhl told me that same day what you had demanded. I saw Hellar immediately and he declared a raid on Marguerite's apartment. But he came himself with only one assistant who is in his confidence, and they boxed the books and carted them off. They will be turned in as contraband volumes, but the report will be falsified; no one will ever know from whence they came."

"Then the books are lost to you," I said; "of that I am sorry, and I worried greatly while I was imprisoned."

"Yes," said Zimmern, "we have lost the books, but you have saved Marguerite. That will more than compensate. For that I can never thank you enough."

"And you were called into the matter, not," I said, "as Marguerite's friend, but as the physician to her mother?"

"They must have looked up the record," replied Zimmern, "but nothing was said to me. I received only a communication from His Majesty commanding me as the physician to Marguerite's mother at the time of Marguerite's birth, to make statement as to her fatherhood."

"But why," I asked, "did you not make this confession before, since it enabled Marguerite to be restored to her rights?"

The old doctor looked pained at the question. "But you forget," he said, "that it is the power of your secret and not my confession that has restored Marguerite. The confession is only a matter of form, to satisfy the wagging tongues of Royal Society."

"Do you mean," I asked, "that she will not be

well received there because she was born out of wedlock? "

" Not at all," replied Zimmern; " it was the failure to confess the father, not the fact of her unwedded motherhood, that brought the punishment. There are many love-children born on the Royal Level and they suffer only a failure of inheritance of wealth from the father. But if they be girls of charm and beauty, and if, as Marguerite now stands credited, they be of rich Royal blood, they are very popular and much sought after. But without the record of the father they cannot be admitted into Royal Society, for the record of the blood lines would be lost, and that, you see, is essential. Social precedent, the value in the matrimonial market, all rest upon it. Marguerite is indeed fortunate; with His Majesty's signature attesting my confession, she has nothing more to fear. But I daresay they shall try their best to win her from you for some shallow-minded prince."

" But when," I asked, " is she to go? His Majesty seemed very gracious, but do you realize that I still possess my secret of the protium formulas? "

" And do you still hesitate to give them up? " asked Marguerite.

" For your freedom, dear, I shall reveal them gladly."

" But," cried Marguerite, " you must not give them up just for me,— if there is any way you can use them for our great plan."

" Nothing," spoke up Zimmern, " could be gained

now by further secrecy but trouble for us all; and by acceding, both you and Marguerite win your places on the Royal Level, where you can better serve our cause. That is, if you are still with us. It may be harder for you, now that you have won the richest privileges that Germany has to offer, to remember those who struggle in the darkness."

" But I shall remember," I said, giving him my hand.

" I believe you will," said Zimmern feelingly, " and I know I can count on Marguerite. You will both have opportunities to see much of the officers of the Submarine Service. The German race may yet be freed from this sunless prison, if you can find one among them who can be won to our cause."

2

I reported the next morning to the Chemical Staff, by whom I was treated with deferential respect. I was immediately installed in my new office, as Director of the Protium Works. While I set about supervising the manufacture of apparatus for the new process, other members of the staff, now furnished with the correct formulas repeated the demonstration without my assistance.

When the report of this had been made to His Majesty, I received my insignia of the social privilege of the Royal Level and a copy of the Royal Society Bulletin announcing Marguerite's restoration to her place in the House of Hohenzollern, with the title of Princess Marguerite, Daughter of Princess Fedora and Count Rudolf. The next day a social secretary from the Royal Level came for Marguerite and conducted her to the Apartments of the Countess Luise, under whose chaperonage she was to make her début into Royal Society.

I, also, was furnished with a social secretary, an obsequious but very wise little man, who took charge of all my affairs outside my chemical work. Under his guidance I was removed to more commodious quarters and my wardrobe was supplied with numerous changes all in the uniform of the Chemical Staff. There was little time to spare from my duties in the Protium Works, but my secretary, ever alert, snatched upon the odd moments to coach me in matters of social etiquette and so prepared me to make my first appearance in Royal Society at the grand ball given by the Countess Luise in honour of Marguerite's début.

Despite the assiduous coaching of my secretary, my ignorance must have been delightfully amusing to the royal idlers who had little other thought or purpose in life than this very round of complicated nothingness. But if I was a blundering amateur in all this, they were not so much discourteous as envious. They knew that I had won my position by my achievements as a chemist and in a vague way they understood that I had saved the empire from impending ruin, and for this achievement I was lionized.

The women rustled about me in their gorgeous gowns and plied me with foolish questions which I had better sense than to try to answer with the slightest degree of truth. But their power of sustained interest in such weighty matters was not great and soon the conversation would drift away, especially if Marguerite was about, when the talk would turn to the romance of her restoration.

One group of vivacious ladies discussed quite frankly with Marguerite the relative advantages of a husband of intellectual genius as compared with one of a high degree of royal blood. Some contended that the added prospect of superior intelligence in the children would offset the lowering of their degree of Hohenzollern blood. The others argued quite as persistently that the " blood " was the better investment.

Through such conversation I learned of the two clans within the Royal House. The one prided themselves wholly in the high degree of their Hohenzollern blood; the other, styling themselves " Royal Intellectuals " because of a greater proportion of outside blood lines, were quite as proud of the fact that, while possessed of sufficient royal blood to be in " the divinity," they inherited supposedly greater intelligence from their mundane ancestors. This latter group, to make good their claims, made a great show of intellectuality, and cultivated most persistently a dilletante dabbling into all sorts of scientific and artistic matters.

Because of Marguerite's high credit in Royal blood she was courted by " purists " by whom I was only tolerated on her account. On the other hand, the " intellectuals " considered me as a great asset for their cause and glorified particularly in the prospects of marriage of an outside scientist to an eighty-degree Hohenzollern princess. This rivalry of the clans of Royal Society made us much sought after and I was flooded with invitations.

It did not take me long to discover, however, that the reason for my popularity was not altogether a matter of respect for my intellectual genius. I had at first been inclined to accept all invitations, innocently supposing that I was being fêted as an honorary guest. But my social secretary advised against this; and, when he began bringing me checks to sign, I realized that the social privileges of Royal Society included the honour of paying the bills for one's own entertainment.

I had already arranged with my banker that a fourth of my income be turned over to Marguerite until her marriage, for she was without income of her own, and it was upon my petition that she had been restored to the Royal Level. At my banker's suggestion I had also made over ten thousand marks a month to the Countess, under whose motherly wing Marguerite was being sheltered. I therefore soon discovered that my income of a million marks a year would be absorbed quite easily by Royal Society. The entire system appeared to me rather sordid, but such matters were arranged by bankers and secretaries and the principals were supposed to be quite innocent of any knowledge of, or concern for, the details.

The Countess Luise, who was permitted to entertain so lavishly at my expense, was playing for the favour of both of the opposing social clans. Possessing a high degree of Hohenzollern blood she stood well with the purists. But her income was not all that could be desired, so she had adroitly discovered in her only son a touch of intellectual genius, and the young man quite dutifully had become a maker of picture plots, hoping by this distinction to win as a wife one of the daughters of some wealthy intellectual interloper. At first I had feared the Countess had designs upon Marguerite as a wife for her son, but as Marguerite had no income of her own I saw that in this I was mistaken, and I developed a feeling of genuine friendliness for the plump and cordial Countess.

"Do you know what I was reading last night?" I remarked one evening, as I chatted with Marguerite and her chaperone.

"Some work on obesity, I hope," sparkled the Countess. Like many of the House of Hohenzollern, among whom there was no weight control, she carried a surplus of adipose tissue not altogether consistent with beauty.

"No, indeed," I said gravely. "Nothing about your material being, but a treatise upon your spiritual nature. I was reading an old school book that I found among my forgotten relics — a book about the Divinity of the House of Hohenzollern."

"Oh, how jolly!" chuckled the Countess. "How very funny that I never thought before that you, Herr von Armstadt, were once taught all those delightful fables."

"And once believed them too," I lied.

"Oh, dear me," replied the Countess, with a ponderous sigh, "so I suppose you did. And what a shock I must have been to you with an eighty centimetre waist."

"You are not quite Junoesque," I admitted.

"The more reason you should use your science, Herr Chemist, to aid me to recover my goddess form."

"What are you folks talking about?" interrupted Marguerite.

"About our divinity, my dear," replied Luise archly.

"But do you feel that it is really necessary," I asked, "that such fables should be put into the helpless minds of children?"

"It surely must be. Suppose your own heredity had proven tricky — it does sometimes, you know — and you had been found incapable of scientific thought. You would have been deranked and perhaps made a record clerk — no personal reflections, but such things do happen — and if you now were filing cards all day you would surely be much happier if you could believe in our divinity. Why else would you submit to a loveless life and the dull routine of toil? Did not all the ancients, and do not all the inferior races now, have objects of religious worship?"

"But the other races," I said, "do not worship

living people but spiritual divinities and the sainted dead.

"Quite so," replied the over-plump goddess, "but that is why their *kulturs* are so inefficient. Surely the worship was useless to the spirits and the dead, whereas we find it quite profitable to be worshipped. But for this wonderful doctrine of the divinity of the blood of William the Great we should be put to all sorts of inconveniences."

"You might even have to work," I ventured.

The Countess bestowed on me one of her most bewitching smiles. "My dear Herr Chemist," she said in sugary tones, "you with your intellectual genius can twit us on our psychic lacks and we must fall back on the divine blood of our Great Ancestor — but would you really wish the slaves of dull toil to think it as human as their own?"

"But to me it seems a little gross," I said.

"Not at all; on the contrary, it is a master stroke of science and efficiency — inferior creatures must worship; they always have and always will — then why waste the worship?"

3

My position as director of the protium works soon brought me into conference with Admiral von Kufner who was Chief of the Submarine Staff. Von Kufner was in his forties and his manner indicated greater talent for pomp and ceremony than for administrative work. His grandfather had been the engineer to whose genius Berlin owed her salvation through the construction of the submarine tunnel. By this service the engineer had won the coveted " von," a princely fortune and a wife of the Royal Level. The Admiral therefore carried Hohenzollern blood in his veins, which, together with his ample fortune and a distinguished position, made him a man of both social and official consequence.

It did not take me long to decide that von Kufner was hopeless as a prospective convert to revolutionary doctrines. Nor did he possess any great knowledge of the protium mines, for he had never visited them. Inheriting his position as an honour to his grandfather's genius, he commanded the undersea vessels from the security of an office on the Royal Level, for journeys in ice-filled waters were entirely too dangerous to appeal to one who loved so well the pleasures and vanities of life.

I had explained to von Kufner the distinctions I had discovered in the various samples of the ore brought from the mines and the necessity of having new surveys of the deposits made on the basis of these discoveries. After he had had time to digest this information, I suggested that I should myself go to make this survey. But this idea the Admiral at once opposed, insisting that the trip through the Arctic ice fields was entirely too dangerous.

" Very well," I replied. " I feel that I could best serve Germany by going to the Arctic mines in person, but if you think that is unwise, will you not arrange for me to consult at once with men who have been in the mines and are familiar with conditions there? "

To this very reasonable request, which was in line with my obvious duties, no objection could be made and a conference was at once called of submarine captains and furloughed engineers who had been in the Arctic ore fields.

I was impressed by the youthfulness of these men, which was readily explained by the fact that one vessel out of every five sent out was lost beneath the Arctic ice floes. With an almost mathematical certainty the men in the undersea service could reckon the years of their lives on the fingers of one hand.

Although the official business of the conference related to ore deposits and not to the dangers of the traffic, the men were so obsessed with the latter fact, that it crept out in their talk in spite of the Admiral's obvious displeasure at such confession of fear. I particularly marked the outspoken frankness of one, Captain Grauble, whose vessel was the next one scheduled to depart to the mines.

I therefore asked Grauble to call in person at my office for the instructions concerning the ore investigations which were to be forwarded to the Director of the Mines. Free from the restraining influence of the Admiral, I was able to lead the Captain to talk freely of the dangers of his work, and was overjoyed to find him frankly rebellious.

That I might still further cultivate his acquaintance I withheld some of the necessary documents;

and, using this as a pretext, I later sought him out at his quarters, which were in a remote and somewhat obscure part of the Royal Level.

The official nature of my call disposed of, I led the conversation into social matters, and found no difficulty in persuading the Captain to talk of his own life. He was a man well under thirty and like most of his fellows in the service was one of the sons of a branch of the Hohenzollern family whose declining fortune denied him all hope of marriage or social life. In the heroic years of his youth he had volunteered for the submarine service. But now he confessed that he regretted the act, for he realized that his death could not be long postponed. He had made his three trips as commander of an ore-bringing vessel.

" I have two more trips," declared Captain Grauble. " Such is the prophecy of statistical facts: five trips is the allotted life of a Captain; it is the law of averages. It is possible that I may extend that number a little, but if so it will be an exception. Trusting to exceptions is a poor philosophy. I do not like it. Sometimes I think I shall refuse to go. Disgrace, of course,— banishment to the mines. Report my treasonable utterances if you like. I am prepared for that; suicide is easy and certain."

" But is it not rather cowardly, Captain? " I asked, looking him steadily in the eye.

Grauble flung out his hand with a gesture of disdain. " That is an easy word for you to pronounce," he sneered. " You have hope to live by, you are on the upward climb, you aspire to marry into the Royal House and sire children to inherit your wealth. But I was born of the Royal House, my father squandered his wealth. My sisters were beautiful and they have married well. My brother was servile; he has attached himself to the retinue of a wealthy Baroness. But I was made of better stuff than that. I would play the hero. I would face danger and gladly die to give Berlin more life and uphold the House of Hohenzollern in its fat and idle existence; and for me they have taken hope away!

"Oh, yes, I was proclaimed a hero. The young ladies of this house of idleness dance with me, but they dare not take me seriously; what one of them would court the certainty of widowhood without a fortune? So why should I not tire of their shallow trifling? I find among the girls of the Free Level more honest love, for they, as I, have no hope. They love but for the passing hour, and pass on as I pass on, I to death, they to decaying beauty and an old age of servile slavery."

Surely, I exulted, here is the rebellious and daring soul that Zimmern and Hellar have sought in vain. Even as they had hoped, I seemed to have discovered a man of the submarine service who was amenable to revolutionary ideas. Could I not get him to consider the myriad life of Berlin in all its barren futility, to grasp at the hope of succour from a free and merciful world, and then, with his aid, find a way out of Berlin, a way to carry the message oi Ger-

many's need of help to the Great God of Humanity
that dwelt without in the warmth and joy of the sun?
The tide of hope surged high within me. I was
tempted to divulge at once my long cherished plan
of escape from Berlin. " Why," I asked, thinking
to further sound his sincerity, " if you feel like this,
have you never considered running your craft to the
surface during the sea passage and beaching her on
a foreign shore? There at least is life and hope and
experience."

" By the Statue of God! " cried Grauble, his body
shaking and his voice quavering, " why do you, in
all your hope and comfort here, speak of that to me?
Do you think I have never been tempted to do that
very thing? And yet you call me a coward. Have
I not breathed foul air for days, fearful to poke up
our air tube in deserted waters lest by the millionth
chance it might lead to a capture? And yet you
speak of deliberate surrender! Even though I destroyed my charts, the capture of a German submarine in those seas would set the forces of the
outer world searching for the passage. If they
found and blocked the passage I should be guilty of
the destruction of three hundred million lives —
Great God! God of Hohenzollern! God of the
World! could this thing be? "

" Captain," I said, placing my hand on the shoulder of the palsied man, " you and I have great secrets and the burden of great sorrows in common.
It is well that we have found each other. It is well
that we have spoken of these things that shake our

souls.   You have confessed much to me and I have much that I shall confess to you.   I must see you again before you leave."

Grauble gave me his hand.   " You are a strange man," he said.   " I have met none before like you. I do not know at what aims you are driving.   If you plotted my disgrace by leading me into these confessions, you have found me easy prey.   But do not credit yourself too much.   I have often vowed I would go to Admiral von Kufner, and say these things to him.   But the formal exterior of that petty pompous man I cannot penetrate.   If I have confessed to you, it is merely because you are a man without that protecting shield of bristling authority and cold formality.   You seemed merely a man of flesh and blood, despite your decorations, and so I have talked.   What is to be made of it by you or by me I do not know, but I am not afraid of you."

" I shall leave you now," I said, " for I have pressing duties, but I shall see you soon again.   So calm yourself and get hold of your reason.   I shall want you to think clearly when I talk with you again. Perhaps I can yet show you a gleam of hope beyond this mathematical law of averages that rattles the dice of death."

CHAPTER XI

I

I HAD delayed in speaking to Grauble of our revolutionary plans, because I wished first to arrange a meeting with Zimmern and Hellar and secure the weight of their calmer minds in initiating Grauble into our plans of sending a message to the World State authorities. I was prevented from doing this immediately by difficulties in the Protium Works. Meanwhile unbeknown to me the sailing date of Grauble's vessel was advanced, and he departed to the Arctic.

Although my position as Director of the Protium Works had been more of an honour than an assignment of active duties, I made it my business to assume the maximum rather than the minimum of the functions of the office as I wished to learn more of the labour situation in Berlin, of which as yet I had no comprehensive understanding.

In a general way I understood that German labour differed not only in being eugenically created as a distinct breed, but that the labour group was also a very distinct caste economically and politically. The labourer, being denied access to the Level of

Free Women, had no need for money or bank credit in any form. This seemed to me to reduce him to a condition of pure slavery — since he received no pay for his services other than the bare maintenance supplied by the state.

Because of this evidence of economic inferiority, I had at first supposed that labour was in every way an inferior caste. But in this I had been gravely mistaken, nor had I been able fully to comprehend my error until this brewing labour trouble revealed in concrete form the political superiority of labour. In my failure to comprehend the true state of affairs I had been a little stupid, for the political basis of German society is revealed to the seeing eye in the Hohenzollern eagle emblazoned on the red flag, the emblem of the rule of labour.

Historically I believe this belies the origin of the red flag for it was first used as the emblem of democratic socialism, a Nineteenth Century theory of a social order in which all social and economic classes were to be blended into a true democracy differing somewhat in its economic organization, but essentially the same politically as the true democracy which we have achieved in the World State. But with the Bolshevist régime in Russia after the First World War, the red flag was appropriated as the emblem of the political supremacy and rule of the proletariat or labour class.

I make these references to bygone history because they throw light on the peculiar status of the German Labour Caste, which is possessed of political superiority combined with social and economic inferiority. It was the Bolshevist brand of socialism that finally overran Germany in the era of loose and ineffective rule of the world by the League of Nations. Though I make no pretence of being an accurate authority on history, the League of Nations, if I remember rightly, was humanity's first timid conception of the World State. Rather weakly born, it was promptly emasculated by the rise in America of a political party founded on the ideas of a great national hero who had just died. The obstructionist policy of this party was inherent in its origin, for it was inspired and held together by the ideas of a dead man, whose followers could only repeat as their test of faith a phrase that has come down to us as an idiom —" What would He do? " " He " being dead could do nothing, neither could he change his mind, but having left an indelible record of his ideas by the strenuous verbiage of his virile and inspiring rhetoric, there was no room for doubt. As in all political and religious faiths founded on the ideas of dead heroes, this made for solidarity and power and quite prevented any adaptation of the form of government to the needs of the world that had arisen since his demise.

I have digressed here from my theme of the political status of the German labour caste, but it is fascinating to trace things to their origin to find the links of the chain of cause and effect. So, if I have read my history aright, the emasculation of the League of Nations by the American obstructionists caused, or at least permitted the rise, and dominance of the Bolshevists in Twentieth-Century Germany. Had the Germans been democrats at heart the pendulum would have swung back as it did with other peoples, and been stayed at the point of equilibrium which we recognized as the stable mean of democracy.

But in the old days before the modern intermingling of the races it seems that there were certain tastes that had become instinctive in racial groups. Thus, just as the German stomach craved the rich flavour of sausage, so the German mind craved the dazzling show of Royal flummery. Had it not been for this the First World War could have never been, for the socialists of that time were bitterly opposed to war and Germany was the world's greatest stronghold of socialism, yet when their beloved imperial poser, William the Great, called for war the German socialists, with the exception of a few whom they afterwards murdered, went forth to war almost without protest.

When I first began to hear of the political rights of Labour, I went to my friend Hellar and asked for an explanation.

" Is not the chain of authority absolute," I asked, " up through the industrial organization direct to the Emperor and so to God himself? "

" But," said Hellar, " the workers do not believe in God! "

" What," I stammered, " workers not believe in

God! It is impossible. Have not the workers simple trusting minds? "

" Certainly," said Hellar, " it is the natural mind of man! Scepticism, which is the basis of scientific reasoning, is an artificial thing, first created in the world under the competitive economic order when it became essential to self-preservation in a world of trade based on deceit. In our new order we have had difficulty in maintaining enough of it for scientific purposes even in the intellectual classes. There is no scepticism among the labourers now, I assure you. They believe as easily as they breathe."

" Then how," I demanded in amazement, " does it come that they do not believe in God? "

" Because," said Hellar, " they have never heard of God.

" The labourer does not know of God because we have restored God since the perfection of our caste system, and hence it was easy to promulgate the idea among the intellectuals and not among the workers. It was necessary to restore God for the intellectuals in order to give them greater respect for the power of the Royal House, but the labourers need no God because they believe themselves to be the source from which the Royal House derives its right to rule. They believe the Emperor to be their own servant ruling by their permission."

" The Emperor a servant to labour! " I exclaimed; " this is absurd."

" Certainly," said Hellar; " why should it be

otherwise? We are an absurd people, because we have always laughed at the wrong things. Still this principle is very old and has not always been confined to the Germans. After the revolutions in the Twentieth Century the American plutocrats employed poverty-stricken European nobility for servants and exalted them to high stations and obeyed them explicitly in all social matters with which their service was concerned.

"The labourers restored William III because they wished to have an exalted servant. He led them to war and became a hero. He reorganized the state and became their political servant, also their emperor and their tyrant. It is not an impossible relation, for it is not unlike the relation between the mother and the child or between a man and his mistress. And yet it is different, more formal, with functions better defined.

"The Emperor is the administrative head of the government and we intellectuals are merely his hirelings. We are merely the feathers of the Royal eagle, our colour is black, we have no part in the red blood of human brotherhood, we are outcasts from the socialistic labour world — for we receive money compensation to which labourers would not stoop. But labour owns the state. This roof of Berlin over our heads and all that is therein contained, is the property of the workers who produced it."

I shook my head in mute admission of my lack of comprehension.

" And who," asked Hellar, " did you think owned Berlin? "

I confessed that I had never thought of that.

" Few of our intellectual class have ever thought of that," replied Hellar, " unless they are well read in political history. But at the time of the Hohenzollern restoration labour owned all property in true communal ownership. They did not release it to the Royal House, but merely turned over the administration of the property to the Emperor as an agent."

These belated explanations of the fundamental ideas of German society quite confused and confounded me, though Hellar seemed in no wise surprised at my ignorance, since as a chemist I had originally been supposed to know only of atoms and valences and such like matters. Seeking a way out of these contradictions I asked: " How is it then that labour is so powerless, since you say that it owns the state, and even the Emperor rules by its permission? "

" Napoleon — have you ever heard of him? "

" Yes," I admitted — and then recalling my rôle as a German chemist I hastened to add —" Napoleon was a directing chemist who achieved a plan for increasing the food supply in his day by establishing the sugar beet industry."

" Is that so? " exclaimed Hellar. " I didn't know that. I thought he was only an Emperor — anyway, Napoleon said that if you tell men they are equal you can do as you please with them. So when

William III was elected to the throne by labour, he insisted that they retain the power and re-elect him every five years.   He was very popular because he invented the armoured city — our new Berlin — some day I will tell you of that — and so of course he was re-elected, and his son after him.   Though most of the intellectuals do not know that it exists the ceremony of election is a great occasion on the labour levels.   The Emperor speaks all day through the horns and on the picture screens.   The workers think he is actually speaking, though of course it is a collection of old films and records of the Royal Voice.   When they have seen and heard the speeches, the labourers vote, and then go back to their work and are very happy."

" But suppose they should sometime fail to re-elect him ? "

" No danger," said Hellar; " there is only one name on the ballot and the ballots are dumped into the paper mill without inspection."

" Most extraordinary," I exclaimed.

" Most ordinary," contradicted Hellar; " it is not even an exclusively German institution; we have merely perfected it.   Voting everywhere is a very useful device in organized government.   In the cruder form used in democracies there were two or more candidates.   It usually made little difference which was elected; but the system was imperfect be-cause the voters who voted for the candidate which lost were not pleased.   Then there was the trouble of counting the ballots.   We avoid all this."

"It is all very interesting," I said, "but who is the real authority?"

"Ah," said Hellar, "this matter of authority is one of our most subtle conceptions. The weakness of ancient governments was in the fact that the line of authority was broken. It came somewhere to an end. But now authority flows up from labour to the Emperor and then descends again to labour through the administrative line of which we are one link. It is an unbroken circuit."

But I was still unsatisfied, for it annoyed me not to be able to understand the system of German politics, as I had always prided myself that, for a scientist, I understood politics remarkably well.

2

I had gone to Hellar for enlightenment because I was gravely alarmed over the rumours of a strike among the labourers in the Protium Works. I had read in the outside world of the murder and destruction of these former civil wars of industry. With a working population so cruelly held to the treadmill of industrial bondage the idea of a strike conjured up in my fancy the beginning of a bloody revolution. With so vast a population so utterly dependent upon the orderly processes of industry the possible terrors of an industrial revolution were horrible beyond imagining; and for the moment all thoughts of escape, or of my own plans for negotiating the surrender of Berlin to the World State, were swept aside by the stern responsibilities that devolved upon me as the Director of Works wherein a terrible strike seemed brewing.

The first rumour of the strike of the labourers in the Protium Works had come to me from the Listening-In-Service. Since Berlin was too complicated and congested a spot for wireless communication to be practical, the electrical conduct of sound was by antiquated means of metal wires. The workers' Free Speech Halls were all provided with receiving horns by which they made their appeals to His Majesty, of which I shall speak presently. These instruments were provided with cut-offs in the halls. They had been so designed by the electrical engineers, who were of the intellectual caste, that not even the workers who installed and repaired them knew that the cut-offs were a blind and that the Listening-In-Service heard every word that was said at their secret meetings, when all but workers were, by law and custom, excluded from the halls.

And so the report came to me that the workers were threatening strike. Their grievance came about in this fashion. My new process had reduced the number of men needed in the works. This would require that some of the men be transferred to other industries. But the transfer was a slow process, as all the workers would have to be examined anatomically and their psychic reflexes tested by the labour assignment experts and those selected re-trained for other labour. That work was proceeding slowly, for there was a shortage of experts because some similar need of transfers existed in one of the metal industries. Moreover, my labour psychologist considered it dangerous to transfer too many men, as they were creatures of habit, and he advised that we ought merely to cease to take on new workers, but wait for old age and death to reduce the number of our men, meanwhile retaining the use of the old extraction process in part of the works.

" Impossible," I replied, " unless you would have your rations cut and the city put on a starvation diet. Do you not know that the reserve store of protium that was once enough to last eight years is now reduced to less than as many months' supply? "

" That is none of my affair," said the labour psychologist; " these chemical matters I do not comprehend. But I advise against these transfers, for our workers are already in a furor about the change of operations in the work."

" But," I protested, " the new operations are easier than the old; besides we can cut down the speed of operations, which ought to help you take care of these surplus men."

" Pardon, Herr Chief," returned the elderly labour psychologist, " you are a great chemist, a very great chemist, for your invention has upset the labour operation more than has anything that ever happened in my long experience, but I fear you do not realize how necessary it is to go slow in these matters. You ask men who have always opened a faucet from left to right to now open one that moves in a vertical plane. Here, I will show you; move your arm so; do you not see that it takes different muscles? "

" Yes, of course, but what of it? The solution flows faster and the operation is easier."

" It is easy for you to say that; for you or me it would make no difference since our muscles have all been developed indiscriminately."

" But what are your labour gymnasiums for, if not to develop all muscles? "

" Now do not misunderstand me. I serve as an interpreter between the minds of the workers and your mind as Director of the Works. As for the muscles developed in the gymnasium, those were developed for sport and not for labour. But that is not the worst of it; you have designed the new benches so low that the mixers must stoop at their work. It is very painful."

" Good God," I cried, " what became of the stools? The mixers are to sit down — I ordered two thousand stools."

" That I know, Herr Chief, but the equipment expert consulted me about the matter and I countermanded the order. It would never do. I did not consult you, it is true, but that was merely a kindness. I did not wish to expose your lack of knowledge, if I may call it such."

" Call it what you please," I snapped, for at the time I thought my labour psychologist was a fool, " but get those stools, immediately."

" But it would never do."

" Why not? "

" Because these men have always stood at their work."

" But why can they not sit down now? "

" Because they never have sat down."

" Do they not sit down to eat? "

" Yes, but not to work. It is very different. You do not understand the psychic immobility of labour. Habits grow stronger as the mentality is simplified. I have heard that there are animals in the zoological garden that still perform useless operations that their remote ancestors required in their jungle life."

" Then do you infer that these men who must stand at their work inherited the idea from their ancestors? "

" That is a matter of eugenics. I do not know, but I do know that we are preparing for trouble with these changes. Still I hope to work it out without serious difficulty, if you do not insist on these transfers. When workmen have already been forced to change their habitual method of work and then see their fellows being removed to other and still stranger work it breeds dangerous unrest."

" One thing is certain," I replied; " we cannot delay the installation of the new method; as fast as the equipment is ready the new operation must replace the old."

" But the effect of that policy will be that there will not be enough work, and besides the work is, as you say, lighter and that will result in the cutting down of the food rations."

" But I have already arranged that," I said triumphantly; "the Rationing Bureau have adjusted the calorie standards so that the men will get as much food as they have been used to."

"What! you have done that?" exclaimed the labour psychologist; "then there will be trouble. That will destroy the balance of the food supply and the expenditure of muscular energy and the men will get fat. Then the other men will accuse them of stealing food and we shall have bloodshed."

"A moment ago," I smiled, "you told me I did not know your business. Now I will tell you that you do not know mine. We ordered special food bulked up in volume; the scheme is working nicely; you need not worry about that. As for the other matter, this surplus of men, it seems to me that the only thing is to cut down the working hours temporarily until the transfers can be made."

The psychologist shook his head. "It is dangerous," he said, "and very unusual. I advise instead that you have the operation engineers go over the processes and involve the operations, both to make them more nearly resemble the old ones, and to add to the time and energy consumption of the tasks."

"No," I said emphatically, "I invented a more economical process for this industry and I do not propose to see my invention prostituted in this fashion. I appreciate your advice, but if we cannot transfer the workers any faster, then the labour hours must be cut. I will issue the order tomorrow. This is my final decision."

I was in authority and that settled the matter. The psychologist was very decent about it and helped me fix up a speech and that next night the workers were ordered to assemble in their halls and I made my speech into a transmitting horn. I told them that they had been especially honoured by their Emperor, who, appreciating their valuable service, had granted them a part-time vacation and that until further notice their six-hour shifts were to be cut to four. I further told them that their rations would not be reduced and advised them to take enough extra exercise in the gymnasium to offset their shorter hours so they would not get fat and be the envy of their fellows.

3

For a time the workers seemed greatly pleased with their shorter hours. And then, from the Listening-In-Service, came the rumour of the strike. The first report of the strike gave me no clue to the grievance and I asked for fuller reports. When these came the next day I was shocked beyond belief. If I had anticipated anything in that interval of terror it was that my workers were to strike because their communications had been shut off or that they were to strike in sympathy for their fellows and demand that all hours be shortened like their own. But the grievance was not that. My men were to go on strike for the simple reason that their hours had been shortened! The catastrophe once started came with a rush, for when I reached the office the next day the psychologist was awaiting me and told me that the strike was on. I rushed out immediately and went down to the works. The psychologist followed me. As I entered the great industrial laboratories I saw all the men at their usual places and going through their usual operations. I turned to my companion who was just coming up, and said: "What do you mean; I thought you told me the strike was on, that the men had already walked out?"

"What do you mean by 'walked out'?" he returned, as puzzled as I.

"Walked out of the works," I explained; "away from their duties, quit work. Struck!"

"But they have struck. Perhaps you have never seen a strike before, but do you not see the strike badges?"

And then I looked and saw that every workman wore a tiny red flag, and the flag bore no imperial eagle.

"It means," I gasped, "that they have renounced the rule of the Royal House. This is not a strike, this is rebellion, treason!"

"It is the custom," said the labour psychologist, "and as for rebellion and treason that you speak of I hardly think you ought to call it that for rebellion and treason are forbidden."

"Then just what does it mean?"

"It means that this particular group of workers have temporarily withdrawn their allegiance to the Royal House, and they have, in their own minds, restored the old socialist régime, until they can make petition to the Emperor and he passes on their grievance. They will do that in their halls tonight. We, of course, will be connected up and listen in."

" Then they are not really on strike? "

" Certainly they are on strike. All strikes are conducted so."

" Then why do they not quit work? "

" But why should they quit work? They are striking because their hours are already too short — pardon, Herr Chief, but I warned you!

" I think I know what you mean," he added after a pause; " you have probably read some fiction of old times when the workers went on strike by quitting work."

" Yes, exactly. I suppose that is where I did get my ideas; and that is now forbidden — by the Emperor? "

" Not by the Emperor, for you see these men wear the flags without the eagle. They at present do not acknowledge his authority."

" Then all this strike is a matter of red badges without eagles and everything else will go on as usual? "

" By no means. These men are striking against the descending authority from the Royal House. They not only refuse to wear the eagle until their grievance is adjusted but they will refuse to accept further education, for that is a thing that descends from above. If you will go now to the picture halls, where the other shift should be, you will find the

halls all empty.   The men refuse to go to the moving pictures."

That night we " listened in." A bull-throated
fellow, whom I learned was the Talking Delegate,
addressed the Emperor, and much to my surprise I
thought I heard the Emperor's own voice in reply,
stating that he was ready to hear their grievance.

Then the bull voice of the Talking Delegate gave
the reason for the strike: " The Director of the
Works, speaking for your Majesty, has granted us
a part time vacation, and shortened our hours from
six to four.   We thank you for this honour but we
have decided we do not like it.   We do not know
what to do during those extra two hours.   We had
our games and amusements but we had our regular
hours for them.   If we play longer we become tired
of play.   If we sleep longer we cannot sleep as well.
Moreover we are losing our appetite and some of us
are afraid to eat all our portions for fear we will
become fat.   So we have decided that we do not
like a four-hour day and we have therefore taken
the eagles off our flags and will refuse to replace
them or to go to the educational pictures until our
hours are restored to the six-hour day that we have
always had."

And now the Emperor's voice replied that he
would take the matter under consideration and report his decision in three days and, that meanwhile
he knew he could trust them to conduct themselves
as good socialists who were on strike, and hence
needed no king.

The next day the psychologist brought a representative of the Information Staff to my office and together we wrote the reply that the Emperor was to make. It would be necessary to concede them the full six hours and introduce the system of complicating the labour operations to make more work. Much chagrined, I gave in, and called in the motion study engineers and set them to the task. Meanwhile the Royal Voice was sent for and coached in the Emperor's reply to the striking workmen, and a picture film of the Emperor, timed to fit the length of the speech, was ordered from stock.

The Royal Voice was an actor by birth who had been trained to imitate His Majesty's speech. This man, who specialized in the Emperor's speeches to the workers, prided himself that he was the best Royal Voice in Berlin and I complimented him by telling him that I had been deceived by him the evening before. But considering that the workers, never having heard the Emperor's real voice, would have no standard of comparison, I have never been able to see the necessity of the accuracy of his imitation, unless it was on the ground of art for art's sake.

CHAPTER XII

I

THE strike that I had feared would be the beginning of a bloody revolution had ended with an actor shouting into a horn and the shadow of an Emperor waving his arms. But meanwhile Capt. Grauble, on whom I staked my hopes of escape from Berlin, had departed to the Arctic and would not return for many months. That he would return I firmly believed; statistically the chances were in his favour as this was his fourth trip, and hope was backing the favourable odds of the law of chance.

So I set myself to prepare for that event. My faith was strong that Grauble could be won over to the cause of saving the Germans by betraying Germany. I did not even consider searching for another man, for Grauble was that one rare man in thousands who is rebellious and fearless by nature, a type of which the world makes heroes when their cause wins and traitors when it fails — a type that Germany had all but eliminated from the breed of men.

But, if I were to escape to the outer world through

Grauble's connivance, there was still the problem of getting permission to board the submarine, ostensibly to go to the Arctic mines. Even in my exalted position as head of the protium works I could not learn where the submarine docks or the passage to them was located. But I did learn enough to know that the way was impenetrable without authoritative permission, and that thoughts of escape as a stowaway were not worth considering. I also learned that Admiral von Kufner had sole authority to grant permission to make the Arctic trip.

The Admiral had promptly turned down my first proposal to go to the Arctic ore fields, and had by his pompous manner rebuffed the attempts I made to cultivate his friendship through official interviews. I therefore decided to call on Marguerite and the Countess Luise to see what chance there was to get a closer approach to the man through social avenues. The Countess was very obliging in the matter, but she warned me with lifted finger that the Admiral was a gay bachelor and a worshipper of feminine charms, and that I might rue the day I suggested his being invited into the admiring circle that revolved about Marguerite. But I laughingly disclaimed any fears on that score and von Kufner was bidden to the next ball given by the Countess.

Marguerite was particularly gracious to the Admiral and speedily led him into the inner circle that gathered informally in the salon of the Countess Luise. I made it a point to absent myself on some of these occasions, for I did not want the Admiral to guess the purpose that lay behind this ensnaring of him into our group.

And yet I saw much of Marguerite, for I spent most of my leisure in the society of the Royal Level, where thought, if shallow, was comparatively free. I took particular pleasure in watching the growth of Marguerite's mind, as the purely intellectual conceptions she had acquired from Dr. Zimmern and his collection of books adjusted itself to the absurd realities of the celestial society of the descendants of William the Great.

It may be that charity is instinctive in the heart of a good woman, or perhaps it was because she had read the Christian Bible; but whatever the origin of the impulse, Marguerite was charitably inclined and wished to make personal sacrifice for the benefit of other beings less well situated than herself. While she was still a resident of the Free Level she had talked to me of this feeling and of her desire to help others. But the giving of money or valuables by one woman to another was strictly forbidden, and Marguerite had not at the time possessed more than she needed for her own subsistence. But now that she was relatively well off, this charitable feeling struggled to find expression. Hence when she had learned of the Royal Charity Society she had straightway begged the Countess to present her name for membership, without stopping to examine into the detail of the Society's activities.

The Society was at that time preparing to hold a bazaar and sent out calls for contributions of cast off clothing and ornaments. Marguerite as yet possessed no clothes or jewelry of Royal quality except the minimum which the demands of her position made necessary; and so she timidly asked the Countess if her clothing which she had worn on the Free Level would suffice as gifts of charity. The Countess had assured her that it would do nicely as the destination of all the clothing contributed was for the women of the Free Level. Thinking that an opportunity had at last arisen for her to express her compassion for the ill-favoured girls of her own former level, Marguerite hastened to bundle up such presentable gowns as she had and sent them to the bazaar by her maid.

Later she had attended the meeting of the society when the net results of the collections were announced. To her dismay she found that the clothing contributed had been sold for the best price it would bring to the women of the Free Level and that the purpose of the sacrifices, of that which was useless to the possessors but valuable to others, was the defraying of the expense of extending the romping grounds for the dogs of the charitably maintained canine garden.

Marguerite was vigorously debating the philosophy of charity with the young Count Rudolph that evening when I called. She was maintaining that human beings and not animals should be the recipients of charity and the young Count was expounding to her the doctrine of the evil effects of charity upon the recipient.

" Moreover," explained Count Rudolph, " there are no humans in Berlin that need charity, since every class of our efficiently organized State receives exactly what it should receive and hence is in need of nothing. Charity is permissible only when poverty exists."

" But there is poverty on the Free Level," maintained Marguerite; " many of the ill-favoured girls suffer from hunger and want better clothes than they can buy."

" That may be," said the Count, " but to permit them gifts of charity would be destructive of their pride; moreover, there are few women on the Royal Level who would give for such a purpose."

" But surely," said Marguerite, " there must be somewhere in the city, other women or children or even men to whom the proceeds of these gifts would mean more than it does to dogs."

" If any group needed anything the state would provide it," repeated the Count.

" Then why," protested Marguerite, " cannot the state provide also for the dogs, or if food and space be lacking why are these dogs allowed to breed and multiply ? "

" Because it would be cruel to suppress their instincts."

Marguerite was puzzled by this answer, but with my more rational mind I saw a flaw in the logic of this statement. " But that is absurd," I said, " for if their number were not checked in some fashion, in a few decades the dogs would overswarm the city."

It was now the Count's turn to look puzzled. "You have inferred an embarrassing question," he stated, "one, in fact, that ought not to be answered in the presence of a lady, but since the Princess Marguerite does not seem to be a lover of dogs, I will risk the explanation. The Medical Level requires dogs for purposes of scientific research. Since the women are rarely good mathematicians, it is easily possible in this manner to keep down the population of the Canine Garden."

"But the dogs required for research," I suggested, "could easily be bred in kennels maintained for that purpose."

"So they could," said the Count, "but the present plan serves a double purpose. It provides the doctors with scalpel practise and it also amuses the women of the Royal House who are very much in need of amusement since we men are all so dull.

"Woman's love," continued Rudolph, waxing eloquent, "should have full freedom for unfoldment. If it be forcibly confined to her husband and children it might burst its bounds and express too great an interest in other humans. The dogs act as a sort of safety valve for this instinct of charity."

The facetious young Count saw from Marguerite's horror-stricken face that he was making a marked impression and he recklessly continued: "The keepers at the Canine Gardens understand this perfectly. When funds begin to run low they put the dogs in the outside pens on short rations, and the brutes do their own begging; then we have another bazaar and everybody is happy. It is a good system and I would advise you not to criticize it since the institution is classic. Other schemes have been tried; at one time women were permitted to knit socks for soldiers — we always put that in historical pictures — but the socks had to be melted up again as felted fibre is much more durable; and then, after the women were forbidden to see the soldiers, they lost interest. But the dog charity is a proven institution and we should never try to change anything that women do not want changed since they are the conservative bulwark of society and our best protection against the danger of the untried."

2

Blocked in her effort to relieve human poverty by the discovery that its existence was not recognized, Marguerite's next adventure in doing good in the world was to take up the battle against ignorance by contributing to the School for the Education of Servants.

The Servant problem in Berlin, and particularly on the Royal Level, had been solved so far as male servants were concerned, for these were a well recognized strain eugenically bred as a division of the intellectual caste. I had once taken Dr. Zimmern to task on this classification of the servant as an intellectual.

"The servant is not intellectual creatively," the

Eugenist replied, " yet it would never do to class him as Labour since he produces nothing. Moreover, the servant's mind reveals the most specialized development of the most highly prized of all German intellectual characteristics — obedience.

" It might interest you to know," continued Zimmern, " that we use this servant strain in outcrossing with other strains when they show a tendency to decline in the virtue of obedience. If I had not chosen to exempt you from paternity when your rebellious instincts were reported to me, and the matter had been turned over to our Remating Board they might have reassigned you to mothers of the servant class. This practice of out-crossing, though rare, is occasionally essential in all scientific breeding."

" Then do you mean," I asked in amazement, " that the highest intellectual strains have servant blood in them? "

" Certainly. And why not, since obedience is the crowning glory of the German mind? Even Royal blood has a dash of the servant strain."

" You mean, I suppose, from illegitimate children? "

" Not at all; that sort of illegitimacy is not recognized. I mean from the admission of servants into Royal Society, just as you have been admitted."

" Impossible! "

" And why impossible, since obedience is our supreme racial virtue? Go consult your social register. The present Emperor, I believe, has admitted none, but his father admitted several and gave them princely incomes. They married well and their children are respected, though I understand they are not very much invited out for the reason that they are poor conversationalists. They only speak when spoken to and then answer, '*Ja, Mein Herr.*' I hear they are very miserable; since no one commands them they must be very bored with life, as they are unable to think of anything to do to amuse themselves. In time the trait will be modified, of course, since the Royal blood will soon predominate, and the strongest inherent trait of Royalty is to seek amusement."

This specialized class of men servants needed little education, for, as I took more interest in observing after this talk with Zimmern, they were the most perfectly fitted to their function of any class in Berlin. But there was also a much more numerous class of women servants on the Royal Level. These, as a matter of economy, were not specially bred to the office, but were selected from the mothers who had been rejected for further maternity after the birth of one or two children. Be it said to the credit of the Germans that no women who had once borne a child was ever permitted to take up the profession of Delilah — a statement which unfortunately cannot be made of the rest of the world. These mothers together with those who had passed the child bearing age more than supplied the need for nurses on the maternity levels and teachers in girls' schools.

As a result they swarmed the Royal Level in all capacities of service for which women are fitted. Originally educated for maternity they had to be re-educated for service. Not satisfied with the official education provided by the masculine-ordered state, the women of the Royal Level maintained a continuation school in the fine art of obedience and the kindred virtues of the perfect servant.

So again it was that Marguerite became involved in a movement that in no wise expressed the needs of her spirit, and from which she speedily withdrew.

The next time she came to me for advice. " I want to do something," she cried. " I want to be of some use in the world. You saved me from that awful life — for you know what it would have been for me if Dr. Zimmern had died or his disloyalty had been discovered — and you have brought me here where I have riches and position but am useless. I tried to be charitable, to relieve poverty, but they say there is no poverty to be relieved. I tried to relieve ignorance, but they will not allow that either. What else is there that needs to be relieved? Is there no good I can do? "

" Your problem is not a new one," I replied, thinking of the world-old experience of the good women yoked to idleness by wealth and position. " You have tried to relieve poverty and ignorance and find your efforts futile. There is one thing more I believe that is considered a classic remedy for your trouble. You can devote yourself to the elimination of ugliness, to the increase of beauty.   Is there no organization devoted to that work? "

" There is," returned Marguerite, " and I was about to join it, but I thought this time I had better ask advice.   There is the League to Beautify Berlin."

" Then by all means join," I advised.   " It is the safest of all such efforts, for though poverty may not exist and ignorance may not be relieved, yet surely Berlin can be more beautiful.   But of course your efforts must be confined to the Royal Level as you do not see the rest of the city."

So Marguerite joined the League to Beautify Berlin and I became an auxiliary member much appreciated because of my liberal contributions.   It proved an excellent source of amusement.   The League met weekly and discussed the impersonal aspects of the beauty of the level in open meetings, while a secret complaint box was maintained into which all were invited to deposit criticisms of more personal matters.   It was forbidden even in this manner to criticize irremedial ugliness such as the matter of one's personal form or features, but dress and manners came within the permitted range and the complaints were regularly mailed to the offenders.   This surprised me a little as I would have thought that such a practice would have made the League unpopular, but on the contrary, it was considered the mainstay of the organization, for the recipient of the complaint, if a non-member, very often joined the League immediately, hoping thereby to gain sweet revenge.

But aside from this safety valve for the desire to make personal criticism, the League was a very creditable institution and it was there that we met the great critics to whose untiring efforts the rare development of German art was due.

Cut off from the opportunity to appropriate by purchase or capture the works of other peoples, German art had suffered a severe decline in the first few generations of the isolation, but in time they had developed an art of their own. A great abundance of cast statues of white crystal adorned the plazas and gardens and, being unexposed to dust or rain, they preserved their pristine freshness so that it appeared they had all been made the day before. Mural paintings also flourished abundantly and in some sections the endless facade of the apartments was a continuous pageant.

But it was in landscape gardening that German art had made its most wonderful advancement. Having small opportunity for true architecture because of the narrow engineering limitations of the city's construction, talent for architecture had been turned to landscape gardening. I use the term advisedly for the very absence of natural landscape within a roofed-in city had resulted in greater development of the artificial product.

The earlier efforts, few of which remained unaltered, were more inclined toward imitation of Nature as it exists in the world of sun and rocks and rain. But, as the original models were forgotten and new generations of gardeners arose, new sorts of nature were created. Artificial rocks, artificial soil, artificially bred and cultured plants, were combined in new designs, unrealistic it is true, but still a very wonderful development of what might be called synthetic or romantic nature. The water alone was real and even in some cases that was altered as in the beautifully dyed rivulets and in the truly remarkable "Fountain of Blood," dedicated to one of the sons of William the Great — I have forgotten his name — in honour of his attack upon Verdun in the First World War.

In these wondrous gardens, with the Princess Marguerite strolling by my side, I spent the happiest hours of my sojourn in Berlin. But my joy was tangled with a thread of sadness for the more I gazed upon this synthetic nature of German creation the more I hungered to tell her of, and to take her to see, the real Nature of the outside world — upon which, in my opinion, with all due respect to their achievements, the Germans had not been able to improve.

3

While the women of the Royal House were not permitted of their own volition to stray from the Royal Level, excursions were occasionally arranged, with proper permits and guards. These were social events of consequence and the invitations were highly prized. Noteworthy among them was an excursion to the highest levels of the city and to the roof itself.

The affair was planned by Admiral von Kufner in Marguerite's honour; for, having spent her childhood elsewhere, she had never experienced the wonder of this roof excursion so highly prized by Royalty, and for ever forbidden to all other women and to all but a few men of the teeming millions who swarmed like larvae in this vast concrete cheese.

The formal invitations set no hour for the excursion as it was understood that the exact time depended upon weather conditions of which we would later be notified. When this notice came the hour set was in the conventional evening of the Royal Level, but corresponding to about three A. M. by solar time. The party gathered at the suite of the Countess Luise and numbered some forty people, for whom a half dozen guides were provided in the form of officers of the Roof Guard. The journey to our romantic destination took us up some hundred metres in an elevator, a trip which required but two minutes, but would lead to a world as different as Mount Olympus from Erebus.

But we did not go directly to the roof, for the hour preferred for that visit had not yet arrived and our first stop was at the swine levels, which had so aroused my curiosity and strained belief when I had first discovered their existence from the chart of my atlas.

As the door of the elevator shaft slid open, a vast

squealing and grunting assaulted our ears. The hours of the swine, like those of their masters, were not reckoned by either solar or sidereal time, but had been altered, as experiment had demonstrated, to a more efficient cycle. The time of our trip was chosen so that we might have this earthly music of the feeding time as a fitting prelude to the visioning of the silent heavens.

On the visitors' gangway we walked just above the reach of the jostling bristly backs, and our own heads all but grazed the low ceiling of the level. To economize power the lights were dim. Despite the masterful achievement of German cleanliness and sanitation there was a permeating odour, a mingling of natural and synthetic smells, which added to the gloom of semi-darkness and the pandemonium of swinish sound produced a totality of infernal effect that thwarts description.

But relief was on the way for the automatic feed conveyors were rapidly moving across our section. First we heard a diminution of sound from one direction, then a hasty scuffling and a happy grunting beneath us and, as the conveyors moved swiftly on, the squealing receded into the distance like the dying roar of a retreating storm.

The Chief Swineherd, immaculately dressed and wearing his full quota of decorations and medals, honoured us with his personal presence. With the excusable pride that every worthy man takes in his work, he expounded the scientific achievements and economic efficiency of the swinish world over which he reigned.   The men of the party listened with respect to his explanations of the accomplishments of sanitation and of the economy of the cycle of chemical transformation by which these swine were maintained without decreasing the capacity of the city for human support.   Lastly the Swineherd spoke of the protection that the swine levels provided against the effects of an occasional penetrating bomb that chanced to fall in the crater of its predecessor before the damage could be repaired.

Pursuant to this fact the uppermost swine level housed those unfortunate animals that were nearest the sausage stage.   On the next lower level, to which we now descended by a spiral stair through a ventilating opening, were brutes of less advanced ages. On the lowest of the three levels where special lights were available for our benefit even the women ceased to shudder and gave expression to ecstatic cries of rapture, as all the world has ever done when seeing baby beasts pawing contentedly at maternal founts.

" Is it not all wonderful? " effused Admiral von Kufner, with a sweeping gesture; " so efficient, so sanitary, so automatic, such a fine example of obedience to system and order.   This is what I call real science and beauty; one might almost say Germanic beauty."

" But I do not like it," replied Marguerite with her usual candour.   " I wish they would abolish these horrid levels."

" But surely," said the Countess, " you would not wish to condemn us to a diet of total mineralism? "

" But the Herr Chemist here could surely invent for us a synthetic sausage," remarked Count Rudolph. " I have eaten vegetarian kraut made of real cabbage from the Botanical Garden, but it was inferior to the synthetic article."

" Do not make light, young people," spoke up the most venerable member of our party, the eminent Herr Dr. von Brausmorganwetter, the historian laureate of the House of Hohenzollern. " It is not as a producer of sausages alone that we Germans are indebted to this worthy animal. I am now engaged in writing a book upon the influence of the swine upon German Kultur. In the first part I shall treat of the Semitic question. The Jews were very troublesome among us in the days before the isolation. They were a conceited race. As capitalists, they amassed fortunes; as socialists they stirred up rebellion; they objected to war; they would never have submitted to eugenics; they even insisted that we Germans had stolen their God!

" We tried many schemes to be rid of these troublesome people, and all failed. Therefore I say that Germany owes a great debt to the noble animal who rid us of the disturbing presence of the Jews, for when pork was made compulsory in the diet they fled the country of their own accord.

" In the second part of my book I shall tell the story of the founding of the New Berlin, for our noble city was modelled on the fortified piggeries of the private estates of William III. In those days of the open war the enemy bombed the stock farms. Synthetic foods were as yet imperfectly developed. Protein was at a premium; the emperor did not like fish, so he built a vast concrete structure with a roof heavily armoured with sand that he might preserve his swine from the murderous attacks of the enemy planes.

" It was during the retreat from Peking. The German armies were being crowded back on every side. The Ray had been invented, but William the III knew that it could not be used to protect so vast a domain and that Germany would be penned into narrow borders and be in danger of extermination by aërial bombardment. In those days he went for rest and consolation to his estates, for he took great pleasure in his thoroughbred swine. Some traitorous spy reported his move to the enemy and a bombing squadron attacked the estates. The Emperor took refuge in his fortified piggery. And so the great vision came to him.

" I have read the exact words of this thoughts as recorded in his diary which is preserved in the archives of the Royal Palace: ' As are these happy brutes, so shall my people be. In safety from the terrors of the sky — protected from the vicissitudes of nature and the enmity of men, so shall I preserve them.'

" That was the conception of the armoured city of Berlin. But that was not all. For the bombardment kept up for days and the Emperor could not escape. On the fourth day came the second idea — two new ideas in less than a week! William III was a great thinker.

" Thus he recorded the second inspiration: ' And even as I have bred these swine, some for bacon and some for lard, so shall the German Blond Brutes be bred the supermen, some specialized for labour and some for brains.'

" These two ideas are the foundation of the kultur of our Imperial Socialism, the one idea to preserve us and the other to re-create us as the superrace. And both of these ideas we owe to this noble animal. The swine should be emblazoned with the eagle upon our flag."

As the Historian finished his eulogy, I glanced surreptitiously at the faces of his listeners, and caught a twinkle in Marguerite's eyes; but the faces of the others were as serious as graven images.

Finally the Countess spoke: " Do I understand, then, that you consider the swine the model of the German race? "

" Only of the lower classes," said the aged historian, " but not the House of Hohenzollern. We are exalted above the necessities of breeding, for we are divine."

Eyes were now turned upon me, for I was the only one of the company not of Hohenzollern blood. Unrelieved by laughter the situation was painful.

" But," said Count Rudolph, coming to my rescue, " we also seek safety in the fortified piggeries."

" Exactly," said the Historian; " so did our noble ancestor."

4

From the piggeries, we went to the green level where, growing beneath eye-paining lights, was a matted mass of solid vegetation from which came those rare sprigs of green which garnished our synthetic dishes. But this was too monotonous to be interesting and we soon went above to the Defence Level where were housed vast military and rebuilding mechanisms and stores. After our guides had shown us briefly about among these paraphernalia, we were conducted to one of the sloping ramps which led through a heavily arched tunnel to the roof above.

Marguerite clung close to my arm, quivering with expectancy and excitement, as we climbed up the sloping passageway and felt on our faces the breath of the crisp air of the May night.

The sky came into vision with startling suddenness as we walked out upon the soft sand blanket of the roof. The night was absolutely clear and my first impression was that every star of the heavens had miraculously waxed in brilliancy. The moon, in the last quarter, hung midway between the zenith and the western horizon. The milky way seemed a floating band of whitish flame. About us, in the form of a wide crescent, for we were near the eastern edge of the city, swung the encircling band of searchlights, but the air was so clear that this stockade of artificial light beams was too pale to dim the points of light in the blue-black vault.

In anticipating this visit to the roof I had supposed it would seem commonplace to me, and had discussed it very little with Marguerite, lest I might reveal an undue lack of wonder. But now as I thrilled once more beneath their holy light, the miracle of unnumbered far-flung flaming suns stifled again the vanity of human conceit and I stood with soul unbared and worshipful beneath the vista of incommensurate space wherein the birth and death of worlds marks the unending roll of time. And at my side a silent gazing woman stood, contrite and humble and the thrill and quiver of her body filled me with a joy of wordless delight.

A blundering guide began lecturing on astronomy and pointing out with pompous gestures the constellations and planets. But Marguerite led me beyond the sound of his voice. "It is not the time for listening to talk," she said. "I only want to see."

When the astronomer had finished his speech-making, our party moved slowly toward the East, where we could just discern the first faint light of the coming dawn. When we reached the parapet of the eastern edge of the city's roof, the stars had faded and pale pink streaked the eastern sky. The guides brought folding chairs from a nearby tunnel way and most of the party sat down on a hillock of sand, very much as men might seat themselves in the grandstand of a race course. But I was so interested in what the dawn would reveal beneath the changing colours of the sky, that I led Marguerite to the rail of the parapet where we could look down into the yawning depths upon the surface of German soil.

My first vision over the parapet revealed but a mottled grey. But as the light brightened the grey land took form, and I discerned a few scraggly patches of green between the torn masses of distorted soil.

The stars had faded now and only the pale moon remained in the bluing sky, while below the land disclosed a sad monotony of ruin and waste, utterly devoid of any constructive work of man.

Marguerite, her gaze fixed on the dawn, was beginning to complain of the light paining her eyes, when one of the guides hurried by with an open satchel swung from his shoulders. " Here are your glasses," he said; " put them on at once. You must be very careful now, or you will injure your eyes."

We accepted the darkened protecting lenses, but I found I did not need mine until the sun itself had appeared above the horizon.

" Did you see it so in your vision? " questioned Marguerite, as the first beams glistened on the surface of the sanded roof.

" This," I replied, " is a very ordinary sunrise with a perfectly cloudless sky. Some day, perhaps, when the gates of this prison of Berlin are opened, we will be able to see all the sunrises of my visions, and even more wonderful ones."

" Karl," she whispered, " how do you know of all

these things? Sometimes I believe you are something more than human, that you of a truth possess the blood of divinity which the House of Hohenzollern claims."

"No," I answered; "not diivnity,— just a little larger humanity, and some day very soon I am going to tell you more of the source of my visions."

She looked at me through her darkened glasses. "I only know," she said, "that you are wonderful, and very different from other men."

Had we been alone on the roof of Berlin, I could not have resisted the temptation to tell her then that stars and sun were familiar friends to me and that the devastated soil that stretched beneath us was but the wasted skeleton of a fairer earth I knew and loved. But we were surrounded by a host of babbling sightseers and so the moment passed and I remained to Marguerite a man of mystery and a seer of visions.

The sun fully risen now, we were led to a protruding observation platform that permitted us to view the wall of the city below. It was merely one vast grey wall without interruption or opening in the monotonous surface.

Amid the more troubled chaos of the ground immediately below we could see fragments of concrete blown from the parapet of the roof. The wall beneath us, we were told, was only of sufficient thickness to withstand fire of the aircraft guns. The havoc that might be wrought, should the defence mines ever be forced back and permit the walls of

Berlin to come within range of larger field pieces, was easily imagined. But so long as the Ray defence held, the massive fort of Berlin was quite impervious to attacks of the world forces of land and air and the stalemate of war might continue for other centuries.

With the coming of daylight we had heard the rumbling of trucks as the roof repairing force emerged to their task. Now that our party had become tired of gazing through their goggles at the sun, our guides led us in the direction where this work was in progress. On the way we passed a single unfilled crater, a deep pit in the flinty quartz sand that spread a protecting blanket over the solid structure of the roof. These craters in the sand proved quite harmless except for the labour involved in their refilling. Further on we came to another, now half-filled from a spouting pipe with ground quartz blown from some remote subterranean mine, so to keep up the wastage from wind and bombing.

Again we approached the edge of the city and this time found more of interest, for here an addition to the city was under construction. It was but a single prism, not a hundred metres across, which when completed would add but another block to the city's area. Already the outer pillars reached the full height and supported the temporary roof that offered at least a partial protection to the work in progress beneath. Though I watched but a few minutes I was awed with the evident rapidity of the building. Dimly I could see the forms below being swung into place with a clock-like regularity and from numerous spouts great streams of concrete poured like flowing lava.

It is at these building sections that the bombs were aimed and here alone that any effectual damage could be done, but the target was a small one for a plane flying above the reach of the German guns. The officer who guided our group explained this to us: these bombing raids were conducted only at times of particular cloud formations, when the veil of mist hung thick and low in an even stratum above which the air was clear. When such formation threatened, the roof of Berlin was cleared and the expected bombs fell and spent their fury blowing up the sand. It had been a futile warfare, for the means of defence were equal to the means of offence.

Our visit to the roof of Berlin was cut short as the sun rose higher, because the women, though they had donned gloves and veils, were fearful of sunburn. So we were led back to the covered ramp into the endless night of the city.

" Have we seen it all? " sighed Marguerite, as she removed her veil and glasses and gazed back blinkingly into the last light of day.

" Hardly," I said; " we have not seen a cloud, nor a drop of rain nor a flake of snow, nor a flash of lightning, nor heard a peal of thunder."

Again she looked at me with worshipful adoration. " I forget," she whispered; " and can you vision those things also? "

But I only smiled and did not answer, for I saw

Admiral von Kufner glaring at me. I had monopolized Marguerite's company for the entire occasion, and I was well aware that his only reason for arranging this, to him a meaningless excursion, had been in the hopes of being with her.

5

But Admiral von Kufner, contending fairly for that share of Marguerite's time which she deigned to grant him, seemed to bear me no malice; and, as the months slipped by, I was gratified to find him becoming more cordial toward me. We frequently met at the informal gatherings in the salon of the Countess Luise. More rarely Dr. Zimmern came there also, for by virtue of his office he was permitted the social rights of the Royal Level. I surmised, however, that this privilege, in his case, had not included the right to marry on the level, for though the head of the Eugenic Staff, he had, so far as I could learn, neither wife nor children.

But Dr. Zimmern did not seem to relish royal society, for when he chanced to be caught with me among the members of the Royal House the flow of his brilliant conversations was checked like a spring in a drought, and he usually took his departure as soon as it was seemly.

On one of these occasions Admiral von Kufner came in as Zimmern sat chatting over cups and incense with Marguerite and me, and the Countess and her son. The doctor dropped quietly out of the conversation, and for a time the youthful Count Ulrich entertained us with a technical elaboration of the importance of the love passion as the dominant appeal of the picture. Then the Countess broke in with a spirited exposition of the relation of soul harmony to ardent passion.

Admiral von Kufner listened with ill-disguised impatience. "But all this erotic passion," he interrupted, "will soon again be swept away by the revival of the greater race passion for world rule."

"My dear Admiral," said the Countess Luise, "your ideas of race passion are quite proper for the classes who must be denied the free play of the love element in their psychic life, but your notion of introducing these ideas into the life of the Royal Level is wholly antiquated."

"It is you who are antiquated," returned the Admiral, "for now the day is at hand when we shall again taste of danger. His Majesty has —"

"Of course His Majesty has told us that the day is at hand," interrupted the Countess. "Has not His Majesty always preserved this allegorical fable? It is part of the formal kultur."

"But His Majesty now speaks the truth," replied the Admiral gravely, "and I say to you who are so absorbed with the light passions of art and love that we shall not only taste of danger but will fight again in the sea and air and on the ground in the outer world. We shall conquer and rule the world."

"And do you think, Admiral," inquired Marguerite, "that the German people will then be free in the outer world?"

" They will be free to rule the outer world," replied the Admiral.

" But I mean," said Marguerite calmly, " to ask if they will be free again to love and marry and rear their own children."

At this naïve question the others exchanged significant glances.

" My dear child," said the Countess, blushing with embarrassment, " your defective training makes it extremely difficult for you to understand these things."

" Of course it is all forbidden," spoke up the young Count, " but now, if it were not, the Princess Marguerite's unique idea would certainly make capital picture material."

" How clever ! " cried the Countess, beaming on her intellectual son. " Nothing is forbidden for plot material for the Royal Level. You shall make a picture showing those great beasts of labour again liberated for unrestricted love."

" There is one difficulty," Count Rudolph considered. " How could we get actors for the parts? Our thoroughbred actors are all too light of bone, too delicate of motion, and our actresses bred for dainty beauty would hardly caste well for those great hulking round-faced labour mothers."

" Then," remarked the Admiral, " if you must make picture plays why not one of the mating of German soldiers with the women of the inferior races ? "

" Wonderful ! " exclaimed the plot maker; " and

practical also. Our actresses are the exact counter-
part of those passionate French beauties. I often
study their portraits in the old galleries. They have
had no Eugenics, hence they would be unchanged.
Is it not so, Doctor? "

" Without Eugenics, a race changes with exceed-
ing slowness," answered Zimmern in a voice devoid
of expression. " I should say that the French
women of today would much resemble their ances-
tral types."

" But picturing such matings of military necessity
would be very disgusting," reprimanded the Countess.

" It will be a very necessary part of the coming
day of German dominion," stated the Admiral.
" How else can we expect to rule the world? It is,
indeed, part of the ordained plan."

" But how," I questioned, " is such a plan to be
executed? Would the men of the World State tolerate it? "

" We will oblige them to tolerate it; the children
of the next generation of the inferior races must be
born of German sires."

" But the Germans are outnumbered ten to one,"
I replied.

" Polygamy will take care of that, among the
white races; the coloured races must be eliminated.
All breeding of the coloured races must cease.
That, also, is part of the ordained plan."

The conversation was getting on rather dangerous
ground for me as I realized that I dare not show

too great surprise at this talk, which of all things I had heard in Germany was the most preposterous. But Marguerite made no effort to disguise her astonishment. "I thought," she said, "that the German rule of the world was only a plan for military victory and the conquering of the World Government. I supposed the people would be left free to live their personal lives as they desired."

"That was the old idea," replied the Admiral, "in the days of open war, before the possibilities of eugenic science were fully realized. But the ordained plan revealed to His Majesty requires not only the military and political rule by the Germans, but the biologic conquest of the inferior races by German blood."

"I think our German system of scientific breeding is very brutal," spoke up Marguerite with an intensity of feeling quite out of keeping with the calloused manner in which the older members of the Royal House discussed the subject.

The Admiral turned to her with a gracious air. "My lovely maiden," he said, "your youth quite excuses your idealistic sentiments. You need only to remember that you are a daughter of the House of Hohenzollern. The women of this House are privileged always to cultivate and cherish the beautiful sentiments of romantic love and individual maternity. The protected seclusion of the Royal Level exists that such love may bloom untarnished by the grosser affairs of world necessity. It was so ordained."

" It was so ordained by men," replied Marguerite defiantly, " and what are these privileges while the German women are prostituted on the Free Level or forced to bear children only to lose them — and while you plan to enforce other women of the world into polygamous union with a conquering race? "

" My dear child," said the Countess, " you must not speak in this wild fashion. We women of the Royal House must fully realize our privileges — and as for the Admiral's wonderful tale of world conquest — that is only his latest hobby. It is talked, of course, in military circles, but the defensive war is so dull, you know, especially for the Royal officers, that they must have something to occupy their minds."

" When the day arrives," snapped the Admiral, " you will find the Royal officers leading the Germans to victory like Atilla and William the Great himself."

" Then why," twitted the Countess, " do you not board one of your submarines and go forth to battle in the sea? "

" I am not courting unnecessary danger," retorted the Admiral; " but I am not dead to the realities of war. My apartments are directly connected with the roof."

" So you can hear the bomb explosions," suggested the Countess.

" And why not? " snapped the Admiral; " we must prepare for danger."

" But you have not been bred for danger," scoffed

the Countess. " Perhaps you would do well to have your reactions to fear tested out in the psychic laboratories; if you should pass the test you might be elected as a father of soldiers; it would surely set a good example to our impecunious Hohenzollern bachelors for whom there are no wives."

The young Count evidently did not comprehend his mother's spirit of raillery. " Has that not been tried? " he asked, turning toward Dr. Zimmern.

" It has," stated the Eugenist, " more than a hundred years ago. There was once an entire regiment of such Hohenzollern soldiers in the Bavarian mines."

" And how did they turn out? " I asked, my curiosity tempting me into indiscretion.

" They mutinied and murdered their officers and then held an election —" Zimmern paused and I caught his eye which seemed to say, " We have gone too far with this."

" Yes, and what happened? " queried the Countess.

" They all voted for themselves as Colonel," replied the Doctor drily.

At this I looked for an outburst of indignation from the orthodox Admiral, but instead he seemed greatly elated. " Of course," he enthused; " the blood breeds true. It verily has the quality of true divinity. No wonder we supermen repudiated that spineless conception of the soft Christian God and the servile Jewish Jesus."

" But Jesus was not a coward," spoke up Marguerite. "I have read the story of his life; it is very wonderful; he was a brave man, who met his death unflinchingly."

"But where did you read it?" asked the Countess. "It must be very new. I try to keep up on the late novels but I never heard of this 'Story of Jesus.'"

"What you say is true," said the Admiral, turning to Marguerite, "but since you like to read so well, you should get Prof. Ohlenslagger's book and learn the explanation of the fact that you have just stated. We have long known that all those great men whom the inferior races claim as their geniuses are of truth of German blood, and that the fighting quality of the outer races is due to the German blood that was scattered by our early emigrations.

"But the distinctive contribution that Prof. Ohlenslagger makes to these long established facts is in regard to the parentage of this man Jesus. In the Jewish accounts, which the Christians accepted, the truth was crudely covered up with a most unscientific fable, which credited the paternity of Jesus to miraculous interference with the laws of nature.

"But now the truth comes out by Prof. Ohlenslagger's erudite reasoning. This unknown father of Jesus was an adventurer from Central Asia, a man of Teutonic blood. On no other conception can the mixed elements in the character of Jesus be explained. His was the case of a dual personality of conflicting inheritance. One day he would say: 'Lay up for yourself treasures'— that was the Jewish blood speaking. The next day he would say: ' I come to bring a sword '— that was the noble German blood of a Teutonic ancestor. It is logical, it must be true, for it was reasoned out by one of our most rational professors."

The Countess yawned; Marguerite sat silent with troubled brows; Dr. Ludwig Zimmern gazed abstractedly toward the cold electric imitation of a fire, above which on a mantle stood two casts, diminutive reproductions of the figures beside the door of the Emperor's palace, the one the likeness of William the Great, the other the Statue of the German God. But I was thinking of the news I had heard that afternoon from my Ore Chief — that Captain Grauble's vessel had returned to Berlin.

CHAPTER XIII

I

ANXIOUS to renew my acquaintance with Captain Grauble at the earliest opportunity, I sent my social secretary to invite him to meet me for a dinner engagement in one of the popular halls of the Free Level.

When I reached the dining hall I found Captain Grauble awaiting me. But he was not alone. Seated with him were two girls and so strange a picture of contrast I had never seen. The girl on his right was an extreme example of the prevailing blonde type. Her pinkish white skin seemed transparent, her eyes were the palest blue and her hair was bright yet pale gold. About her neck was a chain of blue stones linked with platinum. She was dressed in a mottled gown of light blue and gold, and so subtly blended were the colours that she and her gown seemed to be part of the same created thing. But on Grauble's left sat a woman whose gown was flashing crimson slashed with jetty black. Her skin was white with a positive whiteness of rare marble and her cheeks and lips flamed with blood's own red. The sheen of her hair was that of a raven's wing, and her eyes scintillated with the blackness of polished jade.

The pale girl, whom Grauble introduced as Elsa, languidly reached up her pink fingers for me to kiss and then sank back, eyeing me with mild curiosity. But as I now turned to be presented to the other, I saw the black-eyed beauty shrink and cower in an uncanny terror. Grauble again repeated my name and then the name of the girl, and I, too, started in fear, for the name he pronounced was " Katrina " and there flashed before my vision the page from the diary that I had first read in the dank chamber of the potash mine. In my memory's vision the words flamed and shouted: " In no other woman have I seen such a blackness of hair and eyes, combined with such a whiteness of skin."

The girl before me gave no sign of recognition, but only gripped the table and pierced me with the stare of her beady eyes. Nervously I sank into a seat. Grauble, standing over the girl, looked down at her in angry amazement. " What ails you? " he said roughly, shaking her by the shoulder.

But the girl did not answer him and annoyed and bewildered, he sat down. For some moments no one spoke, and even the pale Elsa leaned forward and seemed to quiver with excitement.

Then the girl, Katrina, slowly rose from her chair. " Who are you? " she demanded, in a hoarse, guttural voice, still gazing at me with terrified eyes.

I did not answer, and Grauble again reached over

and gripped the girl's arm. "I told you who he was," he said. "He is Herr Karl von Armstadt of the Chemical Staff."

But, the girl did not sit down and continued to stare at me. Then she raised a trembling hand and, pointing an accusing finger at me, she cried in a piercing voice:

"You are not Karl Armstadt, but an impostor posing as Karl Armstadt!"

We were located in a well-filled dancing café, and the tragic voice of the accuser brought a crowd of curious people about our table. Captain Grauble waved them back. As they pushed forward again, a street guard elbowed in, brandishing his aluminum club and asking the cause of the commotion. The bystanders indicated Katrina and the guard, edging up, gripped her arm and demanded an explanation.

Katrina repeated her accusation.

"Evidently," suggested Grauble, "she has known another man of the same name, and meeting Herr von Armstadt has recalled some tragic memory."

"Perhaps," said the guard politely, "if the gentleman would show the young lady his identification folder, she would be convinced of her error."

For a moment I hesitated, realizing full well what an inquiry might reveal.

"No," I said, "I do not feel that it is necessary."

"He is afraid to show it," screamed the girl. "I tell you he is trying to pass for Armstadt but he is some one else. He looks like Karl Armstadt and at first I thought he was Karl Armstadt, but I know he is not."

I looked swiftly at the surrounding faces, and saw upon them suspicion and accusation. " There may be something wrong," said a man in a militaty uniform, " otherwise why should the gentleman of the staff hesitate to show his folder? "

" Very well," I said, pulling out my folder.

The guard glanced at it. " It seems to be all right," he said, addressing the group about the table; " now will you kindly resume your seats and not embarrass these gentlemen with your idle curiosity? "

" Let me see the folder! " cried Katrina.

" Pardon," said the guard to me, " but I see no harm," and he handed her the folder.

She glanced over it with feverish haste.

" Are you satisfied now? " questioned the guard.

" Yes," hissed the black-eyed girl; " I am satisfied that this is Karl Armstadt's folder. I know every word of it, but I tell you that the man who carries it now is not the real Karl Armstadt." And then she wheeled upon me and screamed, " You are not Karl Armstadt. Karl Armstadt is dead, and you have murdered him! "

In an instant the café was in an uproar. Men in a hundred types of uniform crowded forward; small women, rainbow-garbed, stood on the chairs and peered over taller heads of ponderous sisters of the labour caste. Grauble again waved back the crowd

and the guard brandished his club threateningly toward some of the more inquisitive daughters of labour.

When the crowd had fallen back to a more respectful distance, the guard recovered my identification folder from Katrina and returned it to me.
" Perhaps," he said, " you have known the young
lady and do not again care to renew the acquaintance? If so, with your permission, I shall take her
where she will not trouble you again this evening."

" That may be best," I replied, wondering how I
could explain the affair to Captain Grauble.

" The incident is most unfortunate," said the Captain, evidently a little nettled, " but I think this rude
force unnecessary. I know Katrina well, but I did
not know she had previously known Herr von Armstadt. This being the case, and he seeming not to
wish to renew the acquaintance, I suggest that she
leave of her own accord."

But Katrina was not to be so easily dismissed.
" No," she retorted, " I will not leave until this
man tells me how he came by that identification
folder and what became of the man I loved, whom
he now represents himself to be."

At these words the guard, who had been about
to leave, turned back.

I glanced apprehensively at Grauble who, seeing
that I was grievously wrought up over the affair,
said quietly to the officer, " You had best take her
away."

Katrina, with a black look of hatred at Grauble,

went without further words, and the curious crowd quickly melted away. The three of us who remained at the table resumed our seats and I ordered dinner.

" My, how Katrina frightened me! " exclaimed the fragile Elsa.

" She does have temper," admitted Grauble. " Odd, though, that she would conceive that idea that you were some one else. I have heard of all sorts of plans of revenge for disappointments in love, but that is a new one."

" You really know her? " questioned Elsa, turning her pale eyes upon me.

" Oh, yes, I once knew her," I replied, trying to seem unconcerned; " but I did not recognize her at first."

" You mean you didn't care to," smiled Grauble. " Once a man had known that woman he would hardly forget her."

" But you must have had a very emotional affair with her," said Elsa, " to make her take on like that. Do tell us about it."

" I would rather not; there are some things one wishes to forget."

Grauble chided his dainty companion for her prying curiosity and tried to turn the conversation into less personal channels. But Elsa's appetite for romance had been whetted and she kept reverting to the subject while I worried along trying to dismiss the matter. But the ending of the affair was not to be left in my hands; as we were sitting about our empty cups, we saw Katrina re-enter the café in company with a high official of the level and the guard who had taken her away.

" I am sorry to disturb you," said the official, addressing me courteously, " but this girl is very insistent in her accusation, and perhaps, if you will aid us in the matter, it may prevent her making further charges that might annoy you."

" And what do you wish me to do ? "

" I suggest only that you should come to my office. I have telephoned to have the records looked up and that should satisfy all and so end the matter."

" You might come also," added the official, turning to Grauble, but he waved back the curious Elsa who was eager to follow.

When we reached his office in the Place of Records, the official who had brought us thither turned to a man at a desk. " You have received the data on missing men? " he inquired.

The other handed him a sheet of paper.

The official turned to Katrina. " Will you state again, please, the time that you say the Karl Armstadt you knew disappeared? "

Katrina quite accurately named the date at which the man whose identity I had assumed had been called to the potash mines.

" Very well," said the official, taking up the sheet of paper, " here we have the list of missing men for four years compiled from the weighers' records. There is not recorded here the disappearance of a single chemist during the whole period.   If another man than a chemist should try to step into a chemist's shoes, he would have a rather difficult time of it." The official laughed as if he thought himself very clever.

"But that man is not Karl Armstadt," cried Katrina in a wavering voice. "Do you think I would not know him when every night for —"

"Shut up," said the official, "and get out of here, and if I hear anything more of this matter I shall subtract your credit."

Katrina, now whimpering, was led from the room. The official beamed upon Capt. Grauble and myself.

"Do you see," he said, "how perfectly our records take care of these crazy accusations? The black haired one is evidently touched in the head with jealousy, and now that she has chanced upon you, she makes up this preposterous story, which might cause you no end of annoyance, but here we have the absolute refutation of the charge. Before a man can step into another's shoes, he must step out of his own. Murdered bodies can be destroyed, although that is difficult, but one man cannot be two men!"

We left the official chuckling over his cleverness.

"The Keeper of Records was wise after his kind," mused Grauble, "but it never occurred to him that there might be chemists in the world who are not registered in the card files of Berlin."

Grauble's voice sounded a note of aloofness and suspicion. Had he penetrated my secret? Did I dare make full confession? Had Grauble given me the least encouragement I should have done so, but he seemed to wish to avoid further discussion and I feared to risk it.

My hope of a fuller understanding with Grauble seemed destroyed, and we soon separated without further confidences.

2

When I returned home from my offices one evening some days later, my secretary announced that a visitor was awaiting me.

I entered the reception-room and found Holknecht, who had been my chemical assistant in the early days of my work in Berlin. Holknecht had seemed to me a servile fawning fellow and when I received my first promotion I had deserted him quite brutally for the very excellent reason that he had known the other Armstadt and I feared that his dulled intelligence might at any time be aroused to penetrate my disguise. That he should look me up in my advancement and prosperity, doubtless to beg some favour, seemed plausible enough, and therefore with an air of condescending patronage, I asked what I could do for him.

" It is about Katrina," he said haltingly, as he eyed me curiously.

" Well, what about her? "

" She wants me to bring you to her."

" But suppose I do not choose to go? "

" Then there may be trouble."

" She has already tried to make trouble," I said, " but nothing came of it."

" But that," said Holknecht, " was before she saw me."

" And what have you told her? "

" I told her about Armstadt's going to the mines and you coming back to the hospital wearing his clothes and possessed of his folder and of your being out of your memory."

" You mean," I replied, determined not to acknowledge his assumption of my other identity, " that you explained to her how the illness had changed me; and did that not make clear to her why she did not recognize me at first? "

" There is no use," insisted Holknecht, " of your talking like that. I never could quite make up my mind about you, though I always knew there was something wrong. At first I believed the doctor's story, and that you were really Armstadt, though it did seem like a sort of magic, the way you were changed. But when you came to the laboratory and I saw you work, I decided that you were somebody else and that the Chemical Staff was working on some great secret and had a reason for putting some one else in Armstadt's place. And now, of course, I know very well that that was so, for the other Karl Armstadt would never have become a von of the Royal Level. He didn't have that much brains."

As Holknecht was speaking I had been thinking rapidly. The thing I feared was that the affair of the mine and hospital should be investigated by some one with intelligence and authority. Since Katrina had learned of that, and this Holknecht was also aware that I was a man of unknown identity, it was very evident that they might set some serious investigation going. But the man's own remarks suggested a way out.

"You are quite right, Holknecht," I said; "I am not Karl Armstadt; and, just as you have surmised, there were grave reasons why I should have been put into his place under those peculiar circumstances. But this matter is a state secret of the Chemical Staff and you will do well to say nothing about it. Now is there anything I can do for you? A promotion, perhaps, to a good position in the Protium Works?"

"No," said Holknecht, "I would rather stay where I am, but I could use a little extra money."

"Of course; a check, perhaps; a little gift from an old friend who has risen to power; there would be no difficulty in that, would there?"

"I think it would go through all right."

"I will make it now; say five thousand marks, and if nothing more is said of this matter by you or Katrina, there will be another one like it a year later."

The young man's eyes gloated as I wrote the check, which he pocketed with greedy satisfaction. "Now," I said, "will this end the affair for the present?"

"This makes it all right with me," replied Holknecht, "but what about Katrina?"

"But you are to take care of her. She can only

accept two hundred marks a month and I have given
you enough for that four times over."

" But she doesn't want money; she already has a
full list."

" Then what does she want? "

" Jewels, of course; they all want them; jewels
from the Royal Level, and she knows you can get
them for her."

" Oh, I see. Well, what would please her? "

" A necklace of rubies, the best they have, one
that will cost at least twenty thousand marks."

" That's rather expensive, is it not? "

" But her favourite lover disappeared," fenced
Holknecht, " and his death was never entered on the
records. It may be the Chemical Staff knows what
became of him and maybe they do not; whatever
happened, you seem to want it kept still, so you had
best get the necklace."

After a little further arguing that revealed nothing, I went to the Royal Level, and searching out a
jewelry shop, I purchased a necklace of very beautiful synthetic rubies, for which I gave my check for
twenty thousand marks.

Returning to my apartment, I found Holknecht
still waiting. He insisted on taking the necklace to
Katrina, but I feared to trust a man who accepted
bribes so shamelessly, and decided to go with him
and deliver it in person.

Sullenly, Holknecht led the way to her apartment.

Katrina sensuously gowned in flaming red was awaiting the outcome of her blackmailing venture. She motioned me to a chair near her, while Holknecht, utterly ignored, sank obscurely into a corner.

" So you came," said the lady of black and scarlet, leaning back among her pillows and gazing at me through half closed eyes.

" Yes," I said, " since you have looked up Holknecht and he has explained to you the reason for the disappearance of the man you knew, I thought best to see you and have an understanding."

" But that dumb. fellow explained nothing," declared Katrina, " except that he told me that Armstadt went to the mines and you came back and took his place. He wasn't even sure you were not the other Karl Armstadt until I convinced him, and then he claimed that he had known it all the time; and yet he had never told it. Some men are as dull as books."

" On the contrary, Holknecht is very sensible," I replied. " It is a grave affair of state and one that it is best not to probe into."

" And just what did become of the other Armstadt? " asked Katrina, and in her voice was only a curiosity, with no real concern.

" To tell you the truth, your lover was killed in the mine explosion," I replied, for I thought it unwise to state that he was still alive lest she pursue her inquiries for him and so make further trouble.

" That is too bad," said Katrina. " You see, when I knew him he was only a chemical captain.

And when he deserted me I didn't really care much. But when the Royal Captain Grauble asked me to meet a Karl von Armstadt of the Chemical Staff, at first I could not believe that it was the same man I had known, but I made inquiries and learned of your rapid rise and traced it back and I thought you really were my old Karl. And when I saw you, you seemed to be he, but when I looked again I knew that you were another and I was so disappointed and angry that I lost control of my temper. I am sorry I made a scene, and that official was so stupid — as if I would not know one man from another! How I should like to tell him that I knew more than his stupid records."

" But that is not best," I said; " your former lover is dead and there are grave reasons why that death should not be investigated further —" The argument was becoming a little difficult for me and I hastened to add: " Since you were so discourteously treated by the official, I feel that I owe you some little token of reparation."

I now drew out the necklace and held it out to the girl.

Her black eyes gleamed with triumph at the sight of the bauble. Greedily she grasped it and held it up between her and the light, turning it about and watching the red rays gleaming through the stones. " And now," she gloated, " that faded Elsa will cease to lord it over me — and to think that another Karl Armstadt has brought me this — why that stingy fellow would never have bought me a bluestone ring, if he had been made the Emperor's Minister."

Katrina now rose and preened before her mirror. "Won't you place it round my neck?" she asked, holding out the necklace.

Nor daring to give offence, I took the chain of rubies and attempted to fasten it round her neck. The mechanism of the fastening was strange to me and I was some time in getting the thing adjusted. Just as I had succeeded in hooking the clasp, I heard a curdled oath and the neglected Holknecht hurled himself upon us, striking me on the temple with one fist and clutching at the throat of the girl with the other hand.

The blow sent me reeling to the floor but in another instant I was up and had collared him and dragged him away.

"Damn you both," he whimpered; "where do I come in?"

"Put him out," said Katrina, with a glance of disdain at the cowering man.

"I will go," snarled Holknecht, and he wrenched from my grasp and darted toward the door. I followed, but he was fairly running down the passage and pursuit was too undignified a thing to consider.

"You should have paid him," said Katrina, "for delivering my message."

"I have paid him," I replied. "I paid him very well."

"I wonder if he thought," she laughed, "that I would pay any attention to a man of his petty rank.

Why, I snubbed him unmercifully years ago when the other Armstadt had the audacity to introduce me."

" Of course," I replied, " he does not understand."

And now, as I resumed my seat, I began puzzling my brain as to how I could get away without giving offence to the second member of my pair of blackmailers. But a little later I managed it, as it has been managed for centuries, by looking suddenly at my watch and recalling a forgotten appointment.

" You will come again? " purred Katrina.

" Of course," I said, " I must come again, for you are very charming, but I am afraid it will not be for some time as I have very important duties and just at present my leisure is exceedingly limited."

And so I made my escape, and hastened home. After debating the question pro and con I typed a note to Holknecht in which I assured him that I had not the least interest in Katrina. " Perhaps," I wrote, " when she has tired a bit of the necklace, she would appreciate something else. But it would not be wise to hurry this; but if you will call around in a month or so, I think I can arrange for you to get her something and present it yourself, as I do not care to see her again."

CHAPTER XIV

THE BLACK SPOT IS ERASED FROM THE MAP OF THE
WORLD AND THERE IS DANCING IN THE SUN-
LIGHT ON THE ROOF OF BERLIN

I

THE relative ease with which I had so long
passed for the real Karl Armstadt had
lulled me into a feeling of security. But
now that my disguise had been penetrated, my old
fears were renewed. True, the weigher's records
had seemingly cleared me, but I knew that Grauble
had seen the weak spot in the German logic of the
stupid official, who had so lightly dismissed Katrina's accusations. Moreover, I fancied that Grauble had guessed the full truth and connected this
uncertainty of my identity with the seditious tenor
of the suggestions I had made to him. Even though
he might be willing to discuss rebellious plans with
a German, could I count on him to consider the
treasonable urging coming from a man of another
and an enemy race?

So fearing either to confess to him my identity
or to proceed without confessing, I postponed doing
anything. The sailing date of his fifth trip to the
Arctic was fast approaching; if I was ever to board
a vessel leaving Berlin I would need von Kufner's
permission. Marguerite reported the growing cor-

diality of the Admiral. Although I realized that his infatuation for her was becoming rather serious, with the confidence of an accepted lover, I never imagined that he could really come between Marguerite and myself.

But one evening when I went to call upon Marguerite she was " not at home." I repeated the call with the same result. When I called her up by telephone, her secretary bluntly told me that the Princess Marguerite did not care to speak to me. I hastened to write an impassioned note, pleading to see her at once, for the days were passing and there was now but a week before Grauble's vessel was due to depart.

In desperation I waited two more days, and still no word came. My letters of pleading, like my calls and telephone efforts, were still ignored.

Then a messenger came bearing a note from Admiral von Kufner, asking me to call upon him at once.

" I have been considering," began von Kufner, when I entered his office, " the request you made of me some time ago to be permitted to go in person to make a survey of the ore deposits. At first I opposed this, as the trip is dangerous, but more recently I have reconsidered the importance of it. As others are now fully able to continue your work here, I can quite conceive that your risking the trip to the mines in person would be a very courageous and noble sacrifice. So I have taken the matter up with His Majesty."

With mocking politeness von Kufner now handed me a document bearing the imperial seal.

I held it with a trembling hand as I glanced over the fateful words that commissioned me to go at once to the Arctic.

My smouldering jealousy of the oily von Kufner now flamed into expression. " You have done this thing from personal motives," I cried. " You have revoked your previous decision because you want me out of your way. You know I will be gone for six months at least. You hope in your cowardly heart that I will never come back."

Von Kufner's lips curled. " You see fit," he answered, " to impugn my motives·in suggesting that the order be issued, although it is the granting of your own request. But the commission you hold in your hand bears the Imperial signature, and the Emperor of the Germans never revokes his orders."

" Very well," I said, controlling my rage, " I will go."

2

Upon leaving the Admiral's office my first thought was to go at once to Marguerite. Whatever might be the nature of her quarrel with me I was now sure that von Kufner was at the bottom of it, and that it was in some way connected with this sudden determination of his to send me to the Arctic, hoping that I would never return.

But before I had gone far I began to consider other matters. I was commissioned to leave Berlin

by submarine and that too by the vessel in command
of Captain Grauble, whom I knew to be nursing
rebellion and mutiny in his heart. If deliverance
from Berlin was ever to come, it had come now.
To refuse to embrace it would mean to lose for ever
this fortunate chance to escape from this sunless
Babylon.

I would therefore go first to Grauble and determine without delay if he could be relied on to make
the attempt to reach the outer world.   Once I knew
that, I could go then to Marguerite with an invitation for her to join me in flight — if such a thing
were humanly possible.

But recalling the men who had done so much to
fill me with hope and faith in the righteousness of
my mission, I again changed my plan and sought out
Dr. Zimmern and Col. Hellar and arranged for
them to meet me that evening at Grauble's quarters.

At the hour appointed I, who had first arrived at
the apartment, sat waiting for the arrival of Zimmern.   When he came, to my surprise and bewildered joy he was not alone, for Marguerite was with
him.

She greeted me with distress and penitence in her
eyes and I exulted in the belief that whatever her
quarrel with me might be it meant no irretrievable
loss of her devotion and love.

We sat about the room, a very solemn conclave,
for I had already informed Grauble of my commission to go to the Arctic, and he had sensed at once
the revolutionary nature of the meeting.   I now

gave him a brief statement of the faith of the older men, who from the fulness of their lives had reached the belief that the true patriotism for their race was to be expressed in an effort to regain for the Germans the citizenship of the world.

The young Captain gravely nodded. " I have not lived so long," he said, " but my life has been bitter and full of fear. I am not out of sympathy with your argument, but before we go further," and he turned to Marguerite, " may I not ask why a Princess of the House of Hohenzollern is included in such a meeting as this? "

I turned expectantly to Zimmern, who now gave Grauble an account of the tragedy and romance of Marguerite's life.

" Very well," said Grauble; " she has earned her place with us; now that I understand her part, let us proceed."

For some hours Hellar and Zimmern explained their reasons for believing the life of the isolated German race was evil and defended their faith in the hope of salvation through an appeal to the mercy and justice of the World State.

" Of all this I am easily convinced," said Grauble, " for it is but a logically thought-out conclusion of the feeling I have nourished in my blind rebellion. I am ready to go with Herr von Armstadt and surrender my vessel to the enemy; but the practical question is, will our risk avail anything? What hope can we have that we will even be able to deliver the message you wish to send? How are we to know that we will not immediately be killed?"

The hour had come. "I will answer that question," I said, and there was a tenseness in my tone that caused my hearers to look at me with eager, questioning eyes.

"Barring," I said, "the possibility of destruction before I can gain opportunity to speak to some one in authority, there is nothing to fear in the way of our ungracious reception in the outer world —" As I paused and looked about me I saw Marguerite's eyes shining with the same worshipful wonder as when I had visioned for her the sunlight and the storms of the world outside Berlin —" because I am of that world. I speak their language. I know their people. I never saw the inside of Berlin until I was brought here from the potash mines of Stassfurt, wearing the clothes and carrying the identification papers of one Karl Armstadt who was killed by gas bombs which I myself had ordered dropped into those mines."

At these startling statements the older men could only gasp in incredulous astonishment, but Captain Grauble nodded wisely —" I half expected as much," he said.

I turned to Marguerite. Her eyes were swimming in a mist of tears.

"Then your visions were real memories," she cried,—" and not miracles. I knew you had seen other worlds, but I thought it was in some spirit life." She reached out a trembling hand toward me and then shrinkingly drew it back. "But you are not Karl Armstadt," she stammered, as she realized that I was a nameless stranger.

"No," I said, going to her and placing a reassuring arm about her shoulder, "I am not Karl Armstadt. My name is Lyman de Forrest. I am an American, a chemical engineer from the city of Chicago, and if Captain Grauble does not alter his purpose, I am going back there and will take you with me."

Zimmern and Hellar were listening in consternation. "How is it," asked Hellar, "that you speak German?"

By way of answer I addressed him in English and in French, while he and Zimmern glanced at each other as do men who see a miracle and strive to hold their reason while their senses contradict their logic.

I now sketched the story of my life and adventures with a fulness of convincing detail. One incident only I omitted and that was of the near discovery of my identity by Armstadt's former mistress. Of that I did not speak for I felt that Marguerite, at least in the presence of the others, would not relish that part of the story. Nor did I wish to worry them with the fear that was still upon me that I had not seen the last of that affair.

After answering many questions and satisfying all doubts as to the truth of my story, I again turned the conversation to the practical problem of the escape from Berlin. "You can now see," I declared, "that I deserve no credit for genius or courage. I am merely a prisoner in an enemy city where my life is in constant danger. If any one of you should speak the word, I would be promptly disposed of as a spy. But if you are sincere in your desire to send a message to my Government, I am here to take that message."

"It almost makes one believe that there is a God," cried Hellar, "and that he has sent us a deliverer."

"As for me," spoke up Captain Grauble, "I shall deliver your messenger into the hands of his friends, and trust that he can persuade them to deal graciously with me and my men. I should have made this break for liberty before had I not believed it would be fleeing from one death to another."

"Then you will surely leave us," said Zimmern. "It is more than we have wished and prayed for, but," he added, turning a compassionate glance toward Marguerite, "it will be hard for her."

"But she is going with us," I affirmed. "I will not leave her behind. As for you and Col Hellar, I shall see you again when Berlin is free. But the risks are great and the time may be long, and if Marguerite will go I will take her with me as a pledge that I shall not prove false in my mission for you, her people."

I read Marguerite's answer in the joy of her eyes, as I heard Col. Hellar say: "That would be fine, if it were possible."

But Zimmern shook his head. "No," he said, as if commanding. "Marguerite must not go now even if it were possible. You may come back for her if you succeed in your mission, but we cannot lose her now; she must not go now,—" and his voice trembled with deep emotion. At his words of authority concerning the girl I loved I felt a resurge of the old suspicion and jealousy.

"I am sorry," spoke up Captain Grauble, "but your desire to take the Princess Marguerite with you is one that I fear cannot be realized. I would be perfectly willing for her to go if we could once get her aboard, but the approach of the submarine docks are very elaborately guarded. To smuggle a man aboard without a proper permit would be exceedingly difficult, but to get a woman to the vessel is quite impossible."

"I suppose that it cannot be," I said, for I saw the futility of arguing the matter further at the time, especially as Zimmern was opposed to it.

The night was now far spent and but four days remained in which to complete my preparations for departure. In this labour Zimmern and Hellar could be of no service and I therefore took my leave of them, lest I should not see them again. "Within a year at most," I said, "we may meet again, for Berlin will be open to the world. Once the passage is revealed and the protium traffic stopped, the food stores cannot last longer. When these facts are realized by His Majesty and the Advisory Council, let us hope they will see the futility of resisting. The knowledge that Germany possesses will increase the world's food supply far more than her population will add to the consumptive demands, hence if reason and sanity prevail on both sides there will be no excuse for war and suffering."

3

And so I took my leave of the two men from whose noble souls I had achieved my aspirations to bring the century-old siege of Berlin to a sane and peaceful end without the needless waste of life that all the world outside had always believed would be an inevitable part of the capitulation of the armoured city.

I now walked with Marguerite through the deserted tree-lined avenues of the Royal Level.

"And why, dear," I asked, "have you refused to see me these five days past?"

"Oh, Karl," she cried, "you must forgive me, for nothing matters now — I have been crazed with jealousy. I was so hurt that I could see no one, for I could only fight it out alone."

"And what do you mean?" I questioned. "Jealous? And of whom could you be jealous, since there is no other woman in this unhappy city for whom I have ever cared?"

"Yes, I believe that. I haven't doubted that you loved me with a nobler love than the others, but you told me there were no others, and I believed you. So it was hard, so very hard. The Doctor — I saw Dr. Zimmern this morning and poured out my heart to him — insisted that I should accept the fact that until marriage all men were like that, and it could not be helped. But I never asked you,

Karl, about other women; you yourself volunteered to tell me there were no others, and what you told me was not true. I must forgive you, for now I may lose you, but why does a man ever need to lie to a woman? I somehow feel that love means truth —"

" But," I insisted, " it was the truth. I bear no personal relation to any other woman."

She drew back from me, breathing quickly, faith and doubt fighting a battle royal in her eyes. " But the checks, Karl? " she stammered; " those checks the girl on the Free Level cashes each month, and worse than that the check at the Jeweller's where you bought a necklace for twenty thousand marks? "

" Quite right, there are such checks, and I shall explain them. But before I begin, may I ask just how you came to know about those checks? Not that I care; I am glad you do know; but the fact of your knowledge puzzles me, for I thought the privacy of a man's checking account was one of the unfair privileges that man has usurped for himself and not granted to women."

" But I did not pry into the matter. I would never have thought of such a thing until he forced the facts upon me."

" He? You mean von Kufner? "

" Yes, it was five days ago. I was out walking with him and he insisted on my going into a jewellery store we were passing. I at first refused to go as I thought he wished to buy me something. But he insisted that he merely wanted me to look at things and I went in. You see, I was trying not to offend him."

" Of course," I said, " there was no harm in that. And —"

" The Admiral winked at the Jeweller. I saw him do that; and the jeweller set out a tray of ruby necklaces and began to talk about them, and then von Kufner remarked that since they were so expensive he must not sell many. ' Oh, yes,' said the Jeweller, ' I sell a great number to young men who have just come into money. I sold one the other day to Herr von Armstadt of the Chemical Staff,' and he reached for his sales book and opened it to the page with a record of the sale. He had the place marked, for I saw him remove a slip as he opened the book."

" Rather clever of von Kufner," I commented; " how do you suppose he got trail of it? "

" He admitted his trailing quite frankly," said Marguerite, " for as soon as we were out of the shop, I accused him of preparing the scene. ' Of course,' he said, ' but I had to convince you that your chemist was not so saintly as you thought him. His banker is a friend of mine, and I asked him about von Armstadt's account. He is keeping a girl on the Free Level and evidently also making love to one of better caste, or he would hardly be buying ruby necklaces.' I told von Kufner that he was a miserable spy, but he only laughed at me and said that all men were alike and that I ought to find it out while I was young — and then he asked if I would like him to have the young woman's record sent up from the Free Level for my inspection. I ordered him to leave me at once and I have not seen or heard from him since, until I received a note from him today telling me of the Royal order for you to go to the Arctic."

I first set Marguerite's mind at ease about the checks to Bertha by explaining the incident of the geography, and then told the story of Katrina and the meeting in the café, and the later affair of Holknecht and the necklace.

"And you will promise me never to see her again?"

"But you have forgotten," I said, "that I am leaving Berlin in four days."

"Oh, Karl," she cried, "I have forgotten everything — I cannot even remember that new name you gave us — I believe I must be dreaming — or that it is all a wild story you have told us to see how much we in our simplicity and ignorance will believe."

"No," I said gently, "it is not a dream, though I could wish that it were, for Grauble says that there is no hope of taking you with me; and yet I must go, for the Emperor has ordered me to the Arctic and von Kufner will see to it that I make no excuses. If I once leave Berlin by submarine with Grauble I do not see how I can refuse to carry out my part of this project to which I am pledged, and make the effort to reach the free world outside."

Marguerite turned on me with a bitter laugh.

" The free world," she cried, " your world. You are going back to it and leave me here. You are going back to your own people — you will not save Germany at all — you will never come back for me ! "

" You are very wrong," I said gently. " It is because I have known you and known such men as Dr. Zimmern and Col. Hellar that I do want to carry the message that will for ever end this sunless life of your imprisoned race."

" But," cried Marguerite, " you do not want to take me; you could find a way if you would — you made the Emperor do your bidding once — you could do it again if you wanted to."

" I very much want to take you; to go without you would be but a bitter success."

" But have you no wife, or no girl you love among your own people? "

" No."

" But if I should go with you, the people of your world would welcome you but they would imprison me or kill me as a spy."

" No," and I smiled as I answered, " they do not kill women."

4

During four brief days that remained until Capt. Grauble's vessel was due to depart my every hour was full of hurried preparations for my survey of the Arctic mines. Clothing for the rigours and rough labour of that fearful region had to be obtained and I had to get together the reports of previous surveys and the instruments for the ore analyses that would be needed. Nor was I altogether faithless in these preparations for at times I felt that my first duty might be thus to aid in the further provisioning of the imprisoned race, for how was I to know that I would be able to end the state of war that had prevailed in spite of the generations of pacifist efforts? At times I even doubted that this break for the outer world would ever be made. I doubted that Capt. Grauble, though he solemnly assured us that he was ready for the venture, was acting in good faith. Could he, I asked, persuade his men to their part of the adventure? Would not our traitorous design be discovered and we both be returned as prisoners to Berlin? Granted even that Grauble could carry out his part and that the submarine proceeded as planned to rise to the surface or attempt to make some port, with the best of intentions of surrendering to the World State authorities, might not we be destroyed before we cou'd make clear our peaceful and friendly intentio. ? Could I, coming out of Germany with Germans prove my identity? Would my story be believed? Would I have believed such a story before the days of my sojourn among the Germans? Might I not be consigned to languish in prison as a merely clever German spy, or be consigned to an insanity ward?

At times I doubted even my own desire to escape from Berlin if it meant the desertion of Marguerite, for there could be no joy in escape for me without

her. Yet I found small relish in looking forward
to life as a member of that futile clan of parasitical
Royalty. Had Germany been a free society where
we might hope to live in peace and freedom perhaps
I could have looked forward to a marriage with
Marguerite and considered life among the Germans
a tolerable thing. But for such a life as we must
needs live, albeit the most decent Berlin had to
offer, I could find no relish — and the thought of
escape and call of duty beyond the bomb proof walls
and poisoned soil called more strongly than could
any thought of love and domesticity within the accursed circle of fraudulent divinity.

There was also the danger that lurked for me in
Holknecht's knowledge of my identity and the bitterness of his anger born of his insane and stupid
jealousy.

Rather than remain longer in Berlin I would take
any chance and risk any danger if only Marguerite
were not to be left behind. And yet she must be
left behind, for such a thing as getting a woman
aboard a submarine or even to the submarine docks
had never been heard of. I thought of all the usual
tricks of disguising her as a man, of smuggling her
as a stowaway amidst the cargo, but Grauble's in-
sistence upon the impossibility of such plans had
made it all too clear that any such wild attempt
would lead to the undoing of us all.

If escape were possible with Marguerite —!
But cold reason said that escape was improbable
enough for me alone. For a woman of the House

of Hohenzollern the prison of Berlin had walls of granite and locks of steel.

The time of departure drew nearer. I had already been passed down by the stealthy guards and through the numerous locked and barred gates to the subterranean docks where Grauble's vessel, the *Eitel 3*, rested on the heavy trucks that would bear her away through the tunnel to the pneumatic lock that would float her into the passage that led to the open sea.

My supplies and apparatus were stored on board and the crew were making ready to be off. But three hours were left until the time of our departure and these hours I had set aside for my final leave-taking of Marguerite. I hastened back through the guarded gates to the elevator and was quickly lifted to the Royal Level where Marguerite was to be waiting for me.

With fast beating and rebellious heart I rang the bell of the Countess' apartment. I could scarcely believe I heard aright when the servant informed me that the Princess Marguerite had gone out.

I demanded to see the Countess and was ushered into the reception-room and suffered unbearably during the few minutes till she appeared. To my excited question she replied with a teasing smile that Marguerite had gone out a half hour before with Admiral von Kufner. "I warned you," said the Countess as she saw the tortured expression of my face, "but you would not believe me, when I told you the Admiral would prove a dangerous man."

"But it is impossible," I cried. "I am leaving for the Arctic mines. I have only a couple of hours; surely you are hiding something. Did you see her go? Did she leave no word? Do you know where they have gone or when they will return?"

The Countess shook her head. "I only know," she replied more sympathetically, "that Marguerite seemed very excited all morning. She talked with me of your leaving and seemed very wrought up over it, and then but an hour or so ago she rushed into her room and telephoned — it must have been to the Admiral, for he came shortly afterwards. They talked together for a little while and then, without a word to me they went out, seeming to be in a great hurry. Perhaps she felt so upset over your leaving that she thought it kinder not to risk a parting scene. She is so honest, poor child, that she probably did not wish to send you away with any false hopes."

"But do you mean," I cried, "that you think she has gone out with von Kufner to avoid seeing me?"

"I am sorry," consoled the Countess, "but it looks that way. It was cruel of her, for she might have sent you away with hope to live on till your return, even if she felt she could not wait for you."

I strove not to show my anger to the Countess, for, considering her ignorance of the true significance of the occasion, I could not expect a full understanding.

Miserably I waited for two hours as the Countess

tried to entertain me with her misplaced efforts at sympathy while I battled to keep my faith in Marguerite alive despite the damaging evidence that she had deserted me at the last hour.

I telephoned to von Kufner's office and to his residence but could get no word as to his whereabouts, and Marguerite did not return.

I dared not wait any longer — asking for envelope and paper, I penned a hasty note to Marguerite: " I shall go on to the Arctic and come back to you. The salvation of Berlin must wait till you can go with me. I cannot, will not, lose you."

And then I tore myself away and hastened to the elevator and was dropped to a subterranean level and passed again through the locked and guarded gates.

5

As I came to the vessel no one was in sight but the regular guards pacing along the loading docks. I mounted the ladder to the deck. The second officer stood by the open trap. " They are waiting for you," he said. " The Admiral himself is below. He came with his lady to see you off."

I hastened to descend and saw von Kufner and Marguerite chatting with Captain Grauble.

" Why the delay? " asked von Kufner. " It is nearly the hour of departure, and I have brought the Princess to bid you farewell. We have been showii g her the vessel."

" It is all very wonderful," said Marguerite with a calm voice, but her eyes spoke the feverish excitement of a great adventure.

" The Princess Marguerite," said von Kufner, " is the only woman who has ever seen a submarine since the open sea traffic was closed. But she has seen it all and now we must take our leave for it is time that you should be off."

As he finished speaking the Admiral politely stepped away to give me opportunity for a farewell word with Marguerite. Grauble followed him and, as he passed me, he gave me a look of gloating triumph and then opened the door of his cabin, which the Admiral entered.

" I am going with you," whispered Marguerite. " Grauble understands."

There was the sound of a scuffle and a strangled oath. Grauble's head appeared at the cabin door. " Here, Armstadt; be quick, and keep him quiet."

I plunged into the cabin and saw von Kufner crumpled against the bunk; his hands were manacled behind him and his mouth stuffed with a cloth.

With an exulting joy I threw myself upon the man as he struggled to rise. I easily held him down, and whipping out my own kerchief I bound it tightly across his mouth to more effectively gag him.

Then rolling him over I planted my knee on his back while I ripped a sheet from the bunk and bound his feet.

From without I heard Grauble's voice in command: " Close the hatch." Then I felt the vessel quiver with machinery in motion and I knew that we were moving along the tunnel toward the sea.

Grauble appeared again in the door of the cabin. " The mate understands," he said, " and the crew will obey. I told them that the Admiral was going out with us to inspect the lock. But the presence of a woman aboard will puzzle them. I have placed the Princess in the mate's cabin so no one can molest her. We have other things to keep us occupied."

With Grauble's help I now bound von Kufner to the staunch metal leg of the bunk and we left him alone in the narrow room to ponder on the meaning of what he had heard.

Outside Grauble led me over to the instrument board where the mate was stationed.

" Any unusual message? " asked Grauble.

" None," said the mate. " I think we will go through without interruption at least until we reach the lock; if anything is suspicioned we will be held up there for examination."

" Do you think the guards at the dock suspected anything? " questioned Grauble.

" It is not likely," replied the mate. " They saw him come aboard, but he spoke to none of them. They will presume he is going out to the lock. The presence of a woman will puzzle them; but, as she was with the Admiral, they will not dare interfere or even report the fact."

" Then what do you think we have to fear? " asked Grauble.

" Only the chance that the Admiral's absence may be noted at his office and inquiry be made."

" Of that the Princess could tell us something," said Grauble. " We will talk with her."

Grauble now led me to the mate's snug cabin, where we found Marguerite seated on the bunk, looking very pale and anxious.

" Everything is going nicely, so far," the Captain assured her. " We have only one thing to fear, and that is that inquiry from the Administration Office for the Admiral may be addressed to the Commander of the Lock."

" But how will they know that he is with us? " asked Marguerite. " Will the guards report it? "

" I do not think so," said Grauble, " but does any one at his office know that he came to the docks? "

" I do not see how they could," replied Marguerite; " he was at his apartment when I called him. He came to me at once, not knowing why I wished to see him. I begged him to take me to see you off. I swore that if he did not I should never speak to him again, and he agreed to do so. He seemed to think himself very generous and talked much of the distinctive privilege he was conferring upon me by acceding to my request. But he told no one where we were going. He communicated with no one from the time he came to me until we arrived at the vessel. The guards and gate-keepers let us pass without question."

" That is fine," cried Grauble; " von Kufner often

stays away from his office for days at a time. Unless some chance information leaks back from the guards, he will not be missed. Our chance of being passed speedily out the lock is good — there is a vessel due to lock in this very day and we could not be held back to block the tunnel. That is why the Admiral was impatient when Armstadt failed to appear; he knew our departure ought not be delayed."

"And what," I asked, "do you propose to do with the Admiral?"

"I suppose we must take him with us as a prisoner," replied the Captain. "Your World State Government would appreciate a prisoner of the House of Hohenzollern."

At this suggestion Marguerite shook her head emphatically. "I do not like that," she said. "Is there not some way to leave him behind?"

"I do not like it either," said Grauble, "because I fear his presence aboard may make trouble among my men. I do not think they will object to deserting with us to the free world. Their life in this service is hopeless enough and this is my fifth trip; they have a belief that the Captain's fifth trip is an ill-fated one; not a man aboard but trembles in the dire fear that he will never see Berlin again. They will welcome with joy a proposal to escape with us, but to ask them to make the attempt with the Admiral himself on board as a prisoner is a different thing. These men are cowed by authority and I know not what notions they might have of their fate if they are to kidnap the Admiral."

" But," I questioned, " is there no possible way to leave him behind? "

Grauble sat thinking for a moment. " Yes," he said, " there is one way we might do it. We could shave his beard and clip his hair, dress him in a machinist's garb and smear his hands and face with grease. Then I could drug him and we could carry him off at the lock and put him in a cell. I would report that one of my men had gone raving mad, and I had drugged him to keep him from doing injury to himself and others. It would create no great surprise. Men in this service frequently go mad; and I am provided with a sleep producing drug for just such emergencies."

" Then go ahead," I said.

" But you will lose the satisfaction of delivering him prisoner to your government," smiled Grauble.

" I have no love for the Admiral," I replied, " but I think his punishment will be more appropriately attended to in Berlin. When our escape is known he will indeed have a rather difficult time explaining to His Majesty."

This suggestion of the pompous Admiral's predicament if thus left behind seemed to amuse Grauble and he at once led the way back to his own cabin.

Von Kufner was lying very quietly in his bonds and glared up at us with a weak and futile rage.

Grauble smiled cynically at his prostrate chief. " I had thought to take you along with us," he said, " but I am afraid the excitement of the voyage would be unpleasant for you so I have decided to leave you at the lock to take our farewell back to His Majesty."

Von Kufner, helpless and gagged was given no opportunity to reply, for Grauble, unlocking his medicine case took out a small hypodermic syringe and plunged the needle into the prisoner's thigh.

In a few minutes the Admiral was unconscious. The Captain now brought a suit of soiled mechanic's clothes and a clipper and razor, and in a half hour the prim Admiral in his fancy uniform had been reduced to the likeness of an oiler. His face roughly shaved, but pale and sallow, gave a very good simulation of illness of mind and body.

" He will remain like that for at least twelve hours," said Grauble. " I gave him a heavy dose."

Again we went out, locking the unconscious Admiral in the cabin. " You may go and keep the Princess company," said Grauble, " while I talk with my men and give them an inkling of what we are planning. If there is any trouble at the lock it is better that they comprehend that hope of freedom is in store for them."

Amid tears of joy Marguerite now told me of her belated conception of the desperate plan to induce von Kufner to bring her to the docks to see us depart, and how she had pretended to disbelieve that I was really going and bargained to marry him within sixty days if she could be assured by her own eyes that I had really departed for the Arctic.

As we waited feverishly for the first nerve-racking part of the journey to be over, we spoke of the hopes and dangers of the great adventure upon which we were finally embarked. And so the hours passed. At last we felt the rumble of the motors die and knew that the movement of the vessel had ceased.

6

The voice of the mate spoke at the door: " Remain quiet inside," he said, and a key turned and clicked the bolt of the lock. The tense minutes passed. Again the key turned in the door and the mate stuck his head inside. " Come quick," he said to me.

I followed him into Capt. Grauble's cabin, but saw Grauble nowhere.

" Remove your clothing," said the mate, as he seized a sponge and soap and began washing the blackened oil from the hands and face of the unconscious Admiral. " We must dress him in your uniform. The Commander of the Lock has orders to take you off the vessel. We must pass the Admiral off for you. He will never be recognized. The Commander has never seen you."

Obeying, without fully comprehending, I helped to quickly dress the unconscious man in my own clothing. We had barely finished when we heard voices outside.

" Quick, under the bunk," whispered the mate.

As I obediently crawled into the hiding place, the mate kicked in after me the remainder of the oiler's clothing which I had been trying to put on and pulled the disarranged bedding half off the bunk the better to hide me.   Then he opened the door and several men entered.

"I had to drug him," said Grauble's voice, "because he was so violent with fear when I had him manacled that I thought he might attempt to beat out his brains."

"Let me see his papers," said a strange voice.

After a brief interval the same voice spoke again —"These are identical with the description given by His Majesty's secretary.   There can be no doubt that this is the man they want, but I do not see how an enemy spy could ever pass for a German, even if he had the clothing and identification.   He does not even look like the description in the folder. The chemists must be very stupid to have accepted him as one of them."

"It is strange," replied the voice of Capt. Grauble, "but this man was very clever."

"It is only that most men are very dull," replied the other voice.   "Now I should have suspected at once that the man was not a German.   But he shall answer for his cleverness.   Let him be removed at once.   We have word from the vessel outside that they are short of oxygen, and you must be locked out and clear the passage."

With a shuffling of many feet the form of the third bearer of Karl Armstadt's pedigree was carried from the cabin, and the door was kicked shut. I was still lying cramped in my hiding place when I felt the vessel moving again. Then a sailor came, bringing a case from which I took fresh clothing. As I was dressing I felt my ear drums pain from the increased air pressure, and I heard, as from.a great distance, the roar of the water being let into the lock. From the quiet swaying of the floor beneath me I soon sensed that we were afloat. I waited in the cabin until I felt the quiver of motors, now distinguished by the lesser throb and smoother running, from the drive on the wheeled trucks through the tunnel.

I opened the cabin door and went out. Grauble was at the instrument board. The mate stood aft among the motor controls; all men were at their posts, for we were navigating the difficult subterranean passage that led to the open sea.

As I approached Grauble he spoke without lifting his eyes from his instruments. " Go bring the Princess out of her hiding; I want my men to see her now. It will help to give them faith."

Marguerite came with me and stood trembling at my side as we watched Grauble, whose eyes still riveted upon the many dials and indicators before him.

" Watch the chart," said Grauble. " The red hand shows our position."

The chart before him was slowly passing over rolls. For a time we could only see a straight line thereon bordered by many signs and figures. Then slowly over the topmost roll came the wavy outlines of a shore, and the parallel lines marking the depths of the bordering sea. Tensely we watched the chart roll slowly down till the end of the channel passed the indicator.

Grauble breathed a great sigh of relief and for the first time turned his face towards us. "We are in the open sea," he said, "at a depth of 160 metres. I shall turn north at once and parallel the coast. You had better get some rest; for the present nothing can happen. It is night above now but in six more hours will be the dawn, then we shall rise and take our bearings through the periscope."

I led Marguerite into the Captain's cabin and insisted that she lie down on the narrow berth. Seated in the only chair, I related what I knew of the affair at the locks. "It must have been," I concluded, after much speculation, "that Holknecht finally got the attention of the Chemical Staff and related what he knew of the incident of the potash mines. They had enough data about me to have arrived at the correct conclusion long ago. It was a question of getting the facts together."

"It was that," said Marguerite, "or else I am to blame."

"And what do you mean?" I asked.

"I mean," she said, "that I took a great risk about which I must tell you, for it troubles my conscience. After I had sent for the Admiral and he had promised to come, I telephoned to Dr. Zimmern of my intention to get von Kufner to take me to the docks and my hope that I could come with you.

And it may be that some one listened in on our conversation."

"I do not see," I said, "how such a conversation should lead to the discovery of my identity — the Holknecht theory is more reasonable — but you did take a risk. Why did you do it?"

"I wanted to tell him good-bye," said Marguerite. "It was hard enough that I could not see him." And she turned her face to the pillow and began to weep.

"What is it, my dear?" I pleaded, as I knelt beside her. "It was all right, of course. Why are you crying — you do not think, do you, that Dr. Zimmern betrayed us?"

Marguerite raised herself upon her elbow and looked at me with hurt surprise. "Do you think that?" she demanded, almost fiercely.

"By no means," I hastened to assure her, "but I do not understand your grief and I only thought that perhaps when you told him he was angered — I never understood why he seemed so anxious not to have you go with me."

"Oh, my dear," sobbed Marguerite. "Of course you never understood, because we too had a secret that has been kept from you, and you have been so apologetic because you feared so long to confide in me and I have been even slower to confide in you."

For a moment black rebellion rose in my heart, for though with my reasoning I had accepted the explanation that Zimmern had given for his interest in Marguerite, I had never quite accepted it in my unreasoning heart. And in the depths of me the battle between love and reason and the dark forces of jealous unreason and suspicion had smouldered, to break out afresh on the least provocation.

I fought again to conquer these dark forces, for I had many times forgiven her even the thing which suspicion charged. And as I struggled now the sound of Marguerite's words came sweeping through my soul like a great cleansing wind, for she said — " The secret that I have kept back from you and that I have wanted so often to tell you is that Dr. Zimmern is my father! "

7

In the early dawn of a foggy morning we beached the *Eitel 3* on a sandy stretch of Danish shore within a few kilometres of an airdome of the World Patrol. A native fisherman took Grauble, Marguerite and myself in his hydroplane to the post, where we found the commander at his breakfast. He was a man of quick intelligence. Our strange garb was sufficient to prove us Germans, while a' brief and accurate account of the attempted rescue of the mines of Stassfurt, given in perfect English, sufficed to credit my reappearance in the affairs of the free world as a matter of grave and urgent importance. A squad of men were sent at once to guard the vessel that had been left in charge of the mate. Within a few hours we three were at the seat of the World Government at Geneva.

Grauble surrendered his charts of the secret passage and was made a formal prisoner of state, until the line of the passage could be explored by borings and the reality of its existence verified.

I was in daily conference with the Council in regard to momentous actions that were set speedily a-going. The submarine tunnel was located and the passage blocked. A fleet of ice crushers and exploring planes were sent to locate the protium mines of the Arctic. The proclamation of these calamities to the continued isolated existence of Germany and the terms of peace and amnesty were sent showering down through the clouds to the roof of Berlin.

Marguerite and I had taken up our residence in a cottage on the lake shore, and there as I slept late into the sunlit hours of a July morning, I heard the clatter of a telephone annunciator. I sat bolt upright listening to the words of the instrument —

" Berlin has shut off the Ray generators of the defence mines — all over the desert of German soil men are pouring forth from the ventilating shafts — the roof of Berlin is a-swarm with a mass of men frolicking in the sunlight — the planes of the World Patrol have alighted on the roof and have received and flashed back the news of the abdication of the Emperor and the capitulation of Berlin — the world armies of the mines are out and marching forth to police the city —"

The voice of the instrument ceased.

I looked about for Marguerite and saw her not. I was up and running through the rooms of the cottage. I reached the outer door and saw her in the garden, robed in a gown of gossamer white, her hair streaming loose about her shoulders and gleaming golden brown in the quivering light. She was holding out her hands to the East, where o'er the far-flung mountain craigs the God of Day beamed down upon his worshipper.

In a frenzy of wild joy I called to her —" Babylon is fallen — is fallen! The black spot is erased from the map of the world!"

THE END